TWO OF
A MIND

S M STUART

Matador
9 Priory Business Park
Kibworth Beauchamp
Leicestershire LE8 0RX, UK
Tel: (+44) 116 279 2299
Fax: (+44) 116 279 2277
Email: books@troubador.co.uk
Web: www.troubador.co.uk/matador

ISBN 978 1784621 681

British Library Cataloguing in Publication Data.
A catalogue record for this book is available from the British Library.

Typeset in Aldine and Gill Sans Light by Troubador Publishing Ltd
Printed and bound in the UK by TJ International, Padstow, Cornwall

Matador is an imprint of Troubador Publishing Ltd

PROLOGUE

London: November 2015

"Damn you. You said there were no serious side effects." Lord Simpson struggled to speak through his grotesquely swollen lips.

Despite his exclusive knowledge of its hidden dangers, even Trevalyn couldn't be sure which symptoms were solely attributable to the nano-agent he'd unleashed. He unconsciously touched his arm where the antidote injection had caused a mild irritation. The rash was nothing compared to the potentially fatal reactions to the drug, released soon after the October conference. Many of the worldwide casualties could be explained away, especially now amidst the nuclear war.

"Lord Simpson. I understand the doctor believes your symptoms are those of the latest flu mutation and, therefore, unlikely to be related to the dispersal. Unfortunately, we were caught unawares and haven't had time to develop a new vaccine to counter this virulent strain. I assure you my researchers are currently working on it as a matter of urgency."

Simpson grimaced in pain as he turned to look through the window of his private hospital room. In his heart he knew that Trevalyn Pharmaceuticals were somehow responsible for his dreadful illness but he had lost the will to fight, realising that it wouldn't do much good. The world population was now contaminated by the nano-agent. The damage – alongside the promised benefits – had been done and if the war continued it was all pointless anyway.

"I expect your company to support the government in treating radiation sickness should the need arise," he said. "It's the least you can do."

Trevalyn was about to protest but held back his response in the knowledge that Simpson wouldn't be around much longer.

"Of course," he lied. "We are committed to the welfare of the entire population. It's just unfortunate that the mood-inhibitor didn't have time to take full effect before the first bomb strike. And with this awful flu pandemic I envisage a long, hard, global struggle ahead." He sighed dramatically.

"And how long before your damned drug saves the world, Trevalyn?" Simpson wheezed.

"Reaction periods vary but we should see a marked decrease in hostilities soon. It'll all be over by Christmas."

"Hah! They said that at the beginning of the First World War. We'll have destroyed the whole planet if this goes on as long as that did. God save us all."

Simpson's laboured breathing shuddered to a halt. The monitor by his bed buzzed and a nurse rushed into the room to check the alarm.

"I'm sorry sir. You'll have to leave now," she said, but Trevalyn had already done so.

CHAPTER 1

Ellingham: 24 July 2110

Hell, it's not my fault the damned thing didn't switch on!

The lights dimmed. Everyone stood quietly, waiting for the midnight chimes. My feet ached and my dress stuck to my sweaty back. I just wished for the whole thing to be over and done with.

Why does everyone expect you to be so excited about it? After all, it's just a normal part of growing up, or so they're always telling us. But we can't just let it happen quietly and get on with life – oh no! There has to be a big song and dance – literally. The contracted songwriter has to come up with a natty little number chronicling your life almost from conception to present day – including all the crummy stuff you'd rather forget. After that excruciating torture, you're expected to take to the floor with your father, or nearest equivalent, for the first dance as though you've been waiting your whole life to let him crush each of your toes in turn. *And then*, if you can still stand, you're passed around each of the male participants like a sack of spuds, everyone laughing as you gradually turn a deeper shade of green ready to barf over the most expensive – and most embarrassing – dress that you've ever been forced to wear.

Eventually, the food is served, not that you can stomach any by now, and everyone starts reminiscing about how funny it was when you had that pea stuck up your nose on your second birthday; that you had such a temper at four; broke your leg at six, *blah, blah, blah*.

"Come on," said a calm, familiar voice. "We can hide out over by the pot plants 'til midnight."

"Seth! You're a life-saver!" I followed the one person that I

1

wouldn't have minded dancing with all night. Especially because he hated it more than I did; wicked of me, I know.

Being neighbours and only a couple of months apart in age, we'd spent most of our lives in each other's company. We usually got up to some mischief that landed one, or both, of us in trouble with the 'rents. We weren't bad kids, just enthusiastic, curious and, *okay*, I was a teeny bit rebellious. Seth often took the blame for something that I'd instigated, like the time I managed to jam the Holo-Comms at his house. I still can't work out what I did. Surely just trying to contact my dad when he was abroad on business shouldn't have made it freeze like that? Poor Seth, *his* chip was restricted for a month and *he* had to contribute to the reboot bill by doing extra chores. But, he never once complained to me that it was *my* fault.

The heat of the summer evening sun and the exuberant dancing had loosened my black ringlets, previously pinned to the top of my head "in the most fashionable style", and they now hung in damp tendrils around my shoulders. I felt uncomfortable, ugly and sulky. In this mood, only Seth could get through to me. With his quiet and accepting attitude, he rarely took offence at my behaviour. He could usually calm me down and help me see reason without seeming to criticise. Yet he never let me go too far. He had a way of letting me know when he was disappointed or disapproving without actually saying anything in particular. I once asked if he minded me getting a skin pigment-chip, having chosen an impressive dragon design and thinking myself to be so cool! Seth's simple "No," – his tone not in any way critical – was enough to make me think twice, even though the chip only had a limited-life function.

"Shall I try to tidy you up for the big moment?" he now asked, grinning at my dishevelled appearance.

I looked at his own unruly auburn curls sticking out from his head despite huge quantities of gel.

"If you must," I sighed and suffered a few sharp jabs as he lifted the limp curls from my neck and re-fastened the hairpins. The result wasn't too bad for a lad more interested in the inner workings of antique combustion engines.

"Desirée!" called my mother's shrill voice. "It's almost time, dear."

Instantly, the use of my full name set my teeth on edge. Why, oh why, couldn't she stick to the pet name that everybody else, including Dad, used?

"Patience, Dez!" soothed Seth, feeling the tension in my shoulders. "You're almost done." He eased me out of the shadows, towards the middle of the dance floor where the 'rents waited with beaming smiles.

"Ah, there you are!" Mum put her arm around my shoulders and drew me away from Seth, who melted into the crowd like a wraith.

Mum was the only person in the world who, apparently, didn't care much for Seth. That might be an over-exaggeration – she rarely seemed to notice him. Maybe she was jealous of the time I spent with him but I hated her treatment of him, even if it was unintentional.

"Attention, please! Shush, please everyone!" Mum clapped her hands to silence the partygoers. "We must prepare for the midnight chimes. Does everyone have a glass of champagne for the toast?"

A few hopeful youngsters headed for the wine-waiters but were fobbed off with lemonade. Adults had their glasses refilled and tried to resist the temptations of various nibbles still on offer.

"Don't frown so, Dez," Dad said. "Your mother means well and it spoils your pretty face to pout like that!"

"But Dad, why couldn't I just've had a little family get-together with only our closest friends, like Seth had? It was so cosy and friendly. I feel like the prize exhibit at a freak show. When has anybody *ever* seen me in a fancy get-up like this? They're all laughing at me."

"No, sweetheart, they are simply enjoying the celebration. You are about to embark on the next stage of life and they are here to support and congratulate you." Dad winked as he turned to have his own glass refilled with the amber fizz that was costing him a small fortune.

3

So, there we were. The lights dimmed. Everyone stood quietly, waiting for the midnight chimes. My feet ached and my dress stuck to my sweaty back. I just wished for the whole thing to be over and done with.

"Five, four, three, two, one!" Some loud-mouth in the crowd counted down then the midnight chimes began to ring out.

The beginning of the new day. That of my sixteenth birthday. The one that really was supposed to be the first day of the rest of my life.

"You must be so excited," whispered my mother.

"Can you sense anything?" Dad asked.

"Are they receptive yet?" added Aunt Jennifer.

"Gently, don't force the connection," said Ms Thorogood, the senior Humanities Tutor from the Academy.

What did I hear above their quick fire questioning that hit me like a hail of verbal bullets? Nothing! Not a sound! Well, not counting the incessant buzz of external noise around me, everyone trying to find out who it was. But it wasn't anyone! And it certainly wasn't the one person I'd hoped it would be. What could I say? I was a freak – an Empty. A kid whose telepathic twinning hadn't switched on when it was supposed to. Mum was right to worry all those years when she'd struggled to get pregnant and have a healthy baby. I was the only one she'd managed to bring into the world and now she was never going to have a perfect child.

I frantically looked around trying to find a way to escape the pressing questions and clutching hands. Mum's face started to wear the worried expression that I had seen most of my life. Only for those few hours of the party had she seemed carefree. Dad had finally realised something was wrong and tried to open a path for me.

"She is probably feeling a bit disoriented," he said, "Remember how we all felt. Give her some air, please!" His concern showed in his eyes but he nodded at me, giving his silent consent for me to leave.

"Thank you," I mouthed, as I gradually made it to the foyer and outside to the cooling night air.

I clenched my fists and thumped my head painfully and then I sobbed, as I'd never sobbed before.

And where's Seth when I need him?

CHAPTER 2

Ellingham: 25 July 2110

Omigod, my head aches!

I woke up on my stomach, head twisted to one side with dribble still damp on my face. My custom-made dress was tangled around me tightly and I heard it rip as I tried to straighten out my hot, cramped body. Good job Mum had insisted on the option with coded material that would reweave the torn fibres for a perfect repair – was there anything nano-technology couldn't do?

For a moment, I couldn't remember why I'd been blubbering into my bedding all night then it came rushing back. I tried to tune in but my head was still empty. This wasn't how it was supposed to be! Ms Thorogood had been preparing us over the last eighteen months for this big moment when the switch is thrown and we connect with our very own Psyche-Twin. I remember the excitement of our first "Tele-Prep" lesson. We all felt so grown-up, on the verge of adulthood and way beyond those tiddlers in the lower years at The Academy.

"Settle down kids," Ms Thorogood had said. "Yes, Darius, you *are* still kids for now and some of you always will be, so don't make that face," she'd laughed.

Ms Thorogood lived up to her name. She really was thoroughly good! Cool too. She hadn't seemed much older than we were when she'd joined the Academy staff straight from teacher training. The boys all thought she was hot with her long blonde hair – natural, not coloured – and, no, she wasn't a bimbo! A gorgeous figure; long slim legs, neat little bum, flat belly and natural boobs just the right size for her height. Honestly, I might've fancied her a little too! But she wasn't the 'I'm-stunning-and-I-know-it' type. She was friendly, approachable and kind, and she treated us as though she really enjoyed being with us. Not like those tutors who thought that students just cluttered up the place.

"Right, folks, this is the preparation course for your sixteenth. You might think it'll be a doddle but you'd be surprised how difficult it is to deal with someone else suddenly inside your head."

"Frankie needs someone else, Miss, cos there's no-one in there now!" called Darius, nudging his best friend. Frankie responded by trying to push him off his chair.

"Funny." Ms Thorogood gave Darius and Frankie a withering look and that stopped their antics. They didn't want to get onto her wrong side completely – both of them were besotted – so they tried to look serious and ready to learn.

"As you know, at midnight on the eve of your birthday the process of your telepathy begins. Within a few moments, you should become aware of the connection to your unique Psyche-Twin, I'll call them your PT from now on and you can use that abbreviation in your notes."

There was a sudden scramble for our DataRolls as we took the hint. Most of us had to make do with the old style flexible touch-screens to record our notes but one or two toffs made a big show of tapping their temple to stimulate the latest PILS (personal integrated learning system), a minute implant hotwired directly into the short-term memory and only released onto the market the previous year. There'd been a protest about unfair advantages in school situations so the PILS had to be blocked during assessments and exams. They might've thought their superior recording devices were impressive but the toffs still had to study the subject to fix it into their long-term memory.

Ms Thorogood continued.

"It may not be an immediate complete connection as your PT might not share your birthday. In this case you'll sense their presence, their gender and their approximate location. They'll only fully connect with you when they reach their own sixteenth. This can be quite a blessing for the elder PT as it gives you chance to get used to a partial mental connection before the full onslaught of the younger PT's personality."

"Onslaught sounds like it hurts, Miss," quavered Melanie, the youngest in the year.

"No, not really, Melanie. But it can be quite a shock when you have a complete stranger suddenly having access to your inner thoughts and sharing theirs with you."

"Will it always be a complete stranger?" asked Davy, as he reached towards Jing-Wei's leg under the table. She wriggled away, struggling to keep a straight face.

"Not necessarily, Davy. However, you can't force a connection with your chosen partner no matter how much you stroke her leg!" Davy grinned and Jing-Wei tilted her head forward, using her long curtain of silky, black hair to hide her blushes. The class erupted with cheers and desk thumping. I glanced at Seth but he was looking at his D-Roll so I couldn't see his reaction.

"And whilst it may not be someone you know," Ms Thorogood continued as soon as the noise died down, "they may also be of either gender. He or she may be local or from the other side of the world."

"How will we know what they're saying if they're foreign?" Jing-Wei raised her flushed face.

"Communication between PTs isn't verbal. Language isn't a barrier because the connection is purely telepathic. Think of a Holo-Comms call – the words spoken are digitised to travel through the satellite system then reconstituted by the receiver so that you can hear them clearly. Advances in technology created the current configuration that translates foreign languages automatically. The language centre in the brain has adapted to the telepathic connection in a similar way. When your PT's thoughts and feelings reach your mind it understands the communication on a subconscious level."

"Shame it doesn't sort out our French homework, Miss!"

"Frankie, I hear that your French essays can be very entertaining. You don't need any help finding risqué translations."

We tried to stifle our giggles but Ms Thorogood had a twinkle in her eye.

"What happens if you're a spy? You'd give away all your secrets and your PT might be on the other side!" Tylar fancied a career in the diplomatic service, convinced that it was less about good international relations and more 'cloak-and-dagger'.

"My dad says stuff about your job is automatically kept confidential," I piped up.

"Yeah," Tylar nodded, giving the 'nudge-nudge, wink-wink' gesture, wagging his elbow in my direction and blinking rapidly – he couldn't quite manage the one-eyed wink. I wasn't sure whether he was being serious or snide. My dad did work for the diplomatic service and travelled abroad quite often but it was hardly the stuff of spy stories. Poor old Dad, his ample belly wouldn't be much help if he needed to escape through a secret tunnel or shimmy up a drainpipe. No, I couldn't imagine him as an international spy.

"He's just a civil servant!" I said, then, feeling I needed to defend him, "A *senior* civil servant."

Ms Thorogood smiled at me.

"Your dad's right, Dez. There's a natural mechanism to keep certain aspects of your life private and to protect both you and your PT in the early stages of your connection. Such as work related information; your PT's identity, thoughts and actions; and intimate romantic behaviours." I'm sure she paused for effect. "Yes, okay, I'm talking about sex!"

Once more she waited for the class to settle down.

"Let's have a look at the reasons for this selective block," she said. "Tylar had a good, if somewhat extreme, case. Telepathic-twinning doesn't mean that we automatically have immediate access to all the thoughts and feelings of our connected partner. The temptation would be too great to use the information gleaned. Luckily, no one has that ability. It seems that by good evolutionary design our brains have an inbuilt security system that will only be unlocked under certain circumstances. We call this phenomenon the 'Bloc' – B L O C, without the K. You won't be able to share the identity of your PT until the full telepathic permission evolves.

"We'll be covering it in more detail near the end of the course but imagine if you were connected to one of the Royal Family or a celebrity. Without the Bloc you'd be able to tell others who you had as a PT and, when word got around, you'd be chased by the press looking for juicy gossip!"

"Shame," sighed Mitch, the wheeler-dealer of the class. "I coulda made a fortune dishing the dirt."

"Specially if you'd seen 'em in the act!" Darius laughed.

"Exactly! That's why the brain automatically closes off the connection during the intensely passionate times of your life," Ms Thorogood added. She was the only tutor who openly discussed stuff like sex with us. I suppose she was close enough to our age so she didn't come across as if she'd no idea how we felt. "PTs can sense their partner's extreme feelings but not the specifics. It's rather complicated. You'll probably be able to recognise when your PT is deliriously happy; desperately sad; madly in love or completely distraught, although you're unlikely to be able to eavesdrop on the action. There are some aspects of telepathy that can't be taught, you have to adjust over time once the connection's made, but I'll do my best to prepare you for the changes you can expect when you reach sixteen.

"In the meantime, I'll be coaching you regarding the responsibilities and restrictions that you must follow once you become a full PT. Some of you will be quick to adapt, some will find it a strange and difficult process. These sessions will include joint projects and workshops to encourage trust and mutual support. And I'll be having several individual counselling sessions with each of you to discuss anything you're uncomfortable about."

There were several giggles and exaggerated coughs as we considered what might be uncomfortable when a stranger started to share our thoughts.

"Okay, I'll let you out a little early as you've been *so* well behaved." She winked at the class and waved her hand towards the door. "Go on. Have a good weekend everyone."

"Thanks, Miss!" we chorused and ran for the freedom of a sun-drenched Friday evening.

I wonder if anyone asked her about what to do if the PT connection didn't happen. I certainly never thought to ask during our private sessions and it probably didn't occur to anyone else either. How naïve of us to believe that not one of our classmates might end up being an 'Empty' – MPT: Missing-Psyche-Twin.

So, what happens now?

CHAPTER 3

London: July 2039

"Recent reports suggest that Homo Sapiens have taken a significant evolutionary step forward. Scientists working at the Trevalyn Laboratories in Oxford now believe that many of the mental health issues previously thought to be connected to the 2015 War and the concurrent flu pandemic of that year might have been indicative of changes within the brain, leading to the potential to connect telepathically with another individual…"

"Yes, but why the sudden advancement?" muttered Baroness Julia Simpson.

"Pardon, Grandma?" Matthew paused, his toast halfway to his mouth.

"Oh. Nothing Matt. I was simply thinking out loud. I'm allowed to at my age." She smiled at her grandson. She didn't want the teenager worrying about Grandma's mental health when he already had enough to cope with. "How's your mother this morning?"

"Much the same. The medication seems to help keep her calm but she doesn't sleep much."

"It's so hard for her, poor love. I'll pop up to see her after breakfast."

"It's hard for us too Grandma. You lost Granddad to the flu and then Dad …" Matt choked.

Julia moved to sit by her grandson. She gathered him in her arms and held him close as his tears wet her blouse.

"Yes, we've had our bad times but we've still got each other. Your mother lost her entire family during the flu pandemic. She loves you dearly but your father was her lifeline for a long time before you came along. We can only hope that she remembers we're here for her now. It may take her some time. She was fragile before he … left us." Even the ever-pragmatic Julia couldn't say the words – that her son had taken his own life – it was still too raw a pain.

"Why, Grandma? Why did he do it?"

"I wish I knew, my darling. I wish I knew."

"I'm … I'm scared I'll end up doing it too," Matt whispered.

Julia pushed him upright so that she could see his tear-streaked face.

"What gives you that idea?" Her tone was harsh with worry.

"Since I turned sixteen I've felt I'm going mad. I can't put it into words. When I try, my head hurts like it's going to explode. All I can say is that it feels as if I'm not alone in there any more."

Julia's eyes returned to the vid-screen where the muted news report continued to show images of 3D brain scans and psychic test statistics.

"I'm sure there's an explanation for the changes, love," she said. "Try not to worry. We'll have Dr Armstrong check you over when he comes to see your mother this evening."

The news report had reawakened Julia's suspicions and when Matt left for school she brought out her numerous journals to remind her of her findings over the years. She'd always resisted technology and relied on her hand written notes to bring back the past.

It had been hard to accept the death of her beloved Andrew. Lord Simpson had only been forty-five when he contracted the fatal strain of flu. To help her cope with the loss she had worked tirelessly to assist those worst affected by the pandemic and the War. Her efforts were noticed and she was rewarded with the title of Baroness in the Honours of 2017. Tragically, she hadn't recognised her own son's suffering and depression during the years after his father's death. For that she would always carry the guilt and grief, labelling herself a failed mother. She would not let her family down again.

A sheaf of papers fell from the diary of 2016. Julia bent to retrieve them from the floor, grimacing a little at the twinge in her back. The papers were her hard copy of the King's Speech from the Opening of

Parliament that year. The decimated ranks of all the political parties had, for once, agreed to work together to rebuild the country on a fair and responsible basis. She recalled the hotly debated policies such as abolishing IVF treatments. The staggering increase in birth defects attributed to the nuclear fallout and after effects of the flu pandemic had destabilised the clinical process. Numerous maternal deaths during labour finally tipped the balance towards a blanket ban on fertility treatments. Compulsory genetic screening was introduced to monitor natural conception with many couples being told they would be incompatible.

Julia felt familiar tears welling up. She and Andrew had only managed to conceive Timothy using IVF back in 1999. Her support for the 2016 Bill to abolish the treatment had felt like a betrayal of all those other childless couples but the statistics could not be ignored. The survival of the living and the rehabilitation of the country as a whole had to take precedence. In brutal terms, funds were needed for more urgent projects.

"Julia."

She started from her reverie and turned to respond, "Hello, Rosalind."

"I'm sorry. Did I startle you?"

Julia quickly closed the journal with the speech papers tucked back amongst its pages. "No, I'm fine dear. How are you this morning? Can I get anything for you?"

"I've just put the kettle on for tea and wondered if you'd like one. Or coffee, if you prefer?"

Rosalind's mood seemed to be much improved despite Matt's earlier suggestion and Julia wanted to capitalise on it.

"I'd love a cup of tea and I think we have some fruit teacakes in the cupboard. I could quite fancy one toasted."

As she licked the butter from her fingers, Rosalind began speaking quietly, almost as if she didn't really want to share her thoughts, "I've been so selfish, haven't I? I heard you and Matt talking earlier. He hates me doesn't he?"

"Don't be silly. Of course he doesn't. He's just having a difficult time.

All teenagers go through it." But Julia didn't sound as convincing as she'd have liked. She felt a sensation of déjà vu. Matt was the same age that Timothy had been when his father had died. Was Rosalind doomed to repeat Julia's mistakes?

"It's not hard to imagine what you're thinking. Please, Julia. Help me be my boy's mother again." Rosalind reached out to grasp Julia's arm. The older woman drew her into a comforting hug.

"Of course, my dear," Julia soothed. "We'll work it out together."

CHAPTER 4

Ellingham: 25 July 2110

Can't explain anything until I figure it out for myself.

The thought of telling the 'rents was turning my stomach.

"Dez! Are you coming down for some breakfast?"

"Be there in a minute, Dad."

I grabbed my favourite pair of jeans and a reasonably crease-free T-shirt. Mum regularly complained about the state of my bedroom floor – covered in clothing that should've been neatly tucked away in the wardrobe until I needed to wear it. So what? I was a regular teenager. I have to admit, I did do it simply to wind her up sometimes. She was always finding an excuse to come in, especially if I had friends with me.

The smell of Dad's freshly ground coffee wafted through the house as I came out of my sanctuary. I struggled to hold down the rising panic and threatening tears. A few deep breaths helped slow down my heart and eased the shaking of my hands. As soon as I entered the kitchen, I could sense that the 'rents had been discussing the party. Mum's eyes were red and puffy – I expect my blubbing was just as obvious – and Dad had the set expression that meant he was going to keep calm despite huge provocation.

"Good morning, sweetheart," he said and he kissed the top of my head as I sat down at the table.

"Morning."

I poured a cup of tea, hoping it would settle my stomach. I could tell Mum was desperate to talk about my reaction to the connection last night, but Dad must have said something to keep her at bay so she tried a bright and breezy – and totally false – "Got anything special planned for today, Desirée?"

"Just thought I'd head into town. Spend some of those gift-credits if I see anything nice." My response was equally forced but I had to keep my secret to myself. I couldn't handle the fallout just yet. I needed time to think, something I generally did using my best friend as a sounding board.

And why had Seth deserted me just when I needed him most? In fact, why isn't he knocking at the back door now, checking to see if I'm okay? Huh! I'll go down to the Centre and mooch about all day just to stay away from the 'rents and their enquiring looks. Maybe it'll turn on later today – a sort of delayed reaction. Yeah, that's it. Probably just that I'm not really sixteen until later this afternoon.

I'd conveniently forgotten that the precise time of birth didn't matter. The stroke of midnight to start your sixteenth birthday was the trigger point like all good fairytales. Only this seemed more like a horror story.

"Don't forget we've got a birthday tea party organised."

"Yes, Mum." I tried to be civilised. I even gave her a peck on the cheek as I left the breakfast table, hoping she didn't notice that I hadn't eaten anything.

I looked at myself in the mirror as I cleaned my teeth. The toothbrush buzzed around my mouth making the toothpaste dribble down my chin as I stared at the reflection. I hardly recognised myself. It happens sometimes, when you stare at something familiar for so long it seems to transform into something completely alien. I was looking at a stranger. For a moment I thought; *this is it!* But as I brought the image back into focus I realised it was still just me in the mirror – still just me in my empty head.

People had been generous with their gifts for my sixteenth. I'd have tons of thank you letters to write. Mum still insisted on old-fashioned, formal emails even if I'd said thanks via Holo-Comms, Txt or face-to-face. Oh well, it would give me an excuse to hide in my room for several hours over the next few days. I scanned the gift-credit vouchers onto my wrist-chip, topping-up my spending account; grabbed my retro-denim bag; dragged on a pair of scuffed but comfy ankle boots and picked up a lightweight jumper. They had the air-conditioning set really cool at the shopping centre and whenever I went in there from the warm summer sunshine I always ended up with gooseflesh on my arms.

"See you later," I called over my shoulder as I dashed out of the front door, hoping to avoid further conversation.

"Don't be late!" I heard Mum reply.

The boarding-sensor on the ecotram beeped as it registered my wrist-chip. As the vehicle speaker announced the route, a familiar figure ran alongside the tram and managed to board just before the doors closed. His hair messier than ever, Seth came down the aisle towards my seat.

"How's the hangover birthday girl? You look like you didn't get much sleep."

"And you look like you still haven't managed to work out what to do with a comb!"

A brief expression of confusion crossed Seth's face. His unruly hair was often a source of fun between us but this time he heard anger in my tone. He struggled to smooth his curls down with his hands and then studied the passing landscape rather than trying to find out what was wrong.

Typical!

"Hey! I'm gonna hurl. Open the frikkin' door will ya?" A muscular, dishevelled man was banging on the driver's screen trying to make her engage the override button. The hurler was obviously trying to skip his fare but 'Maddie' wasn't having any of it.

"Sir there are labelled bio-waste bags in the seat pockets if you are feeling unwell," she said via her intercom. "I suggest you return to your seat until the designated stop. I can request a medic to meet us there if you need assistance?" She turned her dainty head and stared the fare-hopper down.

"Frikkin' Holo-Bots!" he muttered as he shuffled back to his seat.

For a few moments there, I'd almost smiled at the comic situation but it wasn't so easy to switch on the happy me. Seth glanced at me to see if my mood was thawing and I recognised his disappointment as he quickly turned back to the window. The rest of the journey passed without further entertainment from 'Mr Hurler' and his wrist-chip must've had enough credit `cos he stepped off the tram at our stop without any problems. Maybe the two security officers who happened to be near the Mall-Stop might've had something to do with his suddenly improved behaviour.

We entered the shopping centre and Seth automatically reached out to hold my bag as I struggled to pull on my jumper. He tried to start our conversation again.

"Can I treat you to a coffee or something? Our own small celebration for your birthday? I know your family have plans for later."

A refusal was on the tip of my tongue. I was still angry with him for his disappearance last night but my conscience was pricking me. *Maybe I should give him chance to explain.*

"Okay," I replied. "Make it tea *and* a muffin and you're on."

His face lit up with a smile and I felt like crying again. When he got to the table with the snacks I was back in control.

"One blueberry muffin – healthy, low-fat variety – and tea for madam. Hot chocolate with whipped cream and a nutty choc-chip cookie pour moi!" He set the tray down. He must've had this planned as there was a single burning candle pushed into the top of the muffin. "Happy birthday!"

"Thank *you*," I said, sarcastically, drooling at sight of the choc-loaded cookie. *He's tormenting me, knowing that I'm trying to keep off the chocolate!*

After a few moments of thoughtful chewing on his cookie and slurping through the mound of whipped cream he asked the inevitable.

"What's the matter, Dez? Come on, tell me."

My throat closed and my eyes filled. I started to shake as I tried to contain my sobs.

"Dez!" Seth became alarmed. "Dez *what is it*?"

"I... it... didn't... it didn't... where were you?" I managed between gulps.

"Sorry?"

"Where were you at midnight? I looked for you and you were gone."

"It's a time for family. I wanted you to savour the moment."

"N-no! You know better than that. I was at your party. I was there at midnight to share it with you. Why was it different for you at mine?"

Seth seemed to deflate. He started to pick at the remains of his cookie.

"Look, I know your mum isn't keen on me being around. I just didn't want to cause any more friction between you. Especially at such an important time for you."

"S'not good enough, Seth." I sniffed and tried to look as though that was all there was to it.

"Sorry, Dez. I really didn't think you'd notice. I didn't mean to hurt you. You know I wouldn't want that."

He put his arm around my shoulder and gave me a squeeze. The feelings of warmth and comfort that his hugs usually brought didn't happen. I shrugged him off and kept my mug of tea in front of my face to hide the disappointment.

"Tell me what to do to put it right," he said.

"I don't know!" I knew I was sulking but I couldn't help it. If I didn't have the nerve to tell my best friend what had happened, how the hell was I going to tell the 'rents? I grabbed my bag and tried to redeem myself.

"For a start, you can help me fritter some of my birthday credits."

We spent the best part of the day idly meandering around the shops but I didn't buy much. My heart wasn't in it. As we sat on the ecotram home, I tried a different approach hoping that I could trick myself into sharing my problem.

"You've never said what your PT's like? Hasn't your Bloc unlocked yet?" I asked.

Seth's face went momentarily blank, like a film on pause. Was he asking his PT if he could tell me about them?

I pressed on, "I haven't asked before 'cos I thought you'd let me know all about them but you've been pretty tight since your party. So, is it 'cos their Bloc won't let you?"

"No. Er, no. It's nothing like that," he stammered. "It's just … it's difficult, you know? We're best mates, aren't we? Don't you think it's strange to have someone else connected to us in a way that we can't be with each other?"

"Yeah, I suppose so," I replied. But I felt short-changed – he hadn't really answered me and now he was hinting that our PTs might come between us, affecting our friendship in ways I hadn't even considered.

At least he's got a bloody PT to share his feelings with!

CHAPTER 5

Ellingham: 25 July 2110

I'm really not in the mood for a damned tea-party!

"S'only me," I called, as I opened the front door and tried to head straight upstairs to my room.

"Just a minute," said Mum from the kitchen door. "Aren't you going to show us what you've bought?"

"Thought you'd want me to get changed for the tea-party."

"We've got time yet. Come on, let me see what you've spent all your credits on."

"Really, Mum, there's nothing exciting. Just a couple of bangles and a t-shirt from 'Q-Tees'."

"Let her be, love," soothed Dad, noticing Mum's cheeks colouring up as she started to lose patience. "She wants to get ready and Jen will be here soon. Come and have a cup of tea before you start charging around after everyone else." He steered her back into the kitchen and winked at me over his shoulder.

I wasn't sure how I was going to cope with another social gathering even if it was going to be just family. Under normal circumstances Aunt Jennifer was a bit of a laugh. She was Dad's younger sister and had been in the same year as Mum at university. Can't imagine how they ended up as best buddies. Mum so old-fashioned, prim and proper and Aunt Jennifer (or Jen as she now insisted on being called) liberal and down-to-earth. Their friendship cooled briefly when Jen got pregnant and refused to tell anyone who the father was. She said that she was "more than capable of bringing up the sprog alone and not going to force a relationship onto a man who wasn't interested in being a father anyway!" The result was Jeremy.

Jeremy was fourteen; a bit of a tear-away and cocky enough to wind up his Aunt Celeste at every given opportunity. He didn't exactly endear himself when he introduced his mother's latest partner: "Dick – as in head!" Mum nearly choked, shocked at her nephew's offensive attitude. Poor Dick just shrugged and gratefully accepted a large whisky from Dad. Jeremy had caught my eye and I'd struggled to keep my mouthful of orange juice from gushing down my nose. He was okay in small doses, I suppose.

I sat on my bed with my eyes closed concentrating like mad. It felt as though I was chasing oxygen in thin air. I knew it had to be there and it was doable but how could I get at it? My head began to ache again as my brows scrunched and my jaw clenched, so I forced myself to relax. Maybe that was my problem, I was trying too hard. It was like that word on the tip of your tongue – it won't come if you keep thinking about it but as soon as you stop worrying it pops into your head.

So I'll just stop worrying and it'll suddenly be there without me even noticing!

I took a deep breath, went to the bathroom to wash my face then changed into my new t-shirt so that Mum could enjoy complaining about the slogan: **"Kiss My A★★"** – even though the cartoon of a donkey beneath showed it was a completely innocent request! Anyway, it'd make her feel better about earlier if she could have a good old tut at me.

By the time I got downstairs Jen, Dick and Jeremy had arrived. I could see from the scowl on Jeremy's face that he'd had alternative plans for the evening but he brightened up when he caught sight of my t-shirt. He was anticipating the inevitable barney.

"How's the hangover, Dez?" Jen grinned as she gave me a hug, hiding the ambiguous slogan for the moment. "You wicked child," she chuckled into my ear.

"Nothing a hair of the dog won't cure," I replied, looking expectantly at Dad.

"Not a chance!" He handed me a non-alcoholic fruit punch. "You know the law, young lady. Leniency for your Sixteenth but until you are eighteen, limited rations!"

Dad was right to keep me off the booze – it would've made me even more belligerent in my current emotional state. And the headache was still hovering so fruit punch was probably all I could stomach anyway.

"Desirée!" Mum wailed.

Oh yeah, forgot about my t-shirt for a minute.

"What on earth possessed you to buy that… that… crude top?" Mum struggled to find the right description.

"What's wrong with kissing a donkey?" asked Jeremy in his most innocent voice. "Mum snogs her horses all the time!"

He earned himself a light-hearted slap from his mother.

Dad's eyes rolled to the ceiling. It was going to be one of *those* evenings! He put on his best diplomatic face and asked Mum if she needed any help in the kitchen. *Well manoeuvred Dad!* She hurried away to stop him messing things up.

"You are such a naughty girl," he said to me, smiling and shaking his head as he went after Mum.

"You look exhausted, Dez," said Jen. "Having trouble sleeping with someone else?" She winked.

"Really, Aunt Jennifer!"

"Jen!"

"Okay – Jen. But tell me, how on earth did you and Mum ever find anything in common?"

"Can't imagine what you mean." Jen stuck out her bottom lip and raised her eyebrows in mock surprise.

"Come on. How did you two end up as best friends? Mum's so up her own … donkey," I whispered.

"She wasn't always like that!" Jen seemed to be going into adult mode but at least she was off the subject of my PT.

"Sorry. I take it back. But it's so frustrating sometimes. I can't do anything right. I'm a huge disappointment to her. All I do is annoy her. I wonder why she tried so hard to have me in the first place!"

The sudden silence alerted me. I turned to see Mum framed in the kitchen doorway holding a plate of smoked salmon mousse, Dad behind her with the curly French toast that always breaks before you can spread anything on it.

Her face was ashen, her lips pressed tightly together in a thin ragged line.

"That looks delicious, Celeste." Dick, bless him, rose to the challenge. He stepped forward to relieve her of the plate so that she could duck back into the kitchen for the sliced lemon, giving her the chance to regain her composure.

I felt like a prize bitch! What was going on with me? I know teenage girls and their mothers often squabble but this was ridiculous. I didn't mean to be hurtful or rude. I just didn't have a talent for tact. I went into the kitchen and reached out to touch Mum's shoulder. My stomach churned with guilt – she was shaking under my hand.

"Sorry, Mum."

She turned to me, her face a twisted mix of emotions. She looked distraught; angry; resigned and despairing all at once.

"¡Yo no sé lo que usted desea de mí más!" The strange, furious words flew at me.

"Pardon?" I was worried. What was that gibberish? Had I tipped her over into a nervous breakdown? I turned to call Dad into the kitchen but she reached out and clutched my arms tightly.

"I don't know what you want from me any more," she gulped. "I try my best to provide you with a secure and loving home. But it's never enough for you. No," she said and held up her hand as I opened my mouth to deny her accusations. "I will not discuss this whilst we have visitors. Please take these through." Uncannily calm now, she handed me the saucer of sliced lemon and a pepper mill. She turned me around towards the door, shooing me out as though I was a little girl getting under her feet in the kitchen.

I was unnerved. *What happens now?* I thought. *Am I supposed to carry on regardless after that?*

Strange as it may seem the evening did pass in a relatively normal fashion. The food was, as always, excellent – although I couldn't taste it for the acid guilt in my mouth. The conversation seemed reasonably relaxed and Jeremy managed to keep on the right side of everyone for once. Had nobody else heard Mum's outburst? Maybe they thought that ignoring both that and my dreadful faux pas would mean that neither had really happened.

As they were leaving, Jen hugged me close once more and whispered, "Take it easy, Dez. Your mum really does love you, even if it sometimes feels otherwise. You're practically an adult now and she's scared of losing you. Call me if you need to talk." She kissed my cheek and hurried out into the night after Jeremy and Dick.

"Celeste, why don't you go up to bed? Dez and I will finish the tidying up. Go on, go get some rest."

Mum didn't seem to have the energy to protest. I watched her shoulders droop as she wearily climbed the stairs and I silently began to cry.

"Come on, sweetheart." Dad pulled me into his embrace and guided me into the kitchen.

I sat at the table while he made some hot chocolate the old-fashioned way – with hot milk, real cocoa, sugar and cinnamon. He'd forgotten my chocolate embargo too, but it didn't seem to matter any more.

"You don't need to say anything," he said, quietly. "I know there's something going on, but you don't have to tell me anything if you can't face it."

Even in speech Dad didn't often use abbreviations and it sounded strange when he did. That was when we knew he was struggling with his own emotions. I felt awful for putting him in this situation. He always tried to avoid getting in the middle of a fight between Mum and me. His diplomatic training didn't equip him to deal with domestic war-zones but he'd always do his best to bring his girls back together again.

"You know we're here for you, no matter what. Don't you?" he continued. "We all get carried away sometimes. Seth is a dependable young man. I'm sure you'll work it out between you."

Omigod! He thinks I'm pregnant!

26

CHAPTER 6

London: January 2060

"Are you sure?" Matt asked. "We can always dodge out early if you're feeling tired."

"My dear boy," Julia answered. "I may be eighty-six but I'm not ready to become a party-pooper yet. Go and dance with Laura. The poor girl looks like she could do with rescuing." She nodded towards her grandson's wife who was glaring wide-eyed in their direction. By her side a small rotund, slightly balding man was chatting animatedly but from Laura's expression his enthusiasm for the subject was certainly not catching. As Matt walked towards her, Laura's features softened with relief and Julia smiled contentedly. She'd been worried during Matt's transition period but he'd finally accepted the connection to his Psyche-Twin, as they were now called. The sadness of his mother's unexpected death ten years previously had been tempered by the support of his PT and the joy of his twin children. They and Laura were the loves of his life. Any tinge of jealousy that Matt was no longer hers alone was quickly overruled by Julia's pride in her little family.

"A splendid occasion, Baroness Simpson."

Her smile became fixed and cold as she recognised the voice but good manners forbade her to ignore the man.

"Good evening Benjamin. Yes. It's a wonderful event. An apt beginning to the Year of Telepathic Twinning."

"Full blown telepathy in two generations! Who would have guessed the ravages of war and disease could trigger such an advance?"

"Who indeed," Julia replied with just a hint of sarcasm. "However, not quite full blown, Benjamin. Merely a single connection with one's

Psyche-Twin, I believe. Although, that is enough to cope with as we've seen. Well, some of us…"

"Ah yes. I heard you'd lost your son to the transition. Tragic. Tragic." Trevalyn shook his head slowly but Julia was unable to accept the sympathetic gesture.

"Most families have suffered tragedy over the last forty years. However, yours seems to have managed a charmed existence. Tell me, Benjamin, what's your secret?" She looked intently into the face of the man she believed somehow responsible for her husband's death. A slight tightening of the skin around his eyes betrayed his anger at the barbed question but he quickly recovered his composure.

"If I knew that, my dear Julia, I could bottle it and make a fortune."

To add to the one you've already amassed, she thought.

CHAPTER 7

Ellingham: 26-28 July 2110

Being pregnant would be easier than being a freak!

Well that's what I thought at the time. I would've gladly had triplets rather than face up to what had – or rather, hadn't – happened. That late night conversation with Dad did give me some breathing space. Although I hadn't responded to his obvious suspicions, he didn't hassle me for an answer and he kept Mum at a distance, soothing her with his 'everything will be fine' routine.

Over the next few days we seemed to settle into some kind of normality. It was summer break from the Academy so I didn't have to find ways to hide my secret from my schoolmates. I needed to get my own reaction sorted out before I could handle anyone else's. My thank-you mails gave me the excuse to keep out of Mum's way for long periods and – much to her surprise – I decided to spring-clean my room. Strangely, it felt good to have a clear out. I'd never expected housework to be so satisfying! Sometimes, though, it threw up memories that I preferred to keep locked away – like the archived news report of Seth's mother's death stored in an old e-diary. I'd probably been looking at that entry and put the gadget away without closing it down properly for as soon as I drew the screen into the light it opened the news page automatically;

"MISSING WOMAN'S BODY FOUND IN ELLINGHAM LAKE."

The headline still seemed to scream from the page even though the audio was switched off.

Elizabeth had been so gentle and considerate with a loving personality that charmed everyone who knew her. Even Mum relaxed in her company. Seth's inherited his mother's beautiful auburn hair but whilst his curls can't be tamed, hers fell in wonderful rich waves of warm autumn tones. She was thirty-nine when she died although, with her slight agile figure, she'd regularly been mistaken for someone much younger. It was only when you looked closely that you'd see a few fine wrinkles between her eyebrows as though she spent most of her time deep in thought. But if you caught her attention she'd smile and her amber-coloured eyes would light up with golden flashes of pleasure to see you. I feel guilty for missing her so much. Poor Seth and his dad are the ones who have to survive without her in their lives anymore.

Occasionally, before the accident, Seth would complain that Elizabeth was in one of her moods but at the time I wasn't very sympathetic, having the experience of my own regularly tetchy mother. According to Seth, Elizabeth would become withdrawn and sometimes on the verge of tears but if Seth or his dad asked her what was upsetting her she'd shake her head and give a little, self-conscious laugh.

"Oh, was I off again?" she'd say. "Don't pay any attention. Just another sad novel I'm reading."

Once I saw her emotional reaction when the evening news reported the brutal death of a boy around our age. He'd gone missing near his home in Australia and a few days later his body was found in dingo territory.

"The poor boy." With tears streaming down her face, she grabbed Seth and hugged him as though she never wanted to let him go.

"Gerroff!" he grumbled. The eleven-year old Seth was trying to be all grown-up – he didn't want to be seen being hugged by his mum, even though I was the only witness. Now, of course, he'd love to be able to hug her and smell her delicate, flowery perfume. Only a year later she was gone and he'd never feel her warmth again.

Now tears were streaming down my face as I closed down the e-diary. I'd been about to ditch it, thinking that the re-charger had failed, and was surprised that it still worked after so long. I hadn't entered much into the memory so it wouldn't have been a great loss but, suddenly, I couldn't bear to throw it away. At that moment I knew I had to tell Seth the truth. He deserved an explanation for my rotten behaviour. I'd been avoiding him since that trip into town. Every time he'd come to the door I'd refused to go out, giving some inadequate excuse about Academy coursework, chores, not feeling well and so on. Even Mum had commented on my rudeness towards him!

I washed my face and raked a brush through my hair. Took a steadying breath and went in search of my best friend.

★★★

"Hello, Dez! How are you?" asked Samuel.

"Fine, thanks, Mr Wallis. Is Seth in, please?"

"SETH!" He turned to shout up the stairs but there was no reply. "Sorry, love. To be honest, I think he might've gone to play football with some of the lads. You two had a bit of a falling-out? Haven't seen you around lately."

"I … erm … sorry to have bothered you, Mr Wallis." I turned to go but he put his hand on my shoulder.

"Come on in, love. Look it's raining now so I'm sure Seth'll be back soon. You can keep me company 'til he gets home."

I couldn't think of a reasonable excuse to refuse without seeming rude, so I followed him into the cluttered kitchen. When Elizabeth was alive, the kitchen had always been a welcoming, cosy haven with fresh baking smells that made my mouth water. She'd greet us with a smile as Seth and I came in breathless after running home from Ellingham Juniors. Then, she'd hand us warm biscuits to dunk in our milk, reminding me not to spoil my appetite or she'd be in trouble with Mum. It was still difficult to sit in that room and not see her preparing a meal or appreciating the latest work of art that Seth had produced with dried pasta and glitter.

31

Despite their efforts, Seth and his dad now lived the bachelor life and the house was slowly losing Elizabeth's little touches. The kitchen, whilst clean, had accumulated a collection of mechanic's tools from the workshop. There was a pile of washing on the floor by the machine, waiting for the weekly catch-up session. Work-overalls currently hung behind the back door, contributing a new aroma from the ingrained engineering fluids. Elizabeth would've given her 'darling boys' a good telling-off, reminding them that the kitchen was for cooking, eating and enjoying company – not an extension of the workshop! She even refused to do her remote-bookkeeping in there, preferring to use a small desk in the corner of the spare bedroom rather than disturbing the heart of her home.

I'd spent most of my free time in that house and it felt natural to start sorting out the washing while Mr Wallis organised the drinks.

"It's not Seth's fault," I said, as I programmed the eco-drive colour-wash. "It's mine. I've come to say sorry and to explain why I've been so awful to him over the past few days."

"He'll be happy just to have you talking to each other again. He's been missing you."

"I've missed him, too. But I needed some time to sort something out on my own."

I thought I saw a similar look on Mr Wallis's face to the one Dad had the other night and before I could stop myself I blurted, "I'm not pregnant!"

"Oh!" He rocked back as though he'd been hit in the chest.

I blushed, realising that he hadn't even considered that option. And I'd just implied that Seth and I were having sex! We'd never even kissed properly. I groaned and buried my head in my hands.

"It's coming out all wrong," I moaned. "We've not ... You know ... But I think my dad thinks we have. And it's nothing like that anyway."

His cheeks were reddening and he was desperately tapping a teaspoon on the kitchen worktop. I clamped my mouth shut, finally realising that I was overstepping the mark. It was really Seth I should be talking to and, luckily, he came through the kitchen door breaking the awkward moment.

"Oh! Hi Dez." His tone sounded flat. Not the usual warm friendly greeting I was used to.

"Seth."

"Do you want a cuppa, son – tea, coffee?" Mr Wallis said with a large smile, obviously relieved to be able to change the subject.

"Thanks, Dad. Whatever's on the go." Seth turned back to me. "Sorry, didn't know you were coming round."

"Spur of the moment," I replied. "Can we talk?"

"It's my night for cooking," he said, and looked at his dad.

"Don't worry, son. I'll make a start on the supper. Do you want to stay, Dez?"

"No thanks, Mr Wallis. Mum'll be expecting me back."

"That's just a polite way to tell me you don't fancy my bangers and mash! And I think we can drop the formalities, eh? Call me Samuel – Mr Wallis makes me feel too old nowadays!" He grinned, showing that the earlier tension was forgotten.

Seth carried the steaming mugs into the sitting room, deposited them on the ceramic coffee table and turned towards me.

"What do you want to talk about?"

In my oversensitive state it sounded like Seth was being patronising. I struggled to stay calm but I couldn't resist a little sarcasm. "The weather! What do you think?"

"Sorry." He raised his hands in surrender. "Dez, I've been trying to give you some space but I just don't know what you want me to do any more."

His unwitting repetition of my mother's response of the other evening stung.

"Yeah, well it's complicated. I'm sorry I've not told you what's going on but I don't really know myself yet."

"Sometimes sharing the hurt helps. At least that's what you told me when I had it hard after Mum went. Sorry if it seems unsympathetic but I can't see what can have upset you so badly at the moment. It all started after your party. Is having a PT causing all this aggro?"

33

"That's just it. That's the problem. I haven't got a bloody PT!"

"Well Ms Thorogood said it might not be a full connection straight away if your PT's younger, remember?"

"It's not that. There's not even a feeling of someone waiting for their birthday. There's just nothing."

"How can you be so sure, Dez? Everyone takes to it differently. Some people find it really difficult to accept the sense of another mind. We talked about it in tele-prep."

"Yeah, I did listen in class you know. THERE'S NOTHING THERE! Stop making me say it over and over."

I was crying now and couldn't understand why Seth didn't believe me. The one person I thought I could trust had let me down yet again. After disappearing at my party and keeping his PT experience to himself, he was now trying to tell me I didn't even know what was going on in my own head! I ran out of the house into the pouring rain neither knowing nor caring where I was going.

Damn Seth. Damn my stupid silent PT. Damn the whole bloody world!

CHAPTER 8

Ellingham: 28/29 July 2110

What? What's going on?

"Dez. Dez, love. Can you hear me? It's Samuel. Seth, keep the rain off her as best you can. I'll call for the medics."

I struggled to open my eyes. My mouth tasted foul; a mixture of blood, tears and gritty soil. My clothes were soaked and I felt chilled to the bone. Despite the warmth of Seth's jacket now covering me I was shivering uncontrollably. I let myself drift back into oblivion.

The next time I woke I couldn't understand where I was. I closed my eyes against the harsh, bright lights. They weren't anything like the subtle glow of my own room. There was a bleeping noise in the background and distant voices. I tried opening my eyes again. The room was pristine white – clinical. One of the walls and the adjacent door were made entirely from opaque glass. A delicate floral fragrance stirred from the crisp sheet as I shifted. I noticed the raised sides of the narrow bed and the full length sensor screen hovering above me.

Oh God! Why am I in hospital?

"Hey …" I tried to call out, but my throat was so dry that I couldn't speak above a whisper and I felt the sharp pain from a split lip.

I tried to sit up but before I could bang my head against the lowered sensor, the door opened and Mum and Dad came in, each holding a cup of steaming coffee.

"See! I told you we shouldn't have gone together for the drinks."

"It's all right Celeste. We were only away for a minute or two." He turned to me, "How are you, sweetheart?"

"I …" I pointed to my throat.

"Just a moment." He left the room. The glass wall and door cleared and the sensor screen lifted towards the ceiling. A male nurse waved at me from the staff station at the centre of the ward. He spoke briefly to Dad, pointing at the monitors and nodding.

"Nurse Bridges says you're doing fine," said Dad, as he stepped back into my room. His relief was obvious from his emotional tone. He helped me to sit up. "Here you go." His hand shook slightly as he poured some chilled water from a Kool-Jug and passed me the half-filled cup. "Just sip it. That's better."

"You gave us such a scare! What on earth were you doing down by the lake? Poor Mr Wallis – as if he doesn't have enough bad memories about that place," Mum said. She started plumping up the pillows and fussing around me.

I felt too tired to retaliate.

"Where's Seth?" I asked, looking to Dad for the answer.

"He's waiting in the family room with his father. Do you want to see them?"

"Yes, please."

Mum looked disapproving but resisted commenting. She finished smoothing the sheet and went to sit on the single chair in the corner of the room. We'd not made up properly since the tea-party row but why couldn't she just give me a hug and tell me everything was going to be all right? I struggled not to cry. After the previous evening, I wasn't sure I had any tears left anyway.

Beyond the glass wall I saw Dad with Seth and Samuel, all deep in conversation as they walked together. Seth and his dad looked worried and both of them had muddy marks on their trousers. Seth's hair was wilder than ever and he had pale streaks through the dirt on his face as though he'd been crying. As I watched them approach my room I suddenly realised that Seth had grown taller than his dad. They hesitated by the door, uncertain of their welcome. Dad gently pushed them in and offered his hand to Mum, signalling that he wanted her to leave with him. She frowned but followed his lead.

"Humph," Samuel coughed in embarrassment. "How are you feeling now, Dez?"

"Bit stupid actually, Mr Wallis. And I'm really very sorry to have put you to so much trouble."

"Samuel, remember? Don't fret, love. Just so long as you're okay, that's all that matters. I'll leave you to it, then," he said. He patted my hand and left to join my parents.

Seth's eyes were brimming with tears. I hadn't seen him so upset since Elizabeth had died. Then it hit me – what Mum had said about me being found by the lake.

"I'm so sorry Seth. I ran out and didn't even consider where I was going. I'd never have put you through that if I'd realised what would happen. You know that, don't you?"

He leaned towards me and we held each other tightly as waves of grief swept over us. When our joint sobbing finally subsided to an occasional shudder I fell back onto my pillow and Seth drew the chair up to the bedside.

"I'm sorry I didn't listen properly earlier, Dez. Please don't try to do anything like that again, I was so scared and it was all my fault."

"No, Seth. I've just told you, I wasn't thinking straight. I needed to get away. It was all too much and you didn't understand what I was saying. I felt let down. Alone. Angry. I still don't know what I'm going to do about this bloody PT thing. How am I going to tell the 'rents?"

"There's no need." He dropped his gaze, fidgeting nervously. "They already know. Dad overheard you shouting about it and he was worried that's what made you want to … When your 'rents arrived at the hospital your mum started giving me the third degree and Dad let slip that it wasn't anything I'd done. You can guess the rest." He dropped his head in his hands.

I felt an overwhelming relief. "Thank you!"

"What?" He straightened up and looked at me in surprise.

"Oh, I don't know, it just feels like a big lump's been taken out of my chest. I could hardly breathe for the fear of telling them. Now I don't have to!"

We started laughing, dissolved into hysterics and ended up hugging again. It felt nice.

"Is it all right to come in?" said Dad from the doorway.

"Yes. Come in." I tried to stifle the giggles. "We're good."

"*That* is debatable!" He smiled, happy to see me laughing for the first time since my party.

"You know what I mean," I said.

"Seriously now, Dez. Do you remember what you were doing by the lake?" He sat on the bed and took my hand.

"Not everything. But I didn't intend to do myself in, honestly." From the corner of my eye I saw Seth frown so I quickly moved on. "I remember running in the rain. I hadn't really set out to go anywhere in particular. I just needed to let off steam, I suppose."

"Excuse me, Mr Hanson?"

"Yes, Seth?"

"It may be that Dez slipped by accident. The grass and mud were all churned up down the banking near where we found her. Does that make sense, Dez?"

"Actually, yes … the grass was slippery with the rain … that'd explain the bruised feeling all over wouldn't it? Surely if I'd meant to kill myself …" Seth winced again. "I'd've just gone straight into the lake."

"Excuse me," Seth said in a choked-up voice and he rushed out of the door.

"That boy thinks the world of you. He wouldn't leave your side until your mother literally dragged him into the family room." Dad's normally calm manner slipped and his eyes glistened.

I couldn't bear to see him on the verge of tears. "I'd've liked to have seen that," I said.

It did the trick and he smiled at the memory. "Yes, it was something to behold – my little Celeste manhandling a resistant young man who's a good six inches taller. Even Samuel had to grin at that."

I tried to stifle a yawn.

"I think you have had enough for now, young lady. You get some rest and we shall come back in the morning." He was in control again – the cultured speech was back.

I looked at his watch before he removed his hand from mine. Two o'clock – the early hours of Tuesday morning!

"Sorry, Dad," I murmured. "I didn't mean to upset you or Mum."

"Don't worry, sweetheart. We can sort everything out tomorrow."

As the duty nurse lowered the lighting in my room I felt myself slipping into the easiest sleep I'd had since my Sixteenth-Eve Party.

★★★

When I woke again the morning was bright and sunny. All the clouds had rained themselves out overnight and it was the start of a beautiful summer's day. I looked in the cupboard, hoping to find my clothes but they weren't there.

Oh no, they can't expect me to wander around in this flimsy disposable gown!

I pressed the call button and saw one of the nurses look towards my room and then at the central monitors. She briefly raised her hand but carried on with whatever she was doing. I checked to make sure the gown was covering all it should then marched out to the staff station.

"Excuse me," I said. "When will my parents be here to take me home?"

The woman's response was cross and impatient. "Your parents will be here later this morning when visiting hours start at ten-thirty. But we don't have any discharge papers for you today so they'll have to leave for the lunch period and any further visits will be from two-thirty to five and seven to nine. Now back to bed, like a good girl."

My mouth fell open and I stepped back as though I'd been slapped.

What does she mean no discharge papers? Who's she calling a good girl?

Because I had no choice I returned to my room but I'd be damned if I was getting back into bed. I sat on the solitary chair, fuming at the indignity of being treated like a child. Later I discovered that Nurse Marion took a dim view of anybody who was, in her words, "one of those selfish individuals who take their own lives without any consideration for others". I think she enjoyed telling me I couldn't go home – miserable cow!

Ten-thirty finally arrived and visitors brought their flowers, fruit and chocolates to their relatives and friends. As they came through the arched doorway, each visitor was sprayed with the clinical dry disinfectant used to keep the bugs out of hospitals. I stood by my door anxiously waiting for sight of Mum and Dad. Maybe Seth would come again.

A few minutes later Dad appeared at the ward entrance. He was followed, not by Mum, but by Ms Thorogood! What was she doing here? I thought she'd be away making the most of the long summer break from the Academy. I would've run up to Dad for a hug if I hadn't been wearing that stupid hospital gown. And Ms Thorogood being there was a bit discouraging too.

"Hello Dez," she said brightly as they reached my room.

"Hello Ms Thorogood," I answered, a little warily.

"Morning sweetheart. Did you sleep well?"

"Yes thanks. Dad. Best night in a while."

There was an awkward pause.

"Ms Thorogood has come in to talk to you about the PT problem, Dez."

"Oh." *Do I take it the whole world knows?*

As if reading my mind – *good trick under the circumstances!* – Ms Thorogood said, "Don't worry Dez. It's not public knowledge. Your father contacted me this morning because of my teaching sessions. He thought I might've come across this phenomenon before."

"Have you?"

"Actually, no. But I have a friend who has and he's had some success in helping those people come to terms with it."

"Come to terms with it? That's it? There's no cure? No switch or drug or anything that can turn it on?" I was beginning to pace around, getting agitated. Surely after having perfected the cancer

40

and HIV vaccines the medical profession could do something for a dodgy PT connection? "You're telling me I'm an Empty freak and I've just got to get used to it?"

Dad raised his hands. "Calm down, Dez. We have to get to grips with this so that we can see a way through."

"What do you mean 'we'? You haven't got a problem with your PT, have you? Claude lets you discuss everything about him. He's not gone into hiding has he?"

The nurses at the staff station were beginning to take notice and one started heading towards my room. Dad waved and shook his head, smiling as if to reassure them that it was all okay in Room 4. But it wasn't. I'd thought that now this was out in the open it could be fixed – not just accepted as the way things were going to be forever.

"Dez, please let me finish," said Ms Thorogood. "We all have your best interests at heart. We're just talking about worst-case scenario – you have to be prepared in case your particular PT connection never happens. It's rare but it's not the end of the world. You'll still be a fully functioning human being."

"How can I be fully functioning if half my brain doesn't work?"

She carried on without responding to the exaggeration. "My friend is a respected psychotherapist and he specialises in the use of hypnotherapy. He really can help you, Dez, if you're prepared to give it a try."

Ms Thorogood and my weary father looked at me expectantly.

"Swinging a watch and making me cluck like a chicken isn't going to find my PT connection is it?"

"Dez, you are being rude now." Dad rarely lost his temper with me. I didn't often give him cause but I was too worked up to hear the warning tone of his voice.

"Come on Dad. You've said yourself they're a load of con artists. In it for the fame and fortune of Saturday night interactive holo-viewing!"

Ms Thorogood looked at me with a mixture of understanding and frustration. "I assure you that Alvin is not a charlatan. He dislikes the entertainment hypnotists too. Hypnotherapy's a trusted and accepted science. It helps you to tap into the strength from your subconscious."

Even now I don't know why, but at that point I lost it. Big time!

"Don't you think I'VE GOT ENOUGH PROBLEMS WITHOUT SOMEONE ELSE MESSING IN MY HEAD!"

As my yelling escalated, I slapped my hands with increasing ferocity against the sides of my head. I didn't appreciate the irony – the problem was that I really *did* want someone else in there. The next thing I knew I was being held down by two orderlies while 'Nasty Nurse Marion' sprayed something up my nose.

"Is that really necessary?" I heard Dad ask through my rage.

"It's the quickest way for this sedative to be absorbed," she explained curtly.

Bet she's enjoying this!

I thrashed about a moment longer until the drug took effect then I lay still, staring at the white ceiling, breathing heavily and letting silent tears dribble into my ears.

I just want to go home.

"I'll see your friend," I whispered, knowing this was the only way to get there.

Ms Thorogood gently patted my shoulder and smiled. "I'll see you soon, Dez. Take care."

As she left Dad came up to the bedside. His face was drawn, his eyes red-rimmed and he looked like he'd aged ten years in two days.

"Dez, sweetheart, you must try to calm down. It breaks my heart to see you like this."

"Why didn't Mum come?"

"She thought it might be too much for you to have all of us visiting together. She's finding it hard to deal with but ..."

"Typical! How hard does she think it is for me? But, it's all about her as usual." Even though my lips stung and my mouth felt like it was full of cotton wool I could still make cutting comments.

"Desirée. That is enough. I will not listen to you talking about your mother in that tone. If you had let me finish I was about to say that she is intending to come in later."

Desirée – that showed I'd really gone too far this time. Would it never stop – this vicious cycle of hurting the ones I loved and hating myself for doing it?

Nurse Marion returned, hovering by the door with another dose of dopey juice. Dad took the hint. He leaned over to kiss my forehead and quietly told me that both he and Mum loved me more than I thought.

The hot, guilty tears continued to flow and as I drifted into a drugged sleep I mourned the loss of my ordinary life. I still wanted to be the over-indulged only child who was the apple of her Daddy's eye. But how long would his patience last if I continued to behave like a spoilt brat?

I've let you down again, haven't I?

CHAPTER 9

London: May 2072

"The business world was shocked today by the untimely death of Jacob Trevalyn. Early indications are that he suffered a massive heart attack during yesterday evening whilst working alone at the Trevalyn Corporation Head Office."

"Yada, yada, yada." Sebastian Trevalyn swiped his hand over the screen to close the news programme. "Stupid idiot!" He was referring to his brother's self-testing of the enhancement drug he'd devised.

Jacob's life-long heart condition had been a family secret and one which their father, Benjamin, was particularly disappointed about. The Trevalyns were infallible as far as Benjamin was concerned and his sons had been nurtured, tutored and moulded into the same self-belief. Unfortunately for Jacob, Mother Nature believed otherwise.

Sebastian had great plans for the Trevalyn Corporation and once the old man was gone he'd have free rein to put them in place – at least until young Victor came of age. He'd have to ensure his nephew would follow the path that 'Uncle Sebastian' laid out for him.

Wiltshire: August 2072

Matt held his grandmother's hand and felt the arthritic bones beneath the paper dry skin. He wanted to hold on tightly but was afraid that it would bring more pain so he gently stroked the back of that beloved hand hoping that she could still sense his presence and the deep love he felt for her.

"Look Dad." Eddie waved a card he'd plucked from Julia's dresser.

"She got her telegram from Buck House just like she said she would. It's even got a personal message from Wills."

Matt chuckled at his son's apparent disrespect. Over the years Baroness Julia Simpson had developed a strong relationship with the royals and, when talking to her family about him, she occasionally lapsed into using the King's pet name.

"Oh, let me see." Jade grabbed her twin-brother's arm to look at the message.

"Shush, you two," their mother said. "You'll disturb Granny Julia."

"It's alright, Laura. Gran will enjoy their chatter." Matt smiled at his wife and gestured for her to sit by him.

"Charles is still available," Julia whispered.

"Gran?" Matt started at the unexpected comment. Julia had been sleeping so soundly that he'd thought she was slipping away already.

"William's grandson – Charles. Jade could do worse." Julia's eyes, though pale and watery held a brief flash of mischief.

The family laughed and gathered around the bed, each of them keen to share the precious little time that Julia had left. Soon the old lady began to tire. Eddie and Jade kissed their great-grandmother and promised to fulfil her wishes that they would follow their dreams. They held tightly to each other's hand as they slipped out of the room. Laura leaned back in her chair to give Matt and Julia the privacy to say their goodbye, but she kept her hand on her husband's back to reassure him he would not be alone.

"I'm sorry Matt, I couldn't finish it."

"What are you talking about Gran?"

"There's a file in my safe. It's not complete yet. You'll have to carry on. It's been so hard to find anything." Julia's breathing became laboured and she frowned with the effort of continuing. "Keep looking, Matthew. Promise you'll keep looking."

Matt had no idea what Julia wanted him to look for but he would have promised her the moon if it helped. "Of course I will," he said, tears now spilling onto his pristine shirt.

Julia smiled then shuddered as her final breath released her troubled spirit at last.

"I can't see what she was looking for." Matt threw the file on to the table in disgust. The printed news cuttings spilled out. "She was obsessed with the damned Trevalyn family. It's all stuff about them and their business dealings. But I can't see anything untoward."

Jade gave her father a comforting hug. "Don't fret, Dad. Granny hadn't managed to solve it in all those years so it's bound to take time for us to work it out. Let me see."

Her father was right, Jade couldn't see what Granny Julia had been searching for either. All the information in the file was from the public domain so it was hardly the stuff of thriller novels but she knew that her great-grandmother wouldn't have wasted her time on something unless she felt it was absolutely necessary.

"Did Granny Julia leave any other documents?" Jade asked.

"Tons," sighed Matt, gesturing towards several old fashioned trunks in the corner of his grandmother's office. "Knock yourself out." He plucked his jacket from the coat stand then tossed a set of keys towards Jade. "I've got a meeting with Gran's solicitor. Will you be home later?"

She deftly caught the keys mid-air. "Yes, I'll be in for supper," she answered, turning towards the trunks with the eagerness of a child about to open her birthday presents. Little did she realise the ultimate cost of that curiosity.

CHAPTER 10

Ellingham Clinic: 30 July 2110

Okay. New day, fresh start. Best behaviour!

My head was still fuzzy. Having been sedated most of the previous day, I wasn't sure whether Mum had actually been to see me. Dreams and reality merged in my memory.

I was now propped up in the hospital bed, still being monitored by the sensor screen – presumably in case they felt I needed another dose of the dopey juice – and trying to put on a happy face for my visitors. It wasn't easy.

"Dez, this is Alvin Grey, the friend that I was talking to you about yesterday. Alvin, this is Dez Hanson." Ms Thorogood introduced us to each other and the handsome black guy held out his hand to me.

"Pleased to meet you Dez – may I call you Dez?" he said.

"Yes, that's fine. Nice to meet you, too," I said, although the circumstances weren't particularly nice. And I would've liked at least to have been dressed in proper clothes to meet such a good-looking bloke, with his sexy retro-specs and stylish clothes. He looked a bit like that actor from way back, the one I drooled over when the classics were being run at the antiquated I-Max, Denzel Washington, yeah, that was him – yum! Grey's handshake was firm, dry and pleasantly cool and his light, spicy cologne lingered as he withdrew to stand at the end of the bed.

Careful, Dez. Do you really want him delving into your darkest secrets?

My flirty thoughts must have given me a flush as Dad commented that I was looking less peaky this morning! I quickly reached for my water and hid behind the cup until I felt more composed.

"Don't worry, Dez. It's normal to feel nervous about hypnotherapy if you haven't experienced it before," said Alvin. "I'll explain the procedure so that you understand what to expect and you can ask about anything you feel unsure or uncomfortable about, okay?"

"Yes. Thank you, Mr Grey."

"To start with you can call me Alvin!" He smiled.

Ooh, what gorgeous white teeth – stop it, Dez!

Ms Thorogood was smiling too. "Alvin, put your charm away or she'll never be able to concentrate." Was I *that* transparent? But the comment broke the tense atmosphere that had lingered since yesterday's episode and I was grateful for the humour.

Dad also seemed to relax a little and offered to get refreshments for everyone. I think it was an excuse for him to give me some privacy with the therapist, knowing that Ms Thorogood was there as a chaperone. He probably wasn't totally convinced that hypnotherapy was going to work but he wouldn't jeopardise anything that might help me.

"Let's start by dispelling some of the myths. Despite what you may have picked up from the media about hypnosis, I can't make you do anything you don't want to do – so, no clucking like a chicken!" He glanced at Ms Thorogood, who winked at me. I blushed again.

"Also," he continued, "even if you sense your mind wandering, you'll be fully aware of your surroundings so you can come back to full consciousness whenever you feel the need. Any questions so far?"

"No. . ," I said tentatively.

He smiled, realising I still needed convincing.

"Hypnotherapy helps you to relax. It closes out the interference of everyday life and allows you to reach a focussed state of concentration. Whilst you're in this trance-like condition I'll use suggestion to modify your customary behaviours, feelings and thoughts."

"You mean, you can change who I am?"

"No, no. The suggestions can only be accepted if you're willing to act on them. For example, if someone wanted to stop biting their nails I wouldn't simply tell them that they must stop biting their nails. The suggestion might be that they imagine a near future when they have beautiful, long, unbitten nails. In some cases, if there is a deep rooted problem for the stress that causes the habit, this must be dealt with first."

I looked down at my ragged fingernails and sore cuticles. I couldn't remember a time when I didn't bite my nails but I was rarely aware when I was actually doing it! Maybe he could help me with that too.

"What do you think is stopping me connecting with my PT?" I asked.

"That's going to take some time to work out. Everyone is unique – and that's not just a cliché. My subconscious deals with things differently from the way yours does. But there are ways to help it behave more uniformly and healthily. Sometimes it's about allowing yourself to be a little selfish, becoming more confident and increasing your self-esteem. Many people feel guilty for wanting those attributes."

I was beginning to feel tearful. He was touching on a nerve – outwardly, I was generally seen as brash, confident, and always game for anything. Inside I was desperate for everyone to like me and, to achieve that, I was willing to make a fool of myself, believing laughter was evidence of acceptance. Lacking a PT had brought the little self-esteem I'd had to an all-time low.

"Do you think you can help me connect then?" I asked, quietly.

"Again, it'll depend on what we discover during our sessions, Dez. I can't make promises that I might not be able to keep. But I'll do my best – *that* I can promise."

Dad's timing was impeccable – or had he been hovering outside the door waiting for a suitable point to bring the drinks in?

"Here we are," he said, handing round the cups. "Sorry I was a while. I had a problem finding a machine that had sweeteners."

"You shouldn't have worried about those," exclaimed Ms Thorogood. "I could have managed without."

"Nonsense. It was no trouble at all. How do you feel about Mr Grey helping you with your PT dilemma, sweetheart?" he asked me brightly, as though it really was up to me to make the decision.

"I'll give it a go. Anything's worth a try, I suppose."

"Dez. You really must want to do this for it to have any chance of success," said Alvin. "It's no good unless you're committed to the therapy."

"Sorry. I didn't mean to be rude, Mr Grey."

"Alvin – remember? Don't worry, Dez. I'm not offended, just worried that you might be damaging your chances if you don't believe in the process. I once treated a woman who told me the sessions weren't helping her. I couldn't understand why. It wasn't a particularly difficult condition to treat. At the third appointment she asked when I was going to hypnotise her. When I asked her what she meant she said I hadn't done it because I hadn't been using a swinging crystal pendant! Although it was against everything I know about hypnotherapy I performed this little ritual for her and … bingo… the treatment worked. Previously, she hadn't believed anything was happening, so it didn't, but once she'd had her 'proper' session it all fell into place." He was chuckling ruefully and shaking his head at the memory.

"Okay," I said. "I'm up for it – one hundred percent!"

Alvin and Ms Thorogood finished their drinks and made arrangements to see me again the following day – either in the clinic or at home as we weren't sure whether I could be discharged yet. When they'd left I delivered my well-rehearsed plea.

"Dad, please let me come home. I'm really sorry for what happened yesterday. It's just that I've never been in hospital before. I was frightened and angry that you'd left me here. I know it was necessary, but I'm fine now, honestly. And I'll do whatever it takes to stay fine. Please?" I could see him wavering, time for the final push. "I miss Mum." As I said it I realised I actually meant it and genuine tears came again.

"All right, sweetheart. I'll see what I can do. Don't get upset again." I could hear the catch in his voice as he held me to his broad, warm chest. His cologne was some ancient woody fragrance and it mixed with the just-washed scent of his shirt. The familiar homely odours made me cling to him harder until the panic of being left in the hospital passed. My Dad, my hero.

★★★

While Dad was convincing the medical staff that I could be trusted not to throw myself under the ten-twenty to Euston I tried to keep my fingernails away from my mouth.

"What's the matter?"

I glanced up to find Seth looking at me from the doorway.

"What do you mean?"

"You were staring at your hands with such a frown on your face. What's up?"

"I'm gonna stop biting my nails!" I declared.

"Oh. Right." Seth seemed uncertain how to react to my suddenly light-hearted mood.

I patted the bed. The sensors and side panels had been retracted for the time being and, although it was against hospital policy for visitors to sit on the bed, I felt the need to flout a rule or two. I was reasonably safe – Nurse Bridges was on duty and he was much more sympathetic than Marion.

"Come on. Tell me what's going on out in the big wide world, then."

Just as Seth was about to sit down, Dad came to the doorway. Seth leapt up again as though the bed was filled with therma-coals! I chuckled to see his face colouring up – Mum never allowed him into my room at home and now my dad had caught him about to sit on my bed.

"Don't mind me, Seth. I was just coming to tell Dez that I have to go and collect some clothes for her. She can come home today!"

Dad blew me a kiss as he almost skipped through the ward towards the exit. I hadn't realised how hard it was for him to deal with all this until I saw how pleased he was that I could leave.

Seth playfully slapped my arm.

"Traitor," he said. "You could've warned me he was coming in."

51

"Sorry," I giggled. "But you did look funny – all rabbit-in-headlights! Anyway, what've you brought?" I pointed to the packet that he was holding close to his chest.

He looked at it as though he'd forgotten he had it then slowly, almost shyly, he handed the parcel to me. His expression was serious, all traces of our earlier laughter gone.

"This must have fallen out of your pocket as you ran out of our house the other evening."

I looked inside the bag. My old e-diary! As the power cell charged under the ward lights the screen lit up on the news report about Elizabeth.

"Thanks," I said. "I'd forgotten all about that. It's what made me come over that night. I needed to tell you everything – why I've been such a rotten mate recently. Thinking about your mum reminded me to take care of our friendship."

"Seeing it like that was a bit weird." He gestured towards the e-diary screen.

"Sorry. I didn't mean to drag up bad memories."

"No, it's not that," he said. "It's just … I found this soon after Mum's funeral." He handed me a small cloth wallet from his back pocket. "I thought, after the other night, it might help you. Dunno if you'll understand it any more than I do but, together, we might work it out."

Inside the wallet was a '*Handi*' – a compact rigid version of my e-diary. The cover was decorated with a marble-effect pattern and the back panel was engraved:

To my darling Lizzy,
For all your memoirs and memories.
Hope they always include me! Yours forever, Sam xx

I looked up at Seth and tried to pass the *Handi* back to him. "I can't, it's private."

"Please," he whispered.

I could see he was struggling to keep himself together so I fought my own emotions and powered-up the *Handi*, feeling like I was walking over Elizabeth's grave.

Using the stylus to choose the appropriate icon, I opened the journal to see Elizabeth's fine calligraphy on the first page:

Journal - Elizabeth Wallis
1/1/2105 – 26/10/2106
So sorry. I love you, my darling boys.

"She liked to use a stylus to write – remember?" said Seth. "She only used the predictive key-screen when she was in a hurry. She must've been in a hurry the night she died." He pointed at the typical computer font that made up the second half of the entry.

I knew I wouldn't have time to read the journal thoroughly before Dad got back. To get an impression of the contents, I skimmed my finger across the screen and quickly glanced at the pages. I saw that Elizabeth's normally exquisite handwriting became untidy in the last quarter, or so, of the journal. Several news reports had been cut from the InfoNet and pasted onto the pages.

"Keep it for now," Seth said. "Take it home and read through it. Then we can talk about it."

"Are you sure? It feels intrusive. Won't your dad mind?"

"Dad doesn't know about it. Don't you see, he never can?" He brought up the title page again: 'So sorry'.

"Oh." I realised what he meant and why he'd thought it might help me. "*No-o*. That could mean anything, she may've felt sorry about something but after the accident you could've overlooked it." Even to my own ears it sounded hollow. "Anyway, I keep telling you, I wasn't trying to…" I tapered off, knowing as I said it that I'd confirmed his fears – he was convinced that his mother had killed herself and he suspected that, in my blind panic, I'd almost followed the same path.

Oh, Seth. When will you believe me?

CHAPTER 11

Ellingham: 30/31 July 2110

Please let Mum be happy to see me!

Dad opened the front door and called out, "We're home!"

He turned towards me and gestured for me to go into the house first. I hesitated. It felt strange to stand on the doorstep, unsure of the welcome that waited for me. Only two days since I'd gone over to visit Seth but it seemed like a lifetime. So much had changed in such a short space of time. My non-connection with a Psyche-Twin was now family knowledge. My temper tantrum and hospitalisation were swiftly becoming old news in the neighbourhood – thankfully! And my best friend had shared his deepest, darkest secret – that he believed his mother had committed suicide and that the reason why was hidden in her journal. I had so much to process and I'd been left pretty much on my own to deal with it.

"Come on, sweetheart," said Dad. "Let's get you inside and have a nice cup of tea."

At that moment, Mum appeared at the end of the hall, wiping her hands on an old-fashioned apron. The smell of home-baked ginger biscuits made my mouth water – my favourites, especially when she put pieces of crystallised ginger in them. She paused, as if she was as nervous as I was, then she smiled.

"Welcome home, Dez." I could see her struggle with my abbreviated name and I appreciated her effort.

"Thanks, Mum." I almost ran down the hall into her embrace. It was a brittle, fragile hug. It felt like she would break if I held her too tightly, but it was surprisingly good to be close to her again. For a moment I felt her tremble as she held herself in check and I couldn't work out whether it was disappointment about my lack of a PT connection or relief that I was safely home again that made her so emotional. I tried to believe it was the latter, but the doubts were there. The hug quickly became awkward and we stepped back from each other. Dad was cheerfully oblivious to the undertones and smiled at the mother and daughter reunion.

"Celeste, you spoil us with those delicious biscuits of yours," he said, rubbing his hands together in anticipation. He was making loud sniffing noises and he gave her a swift kiss on the cheek as he walked past her to the kitchen. "Mmm. 'Good sniffs', as my old grandpa used to say."

Mum's face softened at both the compliment and Dad's chirpy behaviour. Sometimes I got a glimpse of the woman he'd fallen in love with and I wished she could surface more often or – even better – permanently. When she wasn't frowning or fretting Mum was a real stunner, with perfectly defined cheekbones; a delicate, slightly pointed chin; large dark eyes; and a sweet snub little nose. She must have had hordes of boys after her in her youth. I glanced at the photo-shots along the wall. The older ones showed her laughing and happy – all well before I was born. Had I made her change so much? Was I such a terrible child? I swallowed my thoughts, not wanting to fall into another round of resentful feelings. She was making an effort – baking my favourite treats and calling me Dez – the least I could do was meet her half way.

"You've got a spot of flour," I said and used a corner of her apron to clear the smudge from her still-smooth cheek.

"Thank you, dear." And for that instant she held me in a loving gaze that I wished would last forever. The moment passed as she turned to stop Dad demolishing the entire batch of baking. "Jonathan, don't eat all those biscuits. Remember we have visitors tomorrow."

After our tea and biscuits (*"Only two for now, if you don't mind, Jonathan!"*) I felt a sudden wave of exhaustion. It was early evening but I decided I'd head off to bed before the fragile truce between us was broken.

"Are you sure you don't want anything for dinner?"

"No thanks, Mum. The biscuits were enough for now."

"I can bring up a tray for you later. If you like?"

"I'll probably sleep through. But I'll come down if I need anything. Don't worry."

I just wanted to get to my room and take a deep, settling breath. The tension was mounting already. We hadn't talked about what had happened the other night or about my lack of a PT. Did they think that by not saying anything it would go away? Maybe I was jumping the gun. Maybe they've been looking for the right opportunity to broach the subject. Maybe they were waiting for the outcome of my sessions with the hypnotherapist. But now I understood the phrase 'an elephant in the room' – something huge that nobody wants to acknowledge! *Ah, well, I'll just take my elephant to bed, then.*

★★★

I woke early the next morning and, for once, was keen to get out of bed. I was ravenously hungry and desperate for a long, hot shower – the showers had been lukewarm and auto-restricted to three minutes in the clinic, hardly time to get wet never mind wash my hair! Even getting the shampoo in my eyes didn't bother me this morning. I was home and the gorgeous Mr Grey – ahem, Alvin – was coming to sort me out. *Rephrase* – sort out my PT troubles. *Talk about schoolgirl crush!* How was I going to cope with his lusciousness when he got control over my brain? *Hang on the shower's throwing a thermo wobbly – no it's just me having a hot flush. Calm down Dez!*

As if being sixteen wasn't hard enough with all the raging hormones, I now had a non-existent PT and a budding crush on the guy who was supposed to help me find myself. I turned the water to cold, both to close my pores and to cool my flirtatious thoughts. As I stepped out of the shower I knew it was stupid even to consider the therapist in those terms. It was never going to happen. Besides the ethical minefield of patient/practitioner relationship, he was way too old for me anyway! I grinned at my reflection in the *Stay-Clear* mirror and started to detangle my hair. Seth would find all this hilarious. He'd soon put me straight. But just the thought of him made me stop the hairbrush in mid-stroke. My juvenile fantasies about Alvin Grey/Denzel Washington evaporated and something rigid settled in my chest. *Now what? Oh, yeah.* Things were changing between Seth and me now. We had to deal with the serious stuff about his mum and his belief that she – and I – had wanted to die! Trivial, jokey stuff wasn't likely to be on the agenda now. My good mood disappeared along with the fantasies and the resident lump in my chest gave a triumphant twist, choking a couple of dry sobs from me before I got it under control again.

"Dez, sweetheart. Are you all right?" Dad called, as he passed the bathroom door on his way downstairs.

"Yeah. I'm good. Be out in a min."

I quickly pulled my still-damp hair into a loose ponytail, picked up the used towels, hung them over the rail, and opened the window to dispel the lingering steam.

"The solar panels should manage more hot water in an hour or so!" Dad teased, as I hungrily started on my breakfast.

"Sorry," I mumbled around a mouthful of granola. "Just needed to wash away the clinic."

"I was only joking, sweetheart." His brows furrowed as though he was worried that I was going to go off on one again.

Well, I suppose I'll have to get used to that now. I thought. "S'okay, Dad. I know."

His forehead relaxed with obvious relief.

"What time are Ms Thorogood and Alvin coming?" I asked.

"Mr Grey, dear," said Mum.

"He told me to call him Alvin."

"Oh. Well, I suppose if he said so it must be all right then. But I must say it seems rather over-familiar to me."

"Mum. You can be so old fashioned sometimes." I surprised both of us by giving her shoulder a quick squeeze as I walked behind her towards the dishwasher.

57

Sitting back at the kitchen table I asked again, "So what time are they coming then?"

"We settled on ten-thirty. Remember?" Dad answered.

"I knew it was this morning but forgot the time, that's all." I didn't want to admit that Seth's visit had sent everything else straight out of my head. I'd kept his mother's *Handi* out of sight. I instinctively knew that he wanted it to be our secret for now. Seth was convinced his mother's reputation was at risk if it became public knowledge that she'd committed suicide. People could be so narrow-minded. Surely they realised that if you'd got to the point of wanting to end your life you weren't going to be thinking straight. Ms Thorogood had told us that even your PT couldn't overrule your deepest feelings. But what had made Elizabeth so despairing of her life that she felt she had to end it? Whatever it was, it must've been awful – especially as she was adored so openly by her family and friends. It couldn't have been easy to leave her beloved Samuel and Seth behind.

"Dez, sweetheart. Dez? Are you listening?" Dad's voice finally got through my morbid thoughts.

"Mm? Sorry, Dad. What were you saying?"

"I was asking you if you wanted one of us to sit in on your session with Mr Grey?"

"Oh, I'm not sure. No offence, but I'm going to find it hard enough to concentrate on the whole hypnotic trance thing. Anyway, isn't Ms Thorogood coming along? She'll be there to keep an eye on me."

"You're probably right, Desirée. We'd only get in the way."

I could tell by the tone in Mum's voice that she had taken offence even though I'd said not to. Or maybe she was uncomfortable about the hypnotherapy process too. I didn't know her opinion of the treatment – we hadn't had chance to discuss it. Just as I was about to ask her there was a tentative knock on the back door. The silhouette showing through the door's privacy screen was obvious.

"Come in, Seth," I called. Mum frowned. In her opinion it's

polite to greet visitors face-to-face and she hates it when I shout through closed doors.

Seth came in looking bewildered. "How'd you know it was me?"

My exaggerated look towards his head gave him the message. He automatically tried to smooth his hair, with the usual lack of success. We grinned at each other, almost embarrassed by the normal banter but not knowing why.

"Desirée has an appointment this morning," Mum said.

"Yes, I know, Mrs Hanson. Sorry to bother you so early but I was hoping to catch up with her before that. It's a nice morning. I thought a walk in the fresh air might do her some good. If that's okay with you?"

Mum looked at Dad for support but Seth's polite request couldn't be denied without good reason.

"Make sure to be back in good time," Dad said, looking at me and tapping his antique wristwatch.

"Just gotta clean my teeth," I said and ran upstairs to complete my morning routine.

When I returned to the kitchen Seth was still standing by the back door – *honestly, Mum, talk about good manners!*

"Don't start without me," I called over my shoulder and I pushed Seth out onto the garden path. I heard Dad chuckling at my cheekiness as the door closed behind me.

"Good to see you're back to your old self," said Seth.

"Don't bet on it," I replied. "I simply daren't give them an excuse to send me back to the clinic. We're all treading on eggshells in there. It's driving me crazy for real!"

We walked on in silence. Not a strained silence, just the quietness between friends. No need to talk for a while. Seth finally broached the subject he'd come to discuss.

"Have you had chance to think about Mum's journal entries yet?"

"No, not yet. Sorry, I was so tired when we got home yesterday that I went straight to bed. I'll come round to yours later – if I get through this hypno session in one piece that is! We'll look at it together then."

"I don't want to influence your take on it," he said.

"Well I'll read, while you make the cuppas – deal?"

"Deal," he smiled. "So long as you sneak some of your Mum's ginger biscuits over for us."

I punched him on the shoulder and he put his arms around me to defend himself. We wrestled briefly then stood laughing at each other's efforts – well mine mainly, as I tried to break his firm grip with my weak struggles. Without any conscious thought our scuffle became an embrace and I laid my head against his chest, listening to the steady rhythm of his heartbeat.

"Maybe you're not quite back to normal. You'd've tried to knee me by now," he said.

"Careful. I still might," I replied, trying to manoeuvre into a threatening position. "I think those drugs they kept me doped up on must still be in my system. I feel really washed out."

"Come on. Let's get you back home for your appointment. Can't have you dozing off half way through, can we?"

Seth gave me one last squeeze before releasing me. But, instead of our normal brisk pace with an arm's length between us, we remained arm-in-arm and slowly strolled back towards home like an old married couple.

Mm – feels nice!

CHAPTER 12

Val D'Isere: February 2078

"You know, Father, it really is time you handed over the reins while you still have chance to enjoy retirement."

"Sebastian, my boy, I'm as sharp as I ever was up here," Benjamin Trevalyn tapped his temple. "Just because the body's getting a tad decrepit don't think I'm losing my marbles." He raised his whisky glass in a mock toast. He was fully aware of his son's wish to take over the running of the business but with a typical despot's greed he was not ready to bow out even at the advanced age of ninety-three.

Sebastian smiled and returned the gesture. Suddenly Benjamin felt uneasy. The now-empty tumbler slipped from his trembling hand.

"You look cold, Father. I'll go fetch another blanket for you." Sebastian patted Benjamin's shoulder as he walked past and disappeared into the shadows of the chalet.

As an overwhelming weakness spread through his body, Benjamin realised his mistake. He'd held on for too long and Sebastian had grown impatient. What concoction had he just drunk? It had tasted like his favourite Jura Single Malt but what if the toasted peat tones hid a more dangerous distillation? His temperature swiftly dropped and he thought he could see a figure at the end of the veranda. Who was that woman? Why didn't she help? Surely she could see he was having problems breathing? She seemed to be smiling and it wasn't a welcoming smile.

"Has your past finally caught up with you, Benjamin?"

No! She's been dead for six years. I don't believe in ghosts.

"Not a ghost, Trevalyn. Your conscience," whispered the spectre of Julia Simpson.

"Grandpa?" Victor nudged the back of the ice cold figure and it fell forward, slipping from the wheelchair with an awful thud as it hit the wooden decking. He ran around the wheelchair to be confronted by the dull, hard stare of his grandfather and was terrified that he'd pushed the old man too hard. Grandpa must have banged his head when he fell. Victor had killed him! He ran back into the chalet, straight to his room and picked up his latest holo-game pad. When Uncle Sebastian came to tell him that Grandpa had died from a heart attack just like Daddy, twelve-year old Victor knew he'd just got away with murder!

CHAPTER 13

Ellingham: 31 July 2110

Straight face Dez. Don't laugh.

I was sitting in Mum's favourite comfy chair by the patio window overlooking the garden. Alvin sat on an upright ladder-back chair dragged in from the dining room but somehow he still managed to look totally at ease. He'd come into the house all smiles and confidence, oozing so much sex-appeal that Mum actually blushed before hurrying away to make the coffee. My reaction? I was surprised. Yes he was still abso-bloody-lutely gorgeous, but I was totally unfazed! All I could think about was the way I'd felt when Seth had been holding me earlier. Now that did make me feel all warm and gooey. *Nah, don't be daft. He's my best mate that's all.*

"Are you all right, Dez?" asked Alvin.

"Yeah … Yes, thanks." I quickly stopped my daydreaming and looked towards him hoping he couldn't guess what I'd been thinking.

"Before we start do you have any questions or concerns?"

"No. Not really," I said, but I can't have been very convincing as he just looked at me with one eyebrow slightly raised. "Erm. Well I am a bit nervous," I admitted. "A bit keyed up, I suppose."

"That's understandable. We all get anxious when we're trying something new. But I want you to know there's nothing to be worried about. Ms Thorogood and I are completely at your disposal for the next hour, or you can ask us to leave right now if you'd rather not carry on."

Ms Thorogood nodded encouragingly from the far end of the wine-red leather sofa.

"No. I want to do this. I just don't want to disappoint anyone if it doesn't work."

"Do you often feel you are disappointing people, Dez?" Alvin asked.

"Sometimes." I started to pick at one of my ragged cuticles. "I know I'm a big disappointment to Mum."

I expected a patronising denial but Alvin and Ms Thorogood kept quiet.

"She never says I've done well, even when I've tried my best. If I ask her whether I look nice before I go out she tells me not to be vain or she makes a comment like my skirt's too short or my t-shirt's tatty."

Alvin nodded gently in acceptance of what I was saying while he made notes on his palm-pad.

Odd that – normally adults tried to defend each other or justify their take on things. I swallowed the lump of emotion building in my throat and continued, "It's not like I've inherited her amazing looks – I have to work at it. I work hard at the Academy too, 'cos I haven't got Dad's brains either. If I wasn't constantly being reminded about how hard it was for Mum to have me I'd think I was adopted – especially now that my PT connection hasn't turned on!"

I was beginning to feel tearful and Alvin must've sensed my rising tension. He stopped keying into his palm-pad and looked at me.

"Okay, Dez," he said. "Let's get started, shall we? I'd like you to uncross your legs and just let your arms rest alongside your body. You can put your hands in your lap if that feels better for you."

I shuffled around not sure how I really wanted to sit. I was feeling self conscious and desperate not to get the giggles.

"Shall I close my eyes?"

"When you're comfortable. It'll help you to relax."

I closed my eyes, although it was hard not to open them again straight away.

"Now, I'd like you to concentrate on my voice and allow yourself to forget about everything else for the moment. Don't worry about any other noises around you. There's nothing that needs your attention for now."

That wasn't too hard. He had a voice like melting chocolate – rich and warm. It was a comforting voice, soothing and it quickly made me feel safe and not at all giggly.

"Take a nice deep breath. Hold it for a moment then gently breathe out, letting your shoulders drop and allowing your whole body to relax. You can feel the tension slipping away with each breath. Your muscles are gradually relaxing in every part of your body: your face is relaxing, your neck and shoulders are relaxing, your back …"

It was amazing. Until then, I'd never experienced each muscle actually loosen and the tension drain away so physically. It felt like I was sinking into the chair and even though I knew I could move if I needed to I realised I didn't want to. I was enjoying the sense of freedom. My arms and legs, hands and feet were utterly relaxed – I could barely feel them. Then I became aware that I'd let my concentration slide. I tuned back in to what Alvin was saying.

"… to ask you to imagine certain things. Don't worry if you can't picture them or if you find your mind wandering. My voice may fade into the background, but that's fine. Just allow yourself to drift along, completely relaxed."

Every time he said relax I felt myself drift further away. I couldn't believe there was any tension left but at each prompt I sank deeper and deeper into a welcoming semi-conscious state. I'd never felt this safe, this comfortable, not even when Dad used to hold me tightly to his chest after I'd woken from a nightmare.

"Try to imagine, if you can, that you are standing in a park. It's a warm evening with clear skies and a full bright moon lights the path ahead of you. In the distance you can see various coloured lights and hear the music and laughter of a traditional fairground."

A small part of my mind reminded me that I was sitting in our lounge but I could see the lights, hear the old-fashioned pipe music from the merry-go-round and smell the fried onions. I began to walk down the moonlit path, dragging my hand along the park railings, feeling the rhythmic shudder up my arm as I hit each metal post. There was a cheerful elderly man at the gate who scanned my wrist-chip for the entry charge and, with a broad grin and a twinkle in his eye, told me to enjoy the fair.

I wandered though the crowds. There were families, the children holding tightly to helium-filled balloons of all shapes and sizes. Couples walked with their arms draped around each other – the boys strutting, full of testosterone, and the girls cuddling enormous stuffed toys. Groups of boys showed off their expertise at the rifle range while self-assured, predatory girls looked on. I smiled at the stereotypes. My imagination could be really naff sometimes!

The guy at the House of Mirrors called out to me. He bowed extravagantly and gestured for me to enter the darkened doorway. The corridor was lined with mirrors of various types, reflecting my progress in strange and comical forms. I continued along the passage until I reached a room full of mirrors – plain reflections, no distortions but hundreds of images. Or rather hundreds of me! It reminded me of the horror films we'd watch on 'Classics Old & New' but I didn't feel scared, just curious to see where this was leading. I was enjoying the journey that Alvin was guiding me along.

Gradually I became aware of additional reflections materialising in some of the mirrors. In one my mother stood beside me, holding a baby and singing softly while the baby held tightly to her finger. Another had Dad's smiling face just visible behind my left shoulder. Seth's familiar figure strode across the background of one mirror and his mother came forward in another to put her arm around me and give me a friendly squeeze. Eventually, all but one of the mirrors had reflections of my family, friends and memories. I began to feel anxious for in each of those reflections I could sense another identity tied to the family member or friend although I couldn't actually see the extra occupant. In the single reflection of me I was completely alone, no shadows of a third party, no sense of another presence. Just like at my Sixteenth-Eve party – there was nobody there.

"… two, three, four, five." I heard Alvin's voice clearly and opened my eyes.

I stretched like a cat waking from its nap then realised my cheeks were wet. I'd been crying.

"I think we'll leave it at that for today, Dez." Alvin reached out to me with a tissue.

"Thanks," I said, embarrassed by my reaction. "I didn't know I was crying. I'm not really upset. I suppose it just brought stuff back from my sixteenth when my PT connection didn't turn on. Honestly, I feel much better than before. I never realised I could be so relaxed."

The anxious frown left Alvin's face and he smiled reassuringly.

"If you're really up to it we can continue in a couple of days. Or we can leave it until next week if you'd rather."

"No. The sooner the better," I said.

"Good. Debbie, we can manage Saturday morning, can't we?"

"Yes. That'll be fine."

I'd never thought of Ms Thorogood as a Debbie! Then I realised what Alvin had asked her.

"Please don't spoil your weekend. I lost track of what day it is. I'll wait until next week," I said, hurriedly, hoping they didn't think I was being awkward.

"Being self-employed makes me master of my own diary," Alvin said. "Now, Dez. This is just the beginning – don't expect miracles, okay?"

I nodded.

"Sometimes the subconscious can be bit stubborn so have patience. And don't worry about not having a PT connection. There are quite a few folk who haven't got them and they manage to get along just fine. After all, it makes no physiological difference. Telepathic twinning is still a fairly new twist to our evolution. We've only had it for a couple of generations or so and we're still trying to discover how it happened." I must have been showing signs of having lost the thread. "What I'm getting at is that you mustn't feel you're a freak for not having a PT. If anything, you're still the normal one and we're all the freaks!" he said.

"Alvin, please don't start patronising me now," I said. "I can't help how I feel about the telepathic stuff. You only have to see the way non-telepaths are treated to know that they're seen as deficient. Racism and sexism might've died out decades ago but there'll always be someone at the lower end of the pecking order – this time it's us Empties."

There was an uncomfortable silence.

"Omigod. I'm sorry, Alvin. I didn't mean to be offensive," I gasped.

"Don't apologise, Dez. You're right. Making light of the situation was insensitive of me. I'm the one who's sorry. Are you happy to continue with the sessions?"

"Yes. Of course! If there's the slightest chance that we can fix this it's worth the effort. And if not – well, at least you can help me 'come to terms with it'." I looked at Ms Thorogood and winked at her.

"Atta girl!" she whispered.

Just hope I can come to terms with it!

CHAPTER 14

Ellingham: 31 July 2110

Coming to terms with it? Suppose Alvin's right, I'm no different to the person I was before my sixteenth. But isn't that part of the problem?

I gave a jaw breaking yawn and wondered why I was so exhausted after the morning's hypnotherapy session. After all, I'd felt like I'd been sleeping through half of it.

"Desirée. If you're so tired you should cancel your plans to go out and rest here instead."

"Mum, please! I'm old enough to know when I'm ready for bed. I just need some fresh air to blow away the drowsiness from the hypnotherapy. A walk with Seth'll do me more good than moping around the house and getting under your feet."

"Dez is right, Celeste. We shall have a nice quiet afternoon while she gets some exercise," said Dad, as he cleared the lunch plates from the kitchen table.

"I'm just worried that she'll overdo it," said Mum, seeming to forget that I was still in the room.

"I'll be fine," I said.

"And I shall be in the study so you can stretch out on the sofa and get some rest yourself, Celeste." Dad often worked from home.

"Rest? I haven't got time to rest. Do you realise how much work it takes to keep the house looking half-way decent? ..."

I left before Mum's complaining spoiled my relaxed mood from the session with Alvin. I collected my bag from the hallway and stepped out into the afternoon sunshine. For the first time since my sixteenth I felt that it was going to work out, even if the PT never turned on –

I'd manage somehow. The short stroll to Seth's did clear my head, although I was mid-yawn again when he opened the door for me.

"Jeez, Dez! I nearly fell in," he laughed.

He earned himself a second punch of the day. *Oops!* That reminded me why he got the first one.

"Sorry. I forgot the biscuits," I said. "Mum was going into one about all the chores she insists on doing, so I legged it."

"Aw. I've been looking forward to them all day. Now we'll have to make do with shop-bought chewy-nut cookies."

"Well, at least they're not choc-chip!"

We went through to the kitchen, which looked just as it had the other evening. I'm sure the washing pile was exactly how I'd left it. Yes, they'd left the colour-load in the machine – *oh yuck.* I opened the washer door and the smell confirmed it. I recharged the silver detergent ball and set the programme onto a short but intensive wash.

"You're being typical cavemen. You know that don't you?" I scolded.

"Mm," Seth agreed as he poured the tea. "Cookies are on top of the fridge," he said, pointing in the general area of the refrigerator.

I brought the cookie jar to the table and absentmindedly started to munch as I opened Elizabeth's *Handi*. Once again I felt like I was intruding on her private life but Seth nodded for me to continue.

Many of the entries were mundane – appointments with her bookkeeping clients, reminders about Parents' Evenings at the Academy, birthdays, anniversaries etc. There were some saved e-zine snippets about handicrafts, recipes, or gardening tips. She even had some celeb gossip in there, *didn't know she was interested in that.* There was also a wide range of archived news articles; from the legislation effecting her work to political debates and crime reports.

"I'm not sure what I should be looking for," I said. "It all seems fairly ordinary to me. What did you see that made you feel she ... That it wasn't an accident?"

Seth came to sit next to me and leaned close so that he could key commands onto the *Handi* screen.

"Why did she keep these?" he asked, bringing the news archive up on to the screen. "All those horrible murders, deaths and accidents used to really upset her when they came on the news. So why would she remind herself of them? And here…" He started to scroll through the *Handi*'s pages. "There're all sorts of weird quotations throughout the entries. Some even pop up when you're looking at the news reports."

"Maybe she liked to keep a reminder of the things she'd read."

"No. She didn't read all those books. I'm sure of it. Maybe some of the classics but there's some obscure stuff and some of them just aren't her – if you know what I mean. Look."

Seth brought up a page with an orange background and a flashing white exploding text box: 'The rich are the scum of the earth in every country.' The text was in a blocky black font as though the message was being thrown out of the page at the reader. Elizabeth had annotated it with 'Quote: The Flying Inn: G K Chesterton (1874-1936)'

"See? That's not the way Mum thought. She always said there were good and bad in all walks of life, no matter where people came from or how much they had in the bank. You know how tolerant she was of others. And I never heard her speak of G K Chesterton so it's not like he was one of her favourite authors. Why would she keep a quote like that?"

"Seth, I don't know. What're you trying to say?"

"I feel like she's trying to get a message out. But I just can't find it." He scrubbed at his forehead with clenched fists, his shoulders hunching up towards his ears. I reached over to rub his neck and shoulders with large sweeping circles.

"S'okay, Seth. We'll work on it together. We'll suss it out somehow." I felt a tightening in my stomach as I massaged his broad back – I hadn't noticed how muscular he was, he'd always seemed so skinny. He gradually relaxed and turned to look at me. My breath caught as I returned his gaze. His soft brown eyes shimmered with unshed tears and his face was slightly flushed.

"Hmph," he muttered, embarrassed by his reaction. He looked

at the washing-machine and gestured towards it. "Thanks, Dez. I'll just get that lot out while there's still some sunshine. Then we can take another look."

The spell broken, I turned back to the *Handi* while Seth went into the garden with the freshened laundry. He had a point. Some of the entries did seem uncharacteristic of Elizabeth so maybe she was trying to say something. I started from the beginning – a key to the highlighted entries in her diary section: yellow signified client meetings or calls for her bookkeeping business; green for personal reminders such as dental appointments, Academy events and so on; pink was for birthdays and anniversaries. But there was nothing to explain the occasional blue markers, the first of which appeared on Saturday, 31st January 2105.

"Seth," I called through the open back door. "Have you any idea what the blue markers are for?"

"Be there in a minute."

I checked the second year of entries. The blue markers were on different dates so they weren't anything that occurred on a regular basis. But then her client appointments weren't on identical dates either so it probably wasn't a big deal.

The warmth from the afternoon sun shining through the kitchen window was making me drowsy again. I sat with my chin resting on my free hand as I scrolled through the *Handi*'s pages.

"*… do you mean? … started first time yesterday … come on Troy, I said…*"

"What?" My head slipped from my hand as I came back to myself.

"What?" Seth asked from the doorway.

"What? … No, stop," I said. Inside my head was buzzing like that irritating murmur you get in a room full of people all holding different conversations at once. *Must be left over effects of the hypnotherapy.* I thought. *Or those bloody drugs that rotten nurse pumped into me.*

"You okay, Dez?" Seth stepped forward and hesitantly put his hand on my shoulder.

Why is he suddenly so awkward with me?

"Feel a bit queasy," I said. "Can you get me some water, please?"

"Sure. You're not gonna keel over are you?"

"No. I'm fine, promise." I managed a smile. "Just got a bit too hot in the sunshine." I shifted my chair around the table so that I was in the shadier part of the room. But it wasn't the heat that was freaking me out. The murmuring was still there and I kept getting snippets of conversation coming through clearly like a Holo-Comms receiver picking up audio broadcasts. I felt myself shaking my head as though I was trying to dislodge an insect from my ear and Seth was giving me worried look.

"Dez. What *is* going on with you?"

I felt a sudden wave of nausea and headed for the sink.

"Sorry." I broke my promise and crashed down as the buzzing overwhelmed me. When I came round, Seth was bending over me, gently patting my forehead with a damp cloth. His eyes were ringed with dark circles and his lips were clenched tight. I was shivering despite the summer heat and I couldn't seem to get it to stop.

"Come on," he said. "Let's get you home."

He picked me up with only a little stumble as he manoeuvred me into his arms.

When did he get so strong?

"No." I struggled to get my feet to the ground. "I'm fine now, honest."

"Whoa!"

Too late. We both ended up back on the kitchen floor.

"Guess you are!" I could hear the sarcasm in his voice.

"All right. I'm not fine. But I'm not going home."

"Well, tell me what's up."

"I don't really know. I've got this noise in my head. It's making me feel sick and dizzy."

"Sounds like vertigo. My gran used to get it. You need to get something for it, Dez."

"No! I'm not going anywhere near that clinic if I can help it. Ow, it's difficult to concentrate … I … can …hardly …" I just couldn't get any more words out.

Seth picked me up again and took me into the sitting room, carefully lowering me onto the sofa. He went upstairs and came back with a familiar bottle – his mother's lavender oil. Elizabeth was an amateur herbalist, preferring natural remedies to synthetic drugs. He poured a little of the oil into his hand and gently started to dab it onto my temples, lightly tracing circles around my closed eyes and whispering endearments that he probably didn't think I could hear,

"Don't worry. It's okay. I'm here."

His soothing voice and the sweet lavender were helping. The murmuring faded slightly so that I could start to think coherently again and I opened my eyes. Seth's face was so close to mine I could smell the warmth of his skin, the left-over zesty fragrance of his morning shower overlaying the perfumed oil he was massaging into my forehead. I lifted my head to take the kiss that had been hovering between us all afternoon. *Good job I didn't throw up earlier.* I giggled before I could complete my intention and Seth leapt back, embarrassed that he'd been caught so close to me.

"Er. Just about to er … I was er …" he said.

"S'fine. You were just making sure I was okay," I offered.

"Yeah. Yeah. I was just making sure you were okay."

"*Are* you okay now?" he added.

"Feeling much better, thanks. That lavender oil seems to have done the trick." My head had cleared. Maybe the dizzy spell had been brought on by the hypnotherapy session and the hot sun through the kitchen window after all.

"Well I don't think we should do any more today," he said. "I'll take you home before you have another funny turn. We can look at Mum's diary when you're feeling better. Sorry, I shouldn't have pressured you so soon after you got out of the clinic."

"Don't worry, Seth. I'm all right, really I am. But, I *will* go home and have an early night. That hypno stuff must be more tiring than I imagined. I'm whacked."

I packed Elizabeth's *Handi* away into my bag despite Seth's argument that I shouldn't bother myself with it any more. I wanted to look at it alone. Make some notes. See if I could see any pattern to the entries or connections that Seth might've missed. I finally convinced him that I'd be able to handle it without freaking out again.

The afternoon was beginning to cool and, although the shivers were now under control, Seth insisted that I draped his jumper around my shoulders as we started the short stroll to my house. Samuel came around the corner just as we reached the end of their drive.

"Hello, Dez," he said. "Nice to see you out and about. How're you doing?"

"Good thanks, Mr Wa ... Samuel." We all laughed at my stuttered response and I warned Seth with a loaded glance that he wasn't to mention my dizzy spell.

"It'll take me a while to get used to calling you that," I added, turning back to Samuel.

"It's fine, love. You call me whatever you like, as long as it's not late for my dinner!"

"Oh, Dad. That's so lame!"

"I know, Seth. I know." Samuel grinned and winked at me, enjoying the mild embarrassment he was causing his son. "Take care, love. See you later, eh?"

"Yes. I'll be round again tomorrow. And I'll remember the ginger biscuits." Much to Seth's surprise, I took his hand and dragged him out of the drive. Samuel's smile widened when he noticed the gesture.

Now I see where Seth's lovely smile comes from!

CHAPTER 15

Ellingham: May 2089

"She looks adorable."

"You're just saying that because you're her doting granddad!" Jade laughed. "But on this occasion, I'll allow it."

Bethany continued to spin on the spot making her multi-layered skirt flare out almost parallel to the floor. Finally she was too dizzy to stand and collapsed on the floor, giggling uncontrollably.

"Careful." Jade picked up the breathless child. "You'll make yourself sick and ruin the dress before we even get there."

"We'd better be making tracks," Matt said. "Eddie and Trish are meeting us at the church. We'll see you there." He gave his daughter and grand-daughter a proud hug.

Laura watched from the doorway, enjoying the sight of the three generations in a warm embrace.

"Come on," she said. "You know how nervous Jonny is. He'll need his godfather to give him a push towards the altar if he gets stage fright."

"Poor lad, I'd be nervous marrying into the Dévereux family too."

"Be nice. Little ears hear all," Laura whispered, nodding towards Bethany who was now hopping from one foot onto the other, still full of energy and excitement.

Luckily the eight-year old was busy admiring the sparkling sandals that her mother was holding. Too eager about the wedding to listen to Gramps. Being a bridesmaid was a very important job – Aunty Ce-Ce had told her so – and she wasn't going to let Aunty Ce-Ce down. She frowned at her knee, recently grazed and now sporting a lovely, knobbly scab. Mummy had been so careful to keep her indoors for weeks ahead of the wedding but the day before yesterday Bethany ran to the gate to collect a parcel from the postman and promptly tripped on the gravel path. Her loud cries were more to divert Mummy's cross response than from any real pain.

"Don't worry Betty-kins," Jade now soothed, noticing her daughter's sudden change of mood. "Your knee won't be so noticeable under your fancy tights. We just need to be careful we don't scrape off the scab, don't we?"

Jade struggled not to laugh at Bethany's serious nodding then her breath caught as she noticed her child's resemblance to her great-grandmother – still missed after all these years. Jade felt a sudden prod of guilt that she'd been too busy to follow through on her promise to help find out what Julia had been searching for.

"Muuu-mmee!" Bethany's whine brought Jade back to the present.

"Sorry, lovely," she said and continued to smooth the lacy tights over her child's wriggling legs.

***

Despite the groom's nerves everything followed the meticulous planning of his beautiful bride. Laura felt only a brief stab of jealousy that Jade had chosen not to marry Bethany's father, despite numerous proposals. Laura hadn't had the chance to indulge herself as the mother-of-the-bride, however, being godmother of the groom on this occasion had it's advantages. She and Matt were included in all the family portraits of the day so she could enjoy the involvement without the stress of the organisation.

"Remind me again who that couple are with Jen," Matt whispered as the toasts came to an end.

"Samuel went to school with Jen and Celeste and that's his girlfriend Elizabeth."

"Phwar. She's a looker!"

"Matthew Simpson." Laura playfully slapped her husband's arm. "You're old enough to be her father."

"Ah so it's only that you consider me too old for her. Not that you're jealous, at all." Matt smiled as he kissed his wife's pouting lips.

"Behave you two!" Jade interrupted. "Anyone would think it's *your* wedding day."

"I hope that we'll still be just as loving when we reach our thirtieth anniversary," said the new Mrs Hanson, approaching the table.

"My dear girl," Matt said. "I've never seen Jonny happier. He's besotted. Whatever you've been doing together in that office of yours has done the trick." He gave an exaggerated wink and earned another slap from his wife.

Celeste blushed slightly. "If I told you I'd have to kill you," she replied with her own sly wink.

CHAPTER 16

Ellingham: 31 July 2110

Things are getting complicated.

I couldn't work out what was really happening in my relationship with Seth. We were best friends; always had been and, if I had my way, always would be. But I realised that, for me at least, it was developing into something more. I thought about the way he'd cared for me earlier. Was I imagining that the way he felt about me was changing too?

I stretched to relieve the stiffness in my neck and shoulders. I'd been hunched over the desk in my room trying to tune out the white noise in my head that had returned during dinner. I'd made my excuses and left the table before dessert, coming to my room before Mum got into full flow about me going out when she'd said I shouldn't.

So much for improved mother daughter relations! I thought.

As I leaned backwards, Seth's scent wafted up from his jumper, draped over the back of my chair. I'd forgotten to give it back to him when we'd reached my house. I tried to rekindle the relaxed, safe feeling I'd experienced that afternoon when he'd been massaging my face and the noise in my head had diminished. Although the reminder of his smell was comforting it didn't do the trick and the voices continued to chatter incoherently. At least I didn't feel quite so sick this time. Maybe if I concentrated on something else I could ignore the internal racket.

Elizabeth's *Handi* was charging up in the last rays of sunlight on the window ledge. *I'll have another look. See what I can come up with.*

When the unit turned on I chose 'Random Access' – an opportunity to let fate decide where I'd start.

This morning, in a gruesome parody of a Valentine's Day tryst, the bodies of a young couple were found in the gardens of the Théâtre Marigny, Paris. Police wish to speak to anyone in the area of the Square Marigny, Avenue des Champs Élysées, Avenue de Marigny and/or Avenue Gabriél between 9 o'clock yesterday evening and 7 o'clock this morning – the time that the awful discovery was made by one of the groundsmen.

POP-UP: *'How alike are the groans of love to those of the dying.'* Under the Volcano, ch12: Malcolm Lowry (1909-57)
(DOM: 13/02)

Oh great! Just when I was beginning to think about the romantic possibilities with Seth, Fate chooses to throw this up at me. The Pop-Up quote seemed apt enough, although macabre, but what was that notation at the end about? What did it mean? My mind was full of that bloody noise and I couldn't filter it out to work on the riddle of what DOM stood for. I knew it was something obvious. I could feel it on the tip of my tongue but the more I tried to track it down the louder the murmuring voices became.

With a frustrated sigh, I switched off the *Handi*, put it back into my bag and went to bed hoping that a good night's sleep was all I needed to clear my head permanently.

***

The colour of the buildings, smudged monochrome from the past centuries of smoke and exhaust fumes, mirrors the slate grey winter sky. The temperature steadily drops and a light wind chases the Parisians home early from their work and shopping but we're immune to the chill as we walk along the Champs-Élysées arm-in-arm, chattering excitedly about our plans to marry. Tomas chose the ring weeks ago and it fits me so well that I'm amazed he knew the sizing without actually taking my finger to the jewellers! He was too excited to wait until tomorrow – Valentine's Day. I'm glad he didn't wait. Now we can spend the rest of the weekend celebrating. Tomas has managed to get a table at Café Lenôtre, I hate to think how much all this is costing him. He can tell by my expression that I'm worried.

"Don't fret so, ma petite," he says. "I have more good news. I've been promoted to Deputy Research Director. They've given me a bonus of 3000 credits for my past year's performance and my salary goes up by 250 credits per month." He grabs me and spins me around, laughing and kissing me all over my cold face before we enter the welcome warmth of the restaurant.

We eat moules marinières; drink champagne; and share dessert with one spoon. We sit close to each other and kiss at every opportunity. The waiters smile, congratulating us. They can't fail to notice me constantly admiring my ring. As we leave the restaurant we stumble a little – too much champagne! We bump into a man standing by the exit. He's distributing roses to patrons as they leave.

"Excuse me," he says and hands me a rose.

"No. Excuse us!" we giggle, as we both draw in the sweet, heavy scent of the flower.

We decide to walk home along the Avenue de Marigny. In our euphoria, we remain oblivious to the cold. The wintry weather has kept people indoors and it seems as though we are alone in the city. As we approach the junction with Avenue Gabriél, we lean against the wall and enjoy another long, passionate kiss. My hips are pressed up against Tomas's and his hands are squeezing my buttocks. I sense his arousal and a groan escapes me as I anticipate our lovemaking. My rising passion makes my skin tingle. Now there's a hand on my neck but both Tomas's are still gripping my bum. I try to turn to see who is behind me. I can't move. The hand on my neck is strong, keeping my mouth tight on Tomas's. I open my eyes. Tomas has his open too and I see fear in them. What's happening to us? I remember the man at Café Lenôtre – the rose – and I can smell the scent, not sweet now, but sickly, cloying.

"Don't mind me." I recognise that man's voice, even though he is now speaking English. Stupidly, I want to tell him I can understand him, but I can't break away from the kiss. This isn't possible. How can one man hold two people so firmly with only his hands?

81

"The rose was a nice touch, don't you think? I sprayed it with a truly wonderful drug. It breaks down the neurological connections for voluntary movements, only allowing eye activity and, of course, the involuntary mechanisms such as breathing. Naturally I anticipated your immobility and I brought transport along to help move you off the street. We can't have any opportunistic voyeurs watching your passionate antics, now can we?"

He torments us with his snide comment. We're well aware that there are no other people around. No chance of anyone coming to help us. What is he going to do? I'm so scared. Tears spill from my eyes and I can see the anguish in Tomas's.

The man slides a rolling mat under our feet – one like the delivery men use for large parcels – and he pushes us through the darkened gateway into the grounds of the Théâtre Marigny. Tomas's hands remain clasped around my buttocks and what started as a funny, sexy gesture now seems grotesque. Five minutes ago I would've given anything to be able to get in here and fulfil the desires Tomas aroused in me. Now I want to run as far away as possible.

Out of the corner of my eye I see that the clouds have cleared, the moon is bright in a star-filled sky. Such beauty amidst this horror. My gaze returns to Tomas's face. His eyes are closed, possibly to shield me from his own terror.

Why is the Englishman doing this to us? He tapes our bodies together in an even tighter embrace than before, pulling our hips so close that I can feel Tomas's pelvic bones grinding into mine. Oh, I'd wanted him so much but this isn't the way it's supposed to be.

As the Englishman pushes us to the ground the cold creeps into my body from the frozen earth – strange that I can sense that when, otherwise, I'm so numb.

"Almost done," the man says cheerfully. I begin to believe that, despite everything, it's going to be okay after all. Maybe he's just going to leave us here for a sick joke – to teach us that it's not acceptable to make out on street corners. But now he puts a clip on my nose. NO! I scream though no sound emerges. I can't breathe. Please unblock my nose. PLEASE. Tomas suffers the same fate and, eventually, we can't help it – we're trying to breathe through each other's mouth. It won't work. How can it? We have nothing left. I love you, Tomas. I need you to hear me, to read my mind.

Wait – where's Simone? What's happened to our connection? She's only the other side of the river. SIMONE! Phone the police, please. We're … we're … I can't see anything. It's gone dark. My ears buzz. I'm so tired.

★★★

"Dez. Dez! Wake up, sweetheart. It's only a bad dream. Come on. Deep breath now. That's it."

Dad was gently shaking me to rouse me. I was fighting his grip trying to get free, panting and sweating as though I'd run a marathon. My head was fuzzy, I had flashes of light blurring my vision and my chest ached with each breath I pulled in. Finally my vision cleared and I realised where I was. I licked my dry lips, tasting a residual drop of champagne. *Don't be daft! It's just your imagination.*

"S … Sorry, Dad. Didn't mean to disturb you. What time is it?" I looked at my bedside monitor. Only eleven-thirty. It felt like I'd been out for much longer.

"Do you want a drink or something to eat? You didn't have much at dinner."

"A drink would be nice, thanks. My mouth tastes like a badger's arse!" *Where did that come from?*

Dad looked at me with a mixture of shock and bewilderment. I shrugged and put on my 'really sorry' face.

"Oops!"

"I wonder at you sometimes, young lady," he said, shaking his head as he went to get my drink. He still looked puzzled when he returned with a glass of chilled water for me.

"I am sure I have never shared that particular expression of Claude's with you," he said, referring to his own PT. "I am surprised you have heard it at all. It is not one of the more common phrases for today's young people, is it?" He was using his official voice. I wasn't in big trouble yet but he was concerned.

"I'm sorry. I don't know where it came from. Maybe I'm just going frikkin' psycho."

"Desirée this is not funny at all and I suggest you moderate your language before you say anything else."

"I didn't mean to be rude," I protested, crying with frustration, "but I don't know what's going on. The voices in my head – they keep nagging at me. It's so bloody noisy in there I can't think straight any more."

"Voices? What voices? When did this start? Was it before your … accident?"

He sounded angry or was it fear? Whatever it was, I couldn't handle it.

"Can we talk in the morning, please? I've got an awful headache and I'm really tired."

"All right, Desirée. We shall try to get to the bottom of this tomorrow. Good-night."

And, my normally forgiving, understanding father left my room without even a good-night kiss. He'd never done that before. I could see Mum hovering outside my bedroom door. She sighed and shook her head sadly before turning to follow Dad back to their room. Were we ever going to get back to normal – *and what is normal these days anyway?*

I drank the water to try and swill away the choking sensation that lingered in my throat. The noise in my head was subdued but still present – as though it also felt cowed by the seriousness of the situation. That had been more than a dream brought on by reading the news report in Elizabeth's *Handi*. I'd felt every emotion, every sensation. I'd suffocated trying to breathe through the mouth of my lover – *well not technically **my** lover, but that's beside the point.* It was a memory. It was so real. It had to be a memory.

It's fine promising to talk about it. But how do I explain all that?

CHAPTER 17

Ellingham: 1 August 2110

I'd rather have nothing than this constant babble.

A few days ago I was worried that I'd never hook-up with my PT – this morning it felt like I had the whole world chattering in my head. This wasn't the connection that I'd expected from the lessons we'd had with Ms Thorogood.

I sent a message to Seth telling him I was still feeling washed out so needed to stay home – alone. I also managed to avoid further discussions with the 'rents. Dad was called into a big meeting in London and Mum seemed happy to leave me undisturbed in my room all day. I needed the space as I hadn't slept at all for the remainder of that night. I was barely coherent and just lay in bed, restlessly tossing and turning, trying to relax. My head felt as though hundreds of tiny miners were trying to excavate the inside of my skull. I could hardly see through my swollen eyelids, having cried into my pillow for most of the night. It occurred to me that I'd done more crying over this last week than through the entire past year. The peace I'd briefly found during the first hypnotherapy session and afterwards in Seth's arms, was a quickly fading memory. I needed to find it again if I was going to keep my sanity.

Mum would normally have been in the room trying to get me to buck up my ideas and get some chores done to show how sorry I was, but she kept her distance throughout the day then surprised me with a significant change in her behaviour. She brought some supper on a tray and put it on my bedside table – I was never allowed food in my room!

"Here you are, love," she said. "Try to eat. You need something to keep up your strength."

I turned to look at her. She reached forward and stroked the hair away from my damp face. Her expression of concern was so unexpected I couldn't stop the tears from welling up again. When would I run dry? She gathered me in her arms and I'm sure I could feel her sobbing too.

"There, there. We'll sort this out. Don't worry, Dizzy." Mum hadn't used her own, private, pet name for me since I'd started at the Academy. I took a little comfort from the sense that my mum was feeling affectionate towards me for once.

I was exhausted but afraid to sleep. Mum looked intently at me and knew that I was struggling.

"I appreciate that you didn't want to take these when you came home from the clinic," she said, producing a couple of sleeping pills, "but one night's dose won't do you any harm. You need the rest."

Maybe she was right. I swallowed the pills in the hope that they would knock me out so completely that I wouldn't hear the clamouring in my head nor have any more frightening dreams – although I still wasn't convinced that it had been simply a nightmare. I just wanted oblivion for a few hours.

Mum waited with me until I'd eaten enough supper to satisfy her that I wasn't going to fade away through lack of food. Then she picked up the tray, straightened the duvet where she'd been sitting, lightly kissed my forehead and went to the bedroom door.

"We'll talk in the morning. Let's see if Mr Grey can explain things for us tomorrow, shall we?"

"Yes. Thanks, Mum." I held back the sobs that threatened to overwhelm me. This rollercoaster of emotions was exhausting. I had to get myself back under control. Maybe Alvin did have some answers. The drugs began to kick in and I finally managed to slip into a dreamless sleep.

If only it had lasted. I woke in the early hours of the morning, sure that someone had been calling to me. Although I was still slightly groggy, I was convinced I hadn't dreamed the voice. The noise in my head was at a tolerable level, maybe I was getting accustomed to it, but it felt like there was an echo of something above the normal buzz. I was reluctant to chase it while the chatter was manageable. I didn't want to turn up the volume, so I lay still and consciously tried to relax using the breathing technique from my hypno session, thinking about a time when I was truly happy.

We'd been at the Wallis house for a barbeque the Saturday of Seth's eleventh birthday. Mum and Elizabeth were chatting and laughing as they prepared salads and desserts, while Dad and Samuel continued the centuries-old tradition of the men burning sausages on the grill. I don't know how they managed it on the thermasensor-spit, but they did! Summer had started early that year and it was a warm afternoon filled with buzzing insects pollinating the flowers, and twittering birds as they fed their fledglings. Seth and I sat on the bench that surrounded the big oak tree at the bottom of the garden. I nervously gave him my present and a quick peck on the cheek.

"Happy birthday, Seth. Hope you like it."

He carefully unwrapped the gift, smoothing the paper before opening the box I'd retrieved from our recycling. I was pleased with myself for finding one just the right size for the antique binoculars that I'd bought at a house clearance sale. They were the sort that had a focussing wheel and lenses – not the modern satellite enhanced digital-sights.

"Jeez, thanks, Dez. They're genuine Leica Ultravids – look there's an old receipt in the bottom of the case: £1,210 – pre-credits! Hang-on, I can just make out the date, 15th April 2009. They were state-of-the-art back then."

I'd never seen Seth so excited. I knew he was keen on old-fashioned stuff, and binoculars, telescopes and the like were particular favourites. But I hadn't realised how much these would mean to him. He hugged me tightly and gave me a huge, sloppy kiss – on the mouth! – then pulled away embarrassed at his outburst, though still grinning from ear-to-ear. I felt like *I'd* just received the best birthday present of *my* life, instead of being the giver. It wasn't the kiss – still too young to really appreciate that – it was the sheer joy in Seth's face. His boisterous mood was infectious and soon, at his insistence, everyone was taking turns to look at birds, trees, even the neighbour's washing, through his new prized possession.

That blissful afternoon and evening were a cherished memory. Elizabeth was able to ignore her 'moody-blues', as Seth labelled them, and she chased around the garden with us as though she hadn't a care in the world. Mum was slightly less exuberant but happily joined in with the more sedate activities. When they got tired of the party games, Samuel and Dad sat on the tree-bench and enjoyed a glass or two of vintage Chivas Scotch Whisky. Finally, Seth and I stretched out on the grass and watched the day fade to night as the sun set in a peach-coloured sky. The powerful binoculars seemed to bring the glittering stars within reach and we giggled as we tried to grab them. In our little world all was well and we were comfortable and happy in each other's company.

Try as I might I couldn't stop the darkness welling up and obliterating the happy scene. What had happened to make Elizabeth so sad – so desperately miserable that she felt she had to leave her family and friends? She always called Samuel and Seth her 'darling boys' and it didn't sound naff when she said it – it sounded just right. How could she turn away from that much love? The thought reminded me of something I'd seen in her diary and I reached for my bag hanging from my bed-frame. To save time, I opened the *Handi's* index page and entered 'darling boys' in the search box. There it was, an entry in the results for Tuesday 26th October 2106, the day Elizabeth disappeared:

> For my darling boys; *'Golden slumbers kiss your eyes,*
> *Smiles awake you when you rise.'*

As I read the quotation, I tapped my finger against the screen, a habit of mine when concentrating. The connection brought the cursor back into action and I began to doodle, dragging my finger randomly around the page whilst trying to recall the last few times I'd seen Elizabeth. Had she seemed depressed, preoccupied, distant? No, I didn't remember noticing any of those things or maybe she hid her feelings too well. I wasn't really focussing on the *Handi* screen when, by chance, I noticed the cursor temporarily changed shape in one particular area. I carefully traced over that patch and, so briefly that I nearly missed it, the cursor became a teardrop shape. My gut reaction made me click the enter button on the side of the *Handi* and a new handwritten page came into focus:

My darling boys,

If you're reading this then I'm no longer with you and I hope that you can forgive me. I'd give anything for this not to be the case. It's so much harder when I can't even explain why I left this evening. Please believe that if I could have ended the nightmare any other way, I would have done so.

Writing this hurts – physically, as well as emotionally. I'm struggling against barriers that nobody fully understands yet. I know my vagueness is frustrating, but the answers are here if you can find them. This isn't a cruel riddle to hurt you. Please believe me. It's the only way I can get the message to you.

Read my journal. Remember the REAL me. I need you to do this, please. I need you to see why it had to be this way. MOST IMPORTANTLY – REMEMBER, I LOVE YOU WITH ALL MY HEART AND I HATE LEAVING YOU LIKE THIS.

Sam, my love, be brave for our son. Be strong knowing that I've always loved you and that your love has comforted me through my darkest hours. Although I'm envious that I won't be with you, I want you to find love again when this is over. Share your generous heart with someone new. You'll know when you find her and I give you my blessing.

Seth, how can a mother leave such a wonderful son? It's breaking my heart. But I'll be with you in spirit throughout your life. I'll watch you grow into the caring, supportive and warm man that I can already see in you. I'll laugh with you when you're happy – yes, you will be happy again. Dez will help you, she's a wonderful girl and a good friend. I'll cry with you and share your pain and hope that if you feel I'm with you it'll heal quicker. I'll support all your hopes and dreams so don't you dare lose sight of them! I'm already so very proud of you, my dear, sweet boy.

I must go now. I so want to turn back and stay with you but I can't allow the horror to infect our family any longer.

Take care of each other, my darling boys and forgive me, please forgive me. I wish I could have found another way.

E xxx

Yes, I was crying again. Who wouldn't at such an emotional farewell? I didn't think Seth had seen this. He would've pointed it out to me when he first told me of his suspicions that Elizabeth had killed herself. It was obvious that she didn't expect to come home that evening.

Do I have the nerve to show it to him?

CHAPTER 18

Undisclosed Location: January 2094

"*Time to go,*" the Comms unit ordered. Celeste touched her earpiece to activate the response mode, "Received and understood."

She stepped into the cobbled square and mingled with the crowds, constantly glancing around the area to check the position of her team and ensuring they weren't drawing any unwanted attention.

Despite the vast improvement in international relations since telepathic-twinning evolved, there were still a few hot-heads around who thought they could stir the discontented into violent action against the establishment. Occasionally, she was dragged from her cosy office in the City to lead a field operation. Her talents for de-coding, problem solving, and reading people had taken her to a higher grade than simply a desk job and being married to one of the most experienced field officers had its advantages. Often they could be placed in 'couple' scenarios without the need for pretence – it also added an exciting twist to their real marriage!

Celeste smiled and put her hand to her still-flat stomach. When this project was completed, she would have to tell Jonathan, and her bosses, that field work would soon be off the agenda. She couldn't risk another miscarriage. Anyway, a noticeably pregnant woman always attracted too much attention.

Raised voices brought her out of her reverie. *Damn!* She'd let her mind wander and now had lost sight of two of her team. She couldn't risk using the comms link to check their whereabouts. Her instincts were pointing her towards the disturbance but she knew that if she or any other team-members approached the area they would all be at risk. She opened a black parasol and raised it over her head, ostensibly providing shade from the afternoon sun. Her team would recognise the signal to pull back and reassemble at the safe house. She wandered around the square for another five minutes to ensure her action had been noticed by those who understood it.

***

"Does anyone remember seeing Daniel or Nikita leave the square?" Celeste looked at each of the group in turn. Everybody's face wore the same concerned expression. Two team members missing for over three hours without any comms response could only mean they'd been compromised. All their colleagues could hope for now was that they had simply gone to ground until they could find a safe way out. In the meantime, the project would be suspended until Daniel and Nikita's fate was confirmed.

Six weeks later:

"Celeste, it wasn't your fault. How many more times are we going to go through it all?" Jonathan was at the limit of his patience. He'd been her staunch supporter during the investigation which had found no blame attached to any individual for the loss of the two agents during the aborted operation. Daniel and Nikita had been caught up in a brief skirmish that had nothing to do with the team's target. Local authorities were dealing with the issue and the department had to withdraw entirely for fear of being exposed during the clear up.

The official findings meant nothing to Celeste. She would never forgive her momentary lapse in concentration as she'd indulged in her maternal musings. This pregnancy had cost the lives of two of her people – people she was supposed to be protecting.

CHAPTER 19

Ellingham: 2 August 2110

Can't be time to get up already!

"Desirée. Breakfast is ready." Mum was knocking on my bedroom door.

"Coming, Mum." I made sure Elizabeth's *Handi* was safely tucked away in my bag then pushed the bag under my bed. I still hadn't decided if I should share my latest discovery with Seth but I couldn't see how to avoid doing just that. I'm a rubbish liar, even if it's only by omission!

"Morning, Dad," I said, as I sat at the breakfast table. "Sorry. Again. About the other night." I swiftly added hoping that my apology would halt any further discussion – at least until after my hypno session.

"Good morning, Dez."

Good, we're back on pet-name terms. I thought.

"When you have finished with Mr Grey, this morning, I would like to have a chat about that." Dad continued in his formal tone.

Not off the hook then!

"Would you like to sit in on the session to see what Mr Grey makes of it?" I offered politely, hoping he would refuse.

"I might consider that. I shall ask him if he feels it appropriate."

Well done, Dez. That dodge failed spectacularly! I could only hope that Alvin might put Dad off with some excuse about patient/therapist confidentiality but I wasn't too hopeful.

"Dez."

"What?"

"Pardon?" Mum looked at me with a bemused expression.

"Sorry – pardon."

"No, I wasn't correcting your manners," she sighed. "I was wondering what you were asking?"

This was getting confusing. *She'd* said *my* name. She was the one doing the asking – wasn't she? Though when I came to think of it, the voice had sounded odd, not really like Mum's at all. It had been merely a whisper and, now, I couldn't place where it'd come from. I suppose it must've been inside my over-crowded head but it had sounded so real. Maybe it was the same as last night when I'd thought someone had been calling to me in my sleep.

"Sorry, Mum. My mistake. I thought you'd said something to me." I'd be on my guard from now on. I couldn't risk being sent back to the clinic. I had to keep my reactions under control.

Mum raised a finely-shaped eyebrow in silent query but didn't pursue it any further. Our truce was holding and I felt closer to her than I had in a long time.

"*No preocupe a mi amigo. Un día que sabrá el corazón..*" That was definitely in my head and it sounded familiar. Yes, it was like that other night when Mum had been so angry with me and I'd no idea what she was saying. But now I heard it clearly in my own head and how could I understand the meaning? "*Don't worry my friend. One day she will know your heart.*"

"*Thank you, Rosa.*" This *was* Mum but she wasn't speaking – at least not to us. Rosa was her PT – these were their shared thoughts.

Right. Now, I'm getting really freaked. I understand Spanish?

"Excuse me," I said. "I'd better get ready for my session."

I must've looked as queasy as I felt because neither of the 'rents reminded me I hadn't had any breakfast.

This was more than I could take in. I'd thought that maybe I was going out of my mind, hearing voices that didn't exist. Now I discover that I can tap into Mum's thoughts *and* those of her Argentine PT. Did that mean all the voices were real people, having their own PT conversations? I'd become a telepathic eavesdropper? But where was my unique PT? Maybe it was the voice that kept calling to me. Okay. Well that just meant I'd got to find a way of tuning into her – convinced it was female by the tone of the voice. Of course it also meant I had to tune out the rest of them – *Oh, yeah, easy peasy!*

★★★

When Alvin and Ms Thorogood arrived, Dad was in his study taking an important call so missed his opportunity to sit in on my session.

Seems therapists aren't the only ones doing weekend overtime! Fate was on my side for once.

"How've you been?" Alvin asked, gently stirring his coffee. I found myself following his movements, mesmerised by the circular rhythm.

"Dez?" Ms Thorogood's concerned voice got through to me.

"Sorry?" I said. "I was miles away."

"I was asking how you've been since our last session." He put the spoon on the saucer and sat back to sip his coffee.

"Mm … Where to begin!" I tried to keep calm as I went over recent events. When I mentioned the unintentional eavesdropping into Mum's PT conversation – *that* had them looking uncomfortable for a while! But I couldn't bring myself to recount the awful dream/memory of the murdered couple in Paris. That would've brought Elizabeth's diary into the equation and I wasn't going to break Seth's trust.

"Well, I didn't expect a reaction so quickly," said Alvin. "And certainly not one so dramatic! This is new territory for me, I have to admit."

"Oh. Does that mean you can't help me any more?"

"I don't have any experience of this particular situation," he said. "But I haven't heard of anyone else having it either, so I think we're breaking new ground here, Dez. If you want to carry on and you trust me to look after you, I don't see why we shouldn't continue and see if we can rationalise your PT access. It's your decision."

"I can't handle the constant babbling. Not when it gets too loud,

95

anyway. Sometimes it's bearable but often it's just too much. I've got to find a way to control it – or even switch it off again. Please, Alvin, help me be normal."

"And what's your perception of normal?" asked Ms Thorogood.

That made me pause. I'd lost my idea of normality the night of my party when the anticipated PT connection failed and I started down the path of self-indulgent misery, anger and desperation. It was time to set myself back on track and deal with whatever was needed to get things sorted.

"To start with," I answered. "I think I'd feel more normal if I could keep the voices in my head at a reasonable volume. At least, then, I could hear the conversations outside of it!"

We all smiled at my attempt at levity. Alvin asked me to settle down for my next hypno session. He guided me through the relaxation and towards the trance-like state where he could prompt my subconscious to handle the chattering inside. I grinned at the suggested picture of me ushering the uninvited guests into a large room. I could sense my hands shifting in my lap as, mentally, I gently pushed the last one through the door and closed it behind them. Although the murmuring was still present, it was much quieter.

"… four, five." I was awake again, registering Alvin's last words as he counted me back to full consciousness.

"That was quick," I said. I looked at my watch – an hour gone already. "Oh! Not as quick as I thought."

"We did have a lot to try and accomplish today," Alvin said. "I hope it'll help but don't be surprised if it doesn't kick in straight away. It should get easier over time. It's better to handle things in small chunks rather than attempting everything at once. Today I concentrated on dulling the voices. Next time we'll see if we can find a way to isolate your PT if he/she is there. And I've every confidence you do have one, now that we've seen your telepathic abilities. So don't worry. Call me if you have any problems."

"Thanks."

"You're doing really well, Dez," added Ms Thorogood. "You're a natural. Isn't she Alvin?"

"You've certainly taken to the therapy very quickly," said Alvin. "Especially when you consider the swift reaction to your first session. Hopefully, we'll soon have you 'normal' again." This last said with a grin and quote gestures. I smiled in response. I was beginning to understand that there's no such thing as absolute normal – just varying degrees of it.

So long as I get on the scale of normal – that'll do me!

CHAPTER 20

Ellingham: 2 August 2110

Well you needn't look so bloody worried!

I'd just told Seth my latest discovery that I was a telepathic-eavesdropper, amongst the other weird stuff like remembering being murdered! He hadn't taken it as well as expected and was currently pacing around the room, chewing his lip and looking as though he wanted to make a run for it.

"What's the matter with you?" I asked. "I thought you'd be pleased that I'm not actually having a mental breakdown!"

"I am. Really, I am," he protested. "It's just a lot to take in."

He came to a stand-still and looked at me.

"Can you tell what I'm thinking now, then?" he asked, frowning.

"No. It's not like that. Things just come to me. I've avoided deliberately tuning in, in case they all start shouting again." Didn't he trust me with his thoughts? I broke eye contact with him to hide the hurt, but he knew me well enough to sense my feelings.

"Sorry, Dez." He came to sit beside me on the cosy two-seater sofa, a favourite of his mother's. His bulk took up more than half the seat – was he growing bigger on a daily basis? He wrapped his arm around my shoulders and pulled me towards him. With his free hand he threatened to tickle me and I couldn't help squealing.

"Friends?" he asked.

"Only if you don't tickle me!"

"Deal. But stop sulking, okay? It's weeks since I've seen you really laugh, Dez. Even if tickling is a naff way to do it I'm gonna bring the old Dez out."

That did make me smile. If anyone was going to find the old me, it was Seth. I savoured the moment, imagining a future filled with similar comfortable scenes of Seth and me cosied-up together. Samuel came in and wasn't able to hide the brief pained expression as he saw us in a pose that he and Elizabeth had shared on the same sofa. I quickly pulled away from Seth.

"No, don't mind me," Samuel said, gesturing with his hand to keep me sitting where I was. "It's nice to see you two on good terms again."

I wasn't trying to listen but before I knew it Samuel's thoughts were in my head: *God, Lizzie it still hurts.* The pain was so raw, so tangible, it made my chest hurt and my throat burn.

"You all right, love?" Samuel asked. He must've seen my reaction but I didn't dare tell him the truth. Seth realised that I'd probably had another telepathic sound-bite and answered for me.

"She'll be fine, Dad. Just an after-effect of the hypno session. She gets a few emotional tweaks while the treatment settles in."

"Oh! Oh, right then." Samuel nodded, relieved that he hadn't done anything to upset me.

"We're off for a walk. Some fresh air'll do her good, don't you think?" Seth said.

"Yes. Good idea, lad. And when you come back I'll expect you to stay for tea, Dez. It's been a while since you've sampled my delicious 'Cottage-pie a la micro'!"

"Thanks, Samuel. Yum, yum," I laughed, glad that the awkward moment had passed relatively unnoticed.

"See?" said Seth, as we reached the garden gate, "Told you we'd get you laughing again."

"Do you think I'll be sorted in time for next term?" I asked. The summer break wasn't going to last for ever and I was beginning to feel nervous about going back to the Academy if my mind was still going to be susceptible to everyone's thoughts.

"'Course you will," he reassured me. "Whatever happens, you'll cope. Look how well you've managed so far."

"Huh! I've been a miserable, self-absorbed, pain-in-the-arse.

And I'm probably going to stay that way for a while – so be warned."

We walked in companionable silence until we reached the town park. We stopped at the gate and nervously looked at each other. Ellingham Lake was partially within the park boundary and it was this path I'd run along that rainy night.

"Actually…" "Do you …" we said simultaneously.

We both grinned self-consciously.

"Ladies first," Seth offered.

"I was going to say, do you mind if I walk down to the lake on my own – just for a few minutes? I'll be back before you know it," I added quickly, before he got too uncomfortable about the idea.

"And I was going to say, on this occasion, I'd prefer to walk up to the woods. I'll wait on a bench up there if you want to go to the lake," he replied.

"Well, that's settled then. See you in a few."

I realised that I'd been able to keep calm most of the afternoon. The noise in my head had been bearable, almost quiet at times. Was that the hypnotherapy working or just the comforting presence of my best friend keeping it at bay? I wouldn't question the cause, I'd simply enjoy the relative peace. The path meandered along the edge of the park's botanical gardens and finally came to the lakeshore. After the last few dry days the ground was firm underfoot and I felt embarrassed at the thought of my slipping in the rain, rolling down the banking and giving poor Seth and his dad the feeling of déjà-vu when they found me there.

Reflections of the afternoon sun made the lake's surface shimmer like a vast silver-blue cloth studded with countless diamonds. With very little wind to churn the water's surface, it resembled a pool of mercury, lazily lapping at the lakeshore. I could smell the pine resin of the conifer trees and the earthy warmth of the oaks. Despite the awful memories this lakeside held, it was still one of my favourite places – especially when it was so peaceful, so beautiful in the summer sunshine. I sat on the trunk of a fallen spruce tree. One of the park sculptors had worked it into a surprisingly comfortable bench overlooking the lake and the countryside beyond. It was well-used and highly-polished from the years of walkers' backsides resting on it. I could almost ignore the voices chattering in the background of my mind even when one occasionally became clear above the babble. I wouldn't allow myself to take any notice. I'd find a distraction to push it away. That's why I wanted some time here – away from everyone else – where I could practice tuning out the noise.

★★★

The trees are dripping even though it's not raining. I'm glad I have my sturdy waterproof walking boots on. I'll have to remember to keep my head up so that my waxed hat can keep the drips out of my jacket neckline.

The path winds up the valley side under the closely-packed conifers and the mist swirls around the tree trunks like an old horror movie. Under here the daylight barely penetrates. I expect to see werewolves come crashing through the undergrowth at any moment. I shiver at the frightening thought – childish but almost believable in this setting. There's nobody else about at this time of year. The lead mining museum is closed and the woodland is quiet. I feel like we're the only people on the planet.

"How far are we going?" I ask, looking at a couple of fallen trees blocking the path further up the hill. We've already walked several miles and I'm worried about not getting back to civilisation in daylight. There's no artificial lighting out here and a fall could mean a serious injury on this severe slope.

"Not too far," he answers and shifts the backpack more comfortably on his broad shoulders. "Then we'll have our picnic. I've packed some coffee laced with a little something to keep the chills away." He grins.

I smile shyly in return. Why has he chosen me? He can have any girl he wants. Why me? No, I shan't question, I'll just enjoy it while it lasts.

"This looks like a good spot." He gestures towards a hollow. "It'll be sheltered from the dripping trees and the overhang has kept the ground relatively dry, look."

He's right. The pine needles look dry and the lush green sphagnum moss growing over the roof of the hollow makes it look like a tiny eco-cottage, just waiting for someone to brighten it up with a few home comforts.

I giggle like a teenager as I wriggle backwards into the dark recess. He's already taken off the backpack and leans out to open it. A large splat of water hits the back of his neck and he yells in frustration. It startles me to see his swift change of mood, his face so screwed up in anger. But it passes just as quickly and he laughs about the surprise shower he's had.

I sip the coffee gratefully as I'm feeling chilled despite several layers of thermal clothing. January in Upper Weardale – not the most hospitable time or place to come hiking, but it's one of his favourite spots and it sounded so romantic when he offered to whisk me away for the weekend. I can feel the warmth of the coffee radiating from my stomach – odd, I've never felt it so physically before. Wonder what it is he's laced it with, it's certainly doing the trick! I even feel a bit light-headed. Wait 'til I let Valerie in on all this, she'll be so jealous that I've found the perfect gent and she's still looking.

He's looking at me strangely. He's still smiling but now it looks cruel. What's wrong? Why can't I speak? I can't move. He takes the coffee mug out of my paralysed hands and pushes me further back into the shallow cave.

"Don't worry," he says. "You won't feel a thing. You'll soon drift off to sleep. Once hypothermia kicks in it'll break down all traces of the drug so there'll be no forensics to show that this was anything more than a tragic incident – a solo walker lost in the woods, sheltering from the cold. Silly girl hiking in January, tut, tut." He's laughing as he gathers the picnic things back into the rucksack.

Valerie – VALERIE! Where are you? Help me Valerie. Please answer. Why can't I hear you?

He'll not get away with this. Valerie will alert someone if she can't hear me, surely? My wristchip sends out GPS. They'll know where I am.

"I know what you're thinking," he sneers. "This is one of my favourite gadgets." He's holding a pen-drive to my wrist, just like the ones we use at work to back-up data in the labs. "It might look like a pen-drive but it's a sophisticated chip manipulator. It's programming your chip to show that you are now walking towards the road. This evening there will be a transaction at your local grocery registered against your credit balance. Nobody will look for you out here. Not for some time anyway."

Well, the police will have the ground evidence won't they Mister Cleverclogs? But as he walks away whistling cheerfully I see that the treacherous sphagnum moss is just springing back to shape. No tracks, no boot-prints, nothing. Oh, he's been so careful – the bastard!

Why did he choose me? He could've had any girl he wanted. Why me? No, I shan't question, I'll just sleep it off. It's just a bad dream…

★★★

"Dez. Dez, are you okay?" Seth came hurtling down the path and grabbed an overhanging branch to stop himself before he careered down the banking. "I heard you screaming from the other side of the park! What's wrong?"

I was shivering with cold and fear. The apparent reality of another false memory was so strong that I was chilled to the bone, despite the summer sun still being warm overhead. I looked around at the surrounding trees and realised that they weren't the dour dripping woodland of a northern dale. Gradually the terror subsided. Seth wrapped me in his embrace and I soaked up his warmth.

"Jeez, Dez! You're freezing. How the hell did you get so cold?"

"It's all right. I'm fine," I managed through chattering teeth. "Just a bad dream. Must've dozed off in the sun. This hypnotherapy stuff really is tiring."

"Come off it, Dez. People don't freeze having bad dreams. Tell me what happened."

So I did. And as I did, I had a vague feeling of old grief as though I'd already experienced this death but from a different viewpoint. Was it Valerie's bereavement I felt? Did she know how her PT had died? Had the murderer finally been found?

"Come on. We've got to get back. I need to look at your mum's *Handi* again."

Seth looked at me with a quizzical frown then shook his head as if he knew he wouldn't understand the answer. He helped me to my feet and held my hand all the way back to his house. I welcomed his touch and it never occurred to me to look for him in my head. I was busy trying to reassure Valerie, if she could hear me.

Don't worry we'll find the bastard!

103

CHAPTER 21

The Ritz Hotel, London: July 2096

"You didn't need to do this," Sebastian said, sweeping his arm across the table and almost knocking over the three tier cake stand.

"Nonsense, Uncle," replied Victor. "A champagne tea at The Ritz is the least you deserve after all your guidance and support over the years. I hope I can still call on that support now that I'm the new CEO?"

Sebastian ground his teeth, hoping that his nephew couldn't see his frustration at being pushed to one side now that the terms of Benjamin's will enforced Victor's inheritance of the business. Small consolation but at least Victor still seemed to want him involved in the business. The champagne was making him a little drunk and he realised he might be too careless if he didn't ease off. One more couldn't hurt though, could it?

"A toast, dear boy." Sebastian raised his glass. "To the next generation of Trevalyn geniuses – or is that genii? Ha – sounds like something from Aladdin!"

Victor's face was unreadable but he could sense his uncle's increasing tension. He realised that Sebastian loathed the idea of giving up control of the Trevalyn Corporation, despite the huge handshake he was receiving which would keep him amongst the wealthiest in the country. Once again Victor wished the telepathic evolution hadn't stalled at a singular connection. He wanted to know what *everyone* was thinking. How they felt. What they were really like inside. What an advantage that would be in business as well as in personal relationships. His lips twitched into a smile as he sensed his PT recoil at the idea.

'*What's the matter? Will you be jealous if you're not the only one?*' he mentally sneered.

"You still with us, Victor?" Sebastian waved his arm again. The waiter came hurrying across the room to fulfil the guest's wishes only to find his attention wasn't the one the old man had been trying to attract. "Shoo, boy. It's not time for your tip yet." The waiter was too well trained to show his real feelings. He smiled politely, collected the empty champagne bottle and discreetly withdrew. His professionalism had a subtle effect upon the two Trevalyn men. The remainder of the tea-party was a civilised, almost happy occasion. After all, each of them was well aware that accidental death had developed a habit of visiting their family members. Life should be enjoyed while one still had the opportunity to do so.

Sebastian's loud voice and wide gestures hadn't only been noticed by the attentive waiter. A teenage girl had been daydreaming, watching the other guests via the numerous reflections in the mirrored panels of the room. Everyone else was so sedate and relaxed that the man's exaggerated behaviour was out of place amongst the calm surroundings.

"Do you know who that angry man is, Gramps?" she asked.

Matt looked towards the table that Bethany indicated. He held his reaction in check and replied, "It's Sebastian Trevalyn. He runs a big pharmaceutical company. Or rather he did. I heard his nephew is taking over as the boss now."

"Ooh, maybe that's why he's so angry!" Bethany chuckled. "He doesn't look old enough to retire. It can't be nice to be put out to grass before your time."

Matt smiled at his granddaughter's assessment. Her judgement was obviously influenced by the busy life he still led running the charitable foundation created in memory of his father. Sometimes he wished for a quieter life but she was right – he wouldn't like to be forcibly retired either. A brief twinge of sympathy for Sebastian was quickly stifled by the memory of his mother's distrust of the Trevalyn family.

He turned to his daughter, "Did you ever find anything interesting in Granny Julia's files?"

"Sorry, Dad," Jade mumbled, trying to swallow the tiny cake she'd just popped in her mouth. She took a gulp of tea before continuing,

"I've kept meaning to look at them but you know what it's like. Life gets in the way." They both shrugged, disappointed with themselves for allowing their own priorities to overrule their promise to carry on Julia's search for the truth. Although, it was difficult to know *what* truth they were supposed be hunting down!

"I've got lots of time." Bethany's curiosity had been piqued. "Can I help?"

Matt and Jade looked uncertain.

"Plee-ase!" Bethany wheedled. "I've nothing better to do this holiday."

"We're not even sure what Granny Julia was looking for," Jade answered. "Do you remember any hints, Dad? Dad?"

Matt was staring towards the Trevalyn table, lost in memories of his mother's frosty relationship with the old guy – Benjamin. What had he done all those years ago that had upset the Baroness?

"GRAMPS?"

He felt his sleeve being tugged. "What's the matter? Shush now!"

"You didn't hear Mum and you looked weird. I thought you were having a stroke or something!" Bethany was indignant to cover up her fear.

"I'm sorry Betty-kins," Matt replied, hugging her tightly. "I didn't mean to scare you. Tell you what – you can look at Granny's papers and if you find anything interesting I'll ..."

"Book 'Thorny Lyrics' for my Sixteenth-Eve?"

Luckily her family found her interruption amusing but Bethany hoped she could find something worthy of the cheeky request. 'Thorny Lyrics' were *the* biggest band around.

CHAPTER 22

Ellingham: 2 August 2110

Yes. Here it is!

"Look." I pointed at one of the news reports in Elizabeth's *Handi*, "I was remembering this."

> **News Archive:** Tuesday 3 March 2105 (UK)
> The body of a young woman has been found in a wooded area of the Weardale Estates near the Killhope Lead Mining Museum. Ray Barratt (36), an estate and museum worker, found the body during his routine maintenance of the woodland walks. It is believed that she died of hypothermia. The woman's wristchip was corrupted and injuries to the body caused by foraging animals make visual identification virtually impossible. Investigations are underway to identify the woman using DNA comparison with the Missing Persons Register. A police source has confirmed that this appears to be the tragic case of an inexperienced hiker falling victim to bad weather. Anyone who has any information or who believes they can help identify this woman should call …
>
> POP-UP: *'He just had the power to kill her that's all: to destroy her flesh and blood, the tools without which she could not work.' The Girl in a Swing: Richard Adams.*
>
> (DOM: 18/01)

"There's that notation again; DOM. What does that stand for?" I wondered aloud.

"Never mind that. What do you mean, you were remembering this?"

"I'm not sure. But, like the murdered lovers in Paris, it felt more like a memory than a dream. I was there, feeling everything that girl felt. Tasting the coffee. Smelling the damp woods. You said yourself – I was freezing, just like she was."

"How's that even possible?" Seth's expressive features showed his confusion, his concern and a little fear. "How can you remember things that haven't happened to you?"

"Wish I knew!" I sighed and leaned back on the sofa, hoping that he would hold me like he did earlier but he was restless. He stood and began to pace around the room, one hand rubbing the back of his neck and his brow creased in concentration.

"It must be something to do with your open telepathy," he said, snapping his fingers and grinning at the sudden realisation. "Let's see what you're capable of."

"Whoa! What're you suggesting?" I held my hands out in a defensive gesture. "I'm not having anyone else messing with my head, thank you very much indeed! It's bad enough in there as it is."

"Sorry, Dez. I didn't mean to scare you. But you need to understand what's causing these dreaming memories to surface."

"All right. Just let's take it one step at a time." I'd been trying to avoid investigating this latest development in my mental activities, in case it sent me into a psychological free-fall. Even so, Seth was right. We needed to find out where these recollections were coming from. I patted the cushions and he came to sit next to me.

"Take my lead, okay?" I said. "To start with, I think we should see how open this telepathy really is."

"What've you got in mind?"

"Oh, very funny."

Seth frowned, puzzled at my sarcasm – he hadn't heard the pun in his question.

"What've I got 'in mind'?" I said, tapping my temple.

"Ah. I see." His face cleared. "Come on, then. Get on with it – whatever it is," he added.

"We…ell. I thought I'd try to find you," pointing at my head again, "then you could let me know what's happening in your head at the same time." I looked at him with my eyebrows raised in query. It was a lot to ask. I knew he was uncomfortable with my ability so I wasn't sure how he'd take to my idea. His lips tightened and his eyes clouded with doubt at the suggestion but he quickly controlled his expression and nodded his acceptance.

"What do I need to do?" he asked.

"Nothing really. I'll just have a root around in my head to see if I can pick up a sense of you and then try to tune in. Ready?"

He still looked a little unsure but nodded again. "Let's give it a go then," he said.

I thought it'd help to look into his eyes and I placed my hands either side of his head as a tangible attempt to make the connection. The jolt I got wasn't mental it was physical. His eyes were deep pools of smouldering gold, his hair curled softly around my fingers and I saw him catch his bottom lip in his teeth as though to hold back a moan. Before we realised what was happening we were in each others' arms, kissing with an intensity that made me quiver. His tongue explored my mouth and I responded in kind, tracing his even teeth and savouring his taste. I wanted it to last forever but, eventually, we had to come up for air. We looked at each other with shock and lust in equal measure.

"Er … Did you hear anything then?" he whispered, hoarsely.

"Not a thing. I think I was distracted."

"Yeah. Know what you mean. What's going on Dez?" He sounded lost. Why was he so upset? What was wrong with us being together as more than just friends? Before the recent events I would've buried my feelings and made a joke, but now I wanted to clear the air. I was tired of hiding things from the people close to me.

"I think I love you, Seth. No, that's not right. I *do* love you. I realise now that I always have – in a way. You were my big brother when we were younger, you've always been my best friend, but now it's more than that. I'm sorry if it's not what you want from me. I can't help it and I've only just understood it myself." I was near to tears as I finished.

He waited for my ranting to end then he gently took my flushed face in his hands and tilted it so that he could look me straight in the eye,

"Desirée Hanson. I've been in love with you for years but haven't known how to tell you. I was scared that you'd laugh at me. And then you had so much to deal with recently I didn't want to add to your problems by putting this on you too."

My tears did start to fall then. For once, they were happy tears. Seth pulled me into his embrace and we both laughed at the predicament we'd created by masking our feelings.

"That settles it," I said, when we broke off kissing. "We'll stick together for now and see how it goes, yeah?"

"Fine by me, boss!"

I gave him a playful punch then grabbed his shirt and pulled him towards me for some more serious lip-synch action. Everything else faded into the background and we spent a while soaking up the new relationship. I gazed at the angles of his face, loving the sweep of his neck that drew my eye to the hollow at its base. I traced my finger down his shirt and unfastened the buttons so that I could slide my hand across his chest. Funny – I'd spent most of my waking hours in his company and seen him down to his swim-shorts so often I'd lost count but I'd not noticed how well-toned he'd become. As my fingers brushed over his nipple I felt it harden.

"Didn't know that happened to boys too!" I giggled, trying to get his shirt open. He groaned and held my hand still.

"Dez, you're killing me. Stop! We'd better not get carried away. Dad'll be home soon."

I pouted, but realised he was right. Although this was new and exciting, we needed to take things slowly to make sure it was what we really wanted.

"All right," I said, straightening my dishevelled clothing. "Best behaviour for now! What are we going to do about these memories then?"

"How about we ask Alvin if he's any ideas?"

"But that'll mean having to share your mum's journal."

"Not necessarily. We could download the news reports onto an old memory pen. He doesn't need to know where they came from. And we can edit out the pop-up quotes so there'll be no weird riddles for him to worry about."

"If you're sure you don't mind."

"Dez. I'll do anything to help you get things under control. I can't stand it when you're scared and lost, like you were this afternoon. I want you healthy and happy again. We'll comm Alvin now."

Seth launched himself from the sofa and dragged me up with him. *My Seth. My hero!* The thought brought a catch to my throat. Only a few days ago it was my dad who was my hero. I'd sorted out one relationship – it was time to sort out the mess between Dad and me.

"Here you go." Seth interrupted my thoughts by pushing me towards the Holo-Comms unit. "Better call now before my dad gets in."

"You're keen!" I said. "Let's see if he's available."

As I'd suspected, Alvin couldn't take the call so I left a message asking him to contact me when he had the chance. As I closed the connection, Samuel came in from the kitchen.

"Ah, good. You're home," he said. "I'll get washed and then we'll have that Cottage Pie I promised you."

It was great to have a relatively normal dinner for once. The tension between Seth and me had virtually disappeared, although I still felt there was something he was holding back. No worries – I knew I'd get him to open up now that we were a real couple at last. I'm sure Samuel could sense a change too. He was more relaxed than I'd seen him since Elizabeth's death. I occasionally caught him looking at me with a smile, slightly nodding as though in approval.

After helping to clear the dinner things away I decided to head home in good time so that I could talk to Dad before it got too late.

"Thanks for dinner, Samuel," I said. "It's my turn to cook next time."

"It's a deal," he replied. He gave me a quick hug and went out to do a bit of gardening before the light faded.

"I'll walk you home," Seth said.

"I'm only down the road."

"Yeah. But it's what boyfriends do, isn't it?"

"Only the really nice ones!" I earned myself a kiss and we walked to my house with his arm draped over my shoulder.

I could get used to this!

CHAPTER 23

Ellingham: 2 August 2110

Hi Mum and Dad, guess what; I can hear your thoughts and I remember being murdered – twice!

Probably not the best greeting so I settled for "I'm home." I went in to the lounge, breaking my usual habit of running straight up to my bedroom. "Oh. Hi, Aunt Jen."

"Hello, pet. Just popped round to see how you're getting on. And, judging from the glow in your face, I'd say you've perked up nicely." How did she manage to be so perceptive?

"Thanks. How're Jeremy and Dick?"

"Fine. I've left them watching some macho sport together. Hoped it might provide a bit of male bonding. It's a shame Henri can't give me any tips on the inner workings of the male psyche." Jen's French PT couldn't understand her fascination with the 'filthy outdoors and those smelly animals'. And he wasn't always talking about the horses! He came over to visit from time-to-time and, in reality, wasn't nearly as camp as he liked to make out via his telepathic link with Jen. Come to think of it, he'd made some very complimentary comments about Seth on his last trip. *Mm, better keep an eye on him. Seth's mine now!*

"What're you grinning at?" Jen asked me, breaking into my reverie of the afternoon's surprises.

"Sorry? Oh. Just the thought of Henri trying to think of macho stuff for Jeremy and Dick to do. I'm sure his idea of male bonding is something quite different."

"Desirée!" Mum's frown reminded me I was supposed to be behaving myself.

"Sorry, Mum. Sorry, Jen." Although Jen wasn't helping, busy pretending her giggles were a coughing fit. I risked a glance at Dad and was relieved to see even he had a twinkle in his eye.

"Shall I make us all a nice cuppa?" I tried to redeem myself.

"No. I'm fine thanks," said Jen. "I'll be off to check the lads. Make sure they've not broken through the fence again." She was talking about her horses now and not her lads of the two-legged variety. She kissed Mum and Dad goodbye and followed me through to the kitchen. "Good to see you looking a bit brighter, Dez. Sorry I didn't come to see you at the clinic but I thought you'd prefer a bit of space."

"Thanks, Aunt Jen," I said. "You do know it was all simply an accident, don't you?"

"Of course I do, pet. Deep down your mum and dad know it too. They were just in shock for a while thinking they'd lost you. Now, go in there and get on with the making up – I've softened 'em up for you!" She gave me a quick hug. "See you soon," she added from the threshold as she closed the outer door.

I prepared the drinks and took them through to the lounge. The 'rents were in their favourite seats – Mum by the patio door soaking up the warm rays of the evening sun and Dad in the opposite corner with his hobby table across his lap and fitting the pieces in an ancient cardboard jigsaw puzzle.

"Can we talk, please?" They both nodded for me to continue. I paused for a moment, trying to choose my words carefully and I realised that the constant chattering in my head had definitely become less intrusive. *That's a relief.* At least I could start to think more clearly.

"First of all, I want to apologise for the worry I caused you when I ran off the other evening. Please believe me that it wasn't an attempt at suicide. I really did fall by accident but I realise it wouldn't have happened if I hadn't let my temper get the better of me."

"We were worried, Dez. But we now appreciate that it was an accident and we can move on," Dad reassured me. Mum's smile was strained, as though she'd like to disagree but she nodded her acceptance of Dad's response.

"I know I've been a pain since then too and I'll try to explain, though it's hard for me to understand it all myself." My mouth was dry with nerves so I took a quick gulp of tea. Would they accept what I was going to tell them or would they think I needed to go back to the clinic for further psychiatric appraisal? *Here goes!*

"I was scared of letting you down when my PT didn't switch on. I didn't want to be a freak and I got angry that it hadn't happened. I shouldn't have been so cross at you, Mum, but I felt you'd be disappointed in me again."

"But I ... " Mum cut off what she was going to say so that I could carry on.

"Thanks, Mum." I acknowledged her struggle not to react. "I know we've a lot to sort out between us, and we'll not get through it all tonight. I just want to clear up our recent problems."

"Go on," she said.

"The clinic was awful. That nurse was always keen to top up the drugs, simply to keep me quiet. You know the one, Dad. I was so scared." I stopped for another sip of tea to help swallow my rising emotions.

"Don't worry, sweetheart. I have already lodged a complaint to the Trevalyn board of directors. By now, they should be dealing with the shortcomings at their Ellingham clinic. One would think that a corporation of that size could afford to employ better staff." My Dad was still my hero after all.

"After the first session of hypnotherapy my head was suddenly full of noise. Loud, insistent voices. So many that I couldn't make sense of any of them and it felt like I was going mad. That's how I latched on to Claude's saying the other night, Dad. I think it was because I was upset and you were near – it sort of opened up a link to your PT."

"What do you mean, Dez? Are you saying that you can hear our PT connection?" Dad's face wore a similar troubled expression to the one Alvin and Ms Thorogood had that morning. I was beginning to get accustomed to the reaction – even Seth had been worried to hear about my eavesdropping ability.

"Is that why you thought I'd spoken to you earlier today?" Mum asked. This was going to be a difficult bit.

"I was sure I heard someone calling my name. Maybe I do have an PT out there trying to get through to me. But, this morning, I also heard you and Rosa telepathically. I'm sorry I didn't mean to listen in to your conversation. How do I understand Spanish? Ms Thorogood said it would work with our PTs but Rosa's not mine, is she? "

Mum's face had gone pale and she quickly put her cup and saucer on to the side table as though she was afraid of dropping them.

"Don't worry," I hastily added. "Alvin's latest session seems to have helped quieten things down. I haven't had any major connections since the hypnotherapy this morning. Well not of the telepathic sort, anyway." I sneaked a quick look at each of them to see their reactions to that little teaser. Mum turned her attention back into the room from her brief contemplation of the garden and Dad took a deep breath, waiting for the other boot to fall.

"Seth's my boyfriend now." I looked at my dad and thought I'd better put him out of his misery. "Don't worry. I'm not pregnant. We've only just kissed for the first time today. We've not had the nerve to tell each other how we felt and we're taking things nice and slow. It's all very innocent, honestly." I couldn't wait for their reaction and swiftly added, "Well, say something."

"We would if we could get a word in edgeways," said Dad.

"Does Mr Wallis know about this?" Mum asked.

"We haven't said anything but I think he's guessed. He seems pleased. Aren't you?" I was desperate for them to approve of the progression in our relationship but if they didn't it was tough – Seth and I were definitely together now, whatever the 'rents said. I was surprised to see Dad smiling – not so surprised to see Mum with tears in her eyes. *Can't she be happy for me for once?* I thought. Then she did surprise me. She came over to sit by me on the big red sofa and pulled me into a fierce hug.

"Oh, Dizzy. You've grown up so fast," she said. "I'm not ready to stop being a mother yet."

"Don't be daft," I answered shakily, trying to keep my own emotions at bay. "You'll always be my mum. But, I'm sorry that you don't want me getting together with Seth since you don't seem to like him much these days."

"N-no. That's not the case," Mum stuttered through her tears. "I've always been very fond of Seth."

"Look at you two," Dad chuckled and he came to join us on the sofa, wrapping his girls in his arms and gently rocking us back and forth.

Mum gave me a squeeze then sat up straight and began to explain why she'd kept Seth at arm's length.

"Ever since the night Elizabeth disappeared, I've felt guilty for not looking out for her. I saw her going out towards the park that evening but she begged me not to say anything to Samuel. She was in a hurry and said she didn't have time to explain. She was so agitated and kept glancing towards the park as though she was looking for someone. I don't know why but all I could think of was that she was going to meet another man. I was angry. Samuel was … is one of my oldest friends from school. I told her I wouldn't lie for her but that I wouldn't volunteer anything either. My last words to her were: 'Your sordid little secret's safe with me.'" Mum's voice fell to a whisper and her eyes were brimming with tears again. I passed her a tissue from the box on the coffee table. "How can I look Seth in the eye again when I could've stopped his mother going to her death that evening? I should've made her go home and sort things out. I worry that I might let something slip to Samuel or Seth and that would break their hearts all over again."

Dad wrapped his arms around her while she wept uncontrollably. I cried along with her. She'd been carrying around this guilt and pain for almost four years. No wonder she hid behind a wall of severity. She kept herself aloof so that nobody could get close enough to find out her real feelings. Now I understood Jen's comment that Mum hadn't always been this way. The miscarriages had forced her to bury her softer side. She'd had to harden up to keep trying for a baby. Then the circumstances of Elizabeth's death

117

had pushed Mum further into her shell and I'd forgotten the happier times from my childhood when I'd glimpsed her real, loving character.

"Mum. It's not your fault." I reached out to hold her hand.

She shook her head in denial.

"No. Mum, please listen. I can't explain everything yet, we're still working on it. But Elizabeth wasn't having an affair. Seth found her journal and kept it secret from everyone. She had a compact e-diary, you know, one of the *Handi*-types. From the entries I've seen, she loved Seth and Samuel with all her heart. If she was meeting someone it wasn't a lover. And I don't think you could've stopped her if you'd tried anyway. She felt she had to prevent something awful from happening and, whatever she was doing that evening she was fully committed to it. Believe me. You aren't to blame for anything."

Dad turned to me. "Dez. That journal should go to the authorities if it has any bearing on Elizabeth's death. The Coroner ruled that she drowned accidentally but what if she committed suicide in a fit of depression? We know that she sometimes had a dreadful sadness about her that she couldn't, or wouldn't, explain. Your mother's confession is news to me or I would have insisted that she shared her knowledge with the police at the time. And if Elizabeth did meet with someone that night she might even have been murdered! You must take this new information to the authorities. Tomorrow."

"No! Dad, please. Let Seth and me have more time first. He's trusted me with his mother's secret. Please don't drag it into the open yet. I shouldn't have told you, but I couldn't let Mum carry on with all that guilt."

"I shall think about it and let you know my decision in the morning."

"Thank you."

The lighter mood of earlier had dissolved in the floods of tears that Mum and I wept during the evening. And yet the outpouring of grief and worry had finally brought us to an understanding. I took comfort in the thought that Mum and I could have a close relationship after all. It wasn't an instant cure-all and we still had issues to deal with but it was a start. Now I had to hope that I wasn't creating a rift with my beloved father. I knew I would defy him if he tried to insist that we should give Elizabeth's *Handi* to the authorities.

Please, please let us find the truth quickly.

CHAPTER 24

North China Seas: December 2099

Victor was in a good mood. A very good mood. The new century was going to be spectacular.

He stood in front of the wall sized screen admiring the display of normally microscopic biological cells. The cells quivered with activity, growing at a visible rate and dividing just when they seemed to run out of energy. Any that failed to complete the cycle were consumed by their neighbours in the jostling mass.

"Thank you father," Victor murmured, acknowledging the initial work that Jacob Trevalyn had invested in the regenerative drug that his son had now perfected.

Since his appointment as the Chief Executive Officer, Victor had gained access to the massive resources of the Trevalyn Corporation, allowing him to indulge his prodigious scientific knowledge. However, these weren't experiments to benefit the general population. Oh no. These were simply to enhance his own potential. Hence his secret facility off the North China coast. An island so remote that it didn't appear on any tourist guide. It was even too small for satellite mapping to take much notice. But it was perfect for his needs.

After the 2015 Nuke War the area had been declared unsafe but over the years locals had repopulated despite the health risks. A ready-made test group was waiting on the mainland for Victor Trevalyn and his drugs trials when he set-up shop two years previously. China's bureaucracy was still struggling to reassert itself after the decimation of its population from the nukes, the flu pandemic and the economic meltdown. A few individuals from the no-go area could disappear and nobody would notice. Victor could work unhindered and without conscience. These people were dying anyway. Some had slow-burning fallout sickness, some had genetic defects and some had been born with terrible deformities or disabilities. They were glad of the opportunity to find a cure no matter what risks were involved in the process.

And it wasn't just the physical enhancements that Trevalyn was pursuing. He still wanted to further his telepathic ability. He wasn't satisfied with the one PT, despite her being perfect to torment emotionally. She was just so sweet, always trying to get him to be more compassionate about the people he was using. Pushing him to be less self-centred. She'd even allowed her Bloc to ease back so he could experience the love she and her little family had for each other. Didn't she realise that in her own way she was tormenting him in return? What family life had he ever known? His mother had died giving birth to him. A rare occurrence and one his grandfather and Uncle Sebastian blamed on her family genetics, despite the usual pre-conception screening.

At dinner one evening when Victor was about ten years old he made the mistake of asking about Grandmother Trevalyn. Uncle Sebastian had nervously dropped his spoon causing a mini-tsunami in his asparagus soup. Grandfather Benjamin wiped his mouth with his napkin before turning to answer.

"I would prefer it if you never mention that woman again, Victor," he said in a tone that encouraged no argument. "The only useful purpose she served was in providing the next generation of Trevalyns to continue my work. She's likely dead by now, anyway."

With no other female influences, no maternal cosseting, Victor grew up hard and cold. Grandfather Benjamin had indulged him with everything money could buy but was too busy building the Trevalyn Empire to invest any emotion in the relationship. Uncle Sebastian had no family of his own and was also too wrapped up in business matters to take an interest in the young Victor.

Despite being able to share his PT's family feelings he would never understand them.

CHAPTER 25

Ellingham: 3 August 2110

Have I ruined our relationship before it's even got started?

I woke early – not that I'd really slept anyway – feeling desperately worried about what I was going to say to Seth. How would he react when I told him that I'd spilled the beans to my parents? *Only one way to find out I suppose.*

On summer break from the Academy, the days seemed to run into each other and I'd forgotten that it was a Sunday morning. I was showered, dressed and sitting at the kitchen table when the 'rents came in for breakfast.

"Oh! Good morning, Dez!" said Mum, still red around her eyes. "You're not usually down before us. Especially at the weekend. Is something wrong?"

I considered brushing aside the question then decided to confide my fears in the spirit of our new-found closeness. "I'm sure I'll have messed up with Seth. How do I confess that I broke his trust and told you about his mum's diary?"

Mum gently patted my back as reassurance.

"You'll manage it, love. And, if there is something special between you, you'll both get over this upset. You just need to trust your feelings and believe in his."

"Thanks, Mum." I looked at my dad, wondering if the conversation had reminded him of his intention to send us to the authorities. "Dad?"

"All right," he replied. "You can have some time to sort things out with Seth. But you must try to convince him that the police should investigate these new developments. I don't mean to sound patronising, but you are still children, with limited resources. Promise me that you will not take any risks. If Elizabeth was involved with something that led to her death, you could be getting into the sort of trouble you can't handle. Please, at least come to me when you have any further information. *Do not* go chasing after clues on your own."

"Thank you, Daddy!" I squealed and leapt up to give him a big hug. I decided to keep my murder memories to myself for now. *After all they may be something completely unrelated.* Yeah, who was I trying to kid? "Oh, and you won't say anything to Samuel about this, will you?" I quickly added.

"We'll keep quiet," Mum replied. "But you should ask Seth to talk to his father about it. Samuel might be able to offer some insight. Last night I finally realised he's entitled to know the truth even if it is hard to understand."

"I'll see what I can do," I promised. "Don't worry about lunch for me. If I'm back I'll make myself a sandwich."

The walk to Seth's house seemed to stretch far beyond the usual couple of hundred metres yet it was over all too soon. My worrying sent the voices into a frenzied buzz and it was hard to keep them in that mental room I'd created. I kept getting snippets of conversations – all fairly mundane Sunday morning stuff but it bothered me that I could so easily lose my control over them. I was trying to calm my nerves and the chattering as I knocked on Seth's door.

"You're out and about early, Dez," Samuel said, as he ushered me into the kitchen. "Seth's not down yet. Help yourself to a cuppa, there should be one left in the pot. SETH, DEZ IS HERE! Sorry, love, I've got to dash out. One of the trams is stuck up Digby Hill and the remote reset isn't doing the trick. No rest for the wicked, eh?" He grabbed his overalls from the back of the door, picked up his kit, and waved as he left to sort out the town's transport system.

It'd been a frantic but pleasant interval as Samuel rushed around getting ready, but now the kitchen was quiet. I could hear the sparrows chirruping in the gutters outside and the excited barking of a neighbour's dog. Normal everyday sounds that I usually ignored. Now I felt that I had to listen especially hard to hear anything outside my own head. It was all the more special for the extra effort. However, I obviously wasn't listening too well as Seth managed to creep up and give me a huge fright when he grabbed my shoulders from behind.

"Gotcha!" he laughed.

"What the hell are you playing at?" I yelled. My fear making me unreasonably angry.

Stepping back, he held his hands up in surrender, his eyes full of concern, "Sorry. Didn't mean to get you so uptight," he said.

The adrenaline release left me shaking and I struggled not to cry. *I'm really gonna have to stop all this blubbing.* I took a few deep breaths to steady my nerves and started again.

"I'm sorry too, but you frightened me half to death! Anyway, you want a coffee or something to eat?" I'd spent a large part of my life in Seth's kitchen so I was used to helping out during my frequent visits. Actually, I needed the familiarity to bolster my courage before I tore apart our idyll from yesterday.

"Er, thanks," he said, taken aback by my quick mood swing. "I'll have scrambled eggs, please." He sat at the breakfast-bar and tentatively reached for my hand. "Sorry again," he added.

"S'okay." I kissed him on the top of his head as I walked behind him towards the hob. "I'm fine now." I could see that he knew I wasn't fine at all but he didn't argue.

"Did Alvin get back to you last night?" he asked. I'd forgotten that we'd left a message for the therapist.

"Didn't get any calls at home. He might not check his calls at the weekend."

"He came out for a session on a Saturday so why not check his calls?" Seth had a point.

"Hang on, I'll check my messages." I found my earclip in the bottom of my bag, hooked it over my ear and accessed my messages: "You have one new voice message. Received Saturday the 2nd of August at 8.22pm: 'Hi Dez, Alvin returning your call. Hope you haven't developed any further problems from this morning's session. We're away for the rest of the weekend but if there's anything urgent that you need to discuss, please don't hesitate to contact me. I've provisionally booked to see you on Monday morning at ten. Unless I hear from you to the contrary, I'll assume that's okay. Bye for now.' To save the ...." I cut off the recording knowing that it would be saved automatically. Seth looked at me with the curiosity plain in his expression.

"Yes," I answered. "There's a message. He's away but he's booked me in for Monday morning. I think he's worried that I've had an adverse reaction to the hypnotherapy. Better let Dad know there'll be another bill coming."

"Oh gosh, sorry Dez. Never thought about that."

"Don't worry. Remember I'm the spoiled brat of the family. Money is no object," I joked. I was trying to put off the conversation I knew we had to have. I've never been a good liar. It's too much effort to remember the lie and I always manage to trip myself up. Even by trying not to mention the betrayal of Seth's secret I felt I was lying in some way. Time to 'grasp the nettle' as my gran would say.

"Seth. There's something I have to tell you and I'm afraid you're gonna be very upset with me."

"What is it?"

"I told the 'rents about your mum's journal. Not the contents," I added hastily as I saw him frown, "just that one exists and that we're looking at it to see if there're any hints about her ... her... what she was doing that night."

I expected some kind of outburst but the prolonged silence that followed was harder to deal with. Seth's face became a blank mask – emotion completely wiped from it. What was he thinking? How did he feel? *Please say something!*

Finally, in a quiet, hoarse voice he asked; "Why?"

I wasn't sure where to start. How could I justify myself? I thought back to the previous evening and the conversation I'd had with the 'rents.

"It came out when I was telling them about us being a couple, now." I risked a look up into his eyes to see if that was still the case. His deadpan expression didn't flicker; *no hints there.* "Mum was upset and I asked her why she didn't like you. But, apparently it's not like that at all. She said she's uncomfortable around you and your dad 'cos she saw your mum that night."

"What?"

"Your mum was in a hurry and seemed uptight. She asked my mum not to say anything to your dad. Mum jumped to the wrong conclusion, thinking that Elizabeth was having an affair and she made some angry comment about keeping it quiet. It's been eating away at her ever since. She feels really awful for having let Elizabeth go off that night and for not telling you that she'd seen her, but she thought she was saving you from more hurt."

"And how did that lead to you telling them about the diary?" Seth asked, in a flat tone.

"I'm sorry, Seth, I couldn't help it. Mum was in tears. I couldn't let her carry on believing that she was responsible for what happened. I've never seen her in such a state. I said that she wouldn't have been able to stop Elizabeth and, by telling her that, I had to explain how I knew."

"How exactly *do* you know?" His cold questions were frightening me. *I've really screwed up!* I'd forgotten that I hadn't had chance to show him Elizabeth's letter yet. I'd wanted to get him prepared for it and now it was going to be dumped on him in the midst of all this.

"Er … well … I found this on Friday night," I said. I took Elizabeth's *Handi* from my bag, powered it up and opened the page containing the hidden letter. I moved the cursor until it changed shape.

"Click on the teardrop," I said.

I noticed his hand was shaking as he took the *Handi* and read the letter. What little colour had been left in his face drained away and I was worried that he was going to pass out. He blinked rapidly but couldn't stop the tears spilling onto his alabaster cheeks. I swallowed hard to stop my own sobs. I had to be strong for Seth.

He needed the comforting this time. I reached forward and gently laid my hand on his arm where it rested on the kitchen worktop. He drew away from me and it was as though he'd thrust a knife deep into my chest. The pain of that rejection, whether intended or not, was physical and yet I knew I deserved it.

A sudden, furious desire to clean up the kitchen came over me. My coping mechanism. Whenever I feel things getting beyond my control, I start to tidy – whether it's my room, my handbag or a single drawer. Putting stuff away neatly helps me to process my thoughts. 'A place for everything and everything in its place!' I also hoped a burst of activity would chase the suddenly noisy voices back into their 'room' so I began collecting the dirty dishes to stack them in the dishwasher. My anxiety showed in the way the crockery clattered in my hands and I concentrated on stilling the trembling in my arms.

The multitude of connections became suddenly so intense that I dropped the dishes. I clung to the edge of the worktop, my eyes closed, my mind trying to focus on locking them away. When my slight nausea and dizziness from yet another fright had passed, I started to collect up the pieces of a dish that hadn't survived my reaction.

"Leave them," Seth said. "I'll clear up later."

I waited in the hope that he would begin to talk to me again but he just carried on staring at the *Handi* screen. The tension between us continued to build and having my cleaning activity abruptly halted allowed the babbling in my head to intensify. I couldn't ask Seth for any kind of support. I'd lost that option with my loose talk. Now I had to suffer the consequences and hope that time would mend the rupture in our relationship – and if it only restored our friendship, that would have to be enough. But I was terrified that we wouldn't even manage that.

"You might not agree," I said, as I prepared to leave. "But you should tell your dad about the journal, if only to let him see the letter. Your mum wanted to tell him those things too."

I couldn't leave him without some gesture that I was sorry and still wanted to be with him, so I leaned towards him and kissed his tear-streaked cheek. More than the quick peck of a friend, less than the passionate exchanges of the previous day. He looked at me and I saw the pain and resentment competing against the glimpse of love in his soft brown eyes. Outwardly he showed no reaction but in that instant I sensed his feelings of loss and abandonment. Without realising what I was doing I tried to hear his thoughts. There was nothing amongst the babbling of others. I recoiled at my own selfishness. I wouldn't probe further but it was agony to feel so cut off from the one person I'd always been able to communicate with.

Please Seth. Please, don't shut me out now.

CHAPTER 26

Ellingham: 3 August 2110

Great, Dez. You really did a first-rate job of that!

I walked aimlessly towards the park again. The fright of the previous day overshadowed by the more recent emotional upheaval. I found a secluded spot on the embankment leading down to the lake and sat on the dew-damp grass. I wrapped my arms around my legs and bowed my head in surrender, grinding my forehead onto my bony knees as if I could scrape away the pain. I couldn't cope any more. Over the past weeks, too many things had happened that shifted my world to a life now filled with a bewildering onslaught of unfamiliar sensations and instability. I felt like I had my own personal earthquake following me around – tearing everything apart and leaving devastation in its path. Should I ring Alvin or wait until tomorrow to find out whether he had any explanation for what I was going through? Then I realised that, without Elizabeth's *Handi* or Seth's cooperation, I had no references for my dream memories. No matter how bad things were between us, I would have to go back to Seth and ask if he still wanted to know the truth about his mother's death.

"Thought I'd find you here."

I looked up in surprise. "Seth. I ..."

"I know. You're sorry!" He sat beside me. "But that doesn't mean it didn't hurt. It might seem unreasonable, but I was angry that you spoke to your parents without warning me first. I'd only just got used to the idea of *Us* myself. Then, not only do you blab about that, you go on to tell 'em about Mum's diary."

I shuffled awkwardly as he hesitated. My backside was getting chilled from the wet grass but my discomfort wasn't only physical.

"And I was jealous," he said, quietly as though embarrassed to admit it.

"Jealous?"

"Yeah! You still have your mum to confide in. You still have her to argue with and to make up to. And then you tell me that your mum thinks she could've saved mine. 'Course I was jealous – and furious with her. She should've made the effort to find out what was going on – not just been so bloody judgemental. She knew my mum better than that!" He was getting angry again.

"Mum realises that, Seth. If she could go back and do things differently, she would. She was very close to your mum. Don't you remember the barbeques? The Juniors' Sports Days, when they'd get together, bake for Britain and take turns at winning the mums' race? My mum lost her best friend too. Don't you think she'd do anything to change that?"

"Fine. You've made your point. Let's move on shall we? I came to apologise for letting our first disagreement get out of hand."

"Hardly our first disagreement, Seth Wallis."

"As a couple it was."

"I accept your apology on one condition," I said.

"And that is?"

"You accept mine. I should've checked with you before letting on about us and definitely before telling the 'rents about Elizabeth's *Handi*. Am I forgiven?"

"That depends," he said with a lop-sided grin, "on whether you can convince me." He leaned towards me and puckered his lips expectantly. I laughed with relief and tugged him into a full-on, long and lovely kiss.

"Well, it's a start," he said, when we finally came up for air. "Come on, let's get home and you can stand by the stove to dry out your jeans!" He pulled me to my feet and, arms linked, we walked back to his house.

★★★

I looked at the *Handi* while Seth made our brunch – toasted ciabatta with tomato purée and melted mozzarella – basically, home-made pizza. I was still struggling to see why he thought the diary had something significant to tell us about Elizabeth's behaviour. Sometimes the only thing that worked was a good old-fashioned mind-map. I needed to see everything laid out in plain view – flitting between the pages of the compact *Handi* was too disjointed and time-consuming. We launched the Holo-Comms in megascreen mode and synced a couple of digipens so that we each could add comments to the mind-map as it was projected onto the kitchen table.

"Let's see what we've got," I said and powered up the *Handi*. "I think we can ignore the birthday and Academy reminders – so the pink and green highlighted dates are out. That leaves the yellow highlights which your mum used for client appointments and calls, and the blue markers that I asked you about the other day."

"Did you?" Seth looked at me with a raised eyebrow.

"Yes, don't you remember? Oh, hang on a mo. You were out with the washing and then I started hearing the voices." I rolled my eyes in an attempt at dramatic expression then found myself laughing instead. Maybe it was the relief of having Seth on my side again when I'd expected him to hate me, I just had an uncontrollable urge to grin and giggle. Even the ever-present murmuring in my head couldn't dampen my good mood. It was insensitive, we were dealing with Seth's serious concerns about his mum but he smiled and put his arm around me while he looked at the *Handi's* calendar pages. *Mm. That's better.*

"You mean these?" He pointed at the appropriate dates. "No idea what they are. Can't think of anything significant about those dates."

"I'll list them out separately for now. Maybe something'll come to mind later."

As I scrolled through the calendar to find the first marker, the cursor changed to a skull icon as it reached that date: 18th January 2105. I tapped on the date to enter the page and the news report of

131

the girl in the woods came on screen. I shuddered as I remembered the telepathic experience of freezing to death.

"Got it!" Seth's sudden loud outburst made me jerk back to reality.

"W-what?"

"That notation thing – DOM. Date of … M … You know, like DOB is date of birth. But what does the M stand for?"

"Murder," I whispered. "Look, the quotation says it all: '… *He just had the power to kill her that's all:…*' And I was there, remember? The bastard murdered her and got away with it."

"So, if that's what DOM means, do all the reports tally with the dates highlighted blue in the calendar?"

We spent the next hour matching the marked dates to the news reports that had corresponding DOM notations and pop-up quotations. The result was a depressing list of apparently unrelated incidents and accidents. Deaths of various individuals, a group of hikers, even a busload of school kids, and the only connection was that Elizabeth had highlighted them.

"Now what?" Seth's frustration was obvious as he ran his hands through his hair and blew out his cheeks in a long sigh.

"I think we're coming at it from the wrong angle," I said. "We're looking for the common thread in the way these people died, but there isn't one. The deaths were all different. If they were murders committed by the same killer, he kept changing the way he did it – switching his M.O. so they wouldn't be recognised as a series."

"You sound like a classic re-run of 'CSI-2015'."

"Oh, ha, ha. No, listen. What's the only link to these events?"

"I give in."

"Seth! You're not even trying. It's your mum."

"Yeah, I know. They're in my mum's diary. So what's the connection?"

"You still don't get it – that *is* the connection – they're in your mum's diary. She linked the news reports to the dates marked in blue – with a skull-shaped icon, for goodness' sake!"

"O-kay." Seth drew out his reply as though he was trying to

think it through as he spoke. "You're saying that *because* Mum linked them, there *has* to be a connection. So what is it and why didn't she just go to the police?"

"Not sure." I switched on the hard-copier and transmitted a command from the *Handi* to get a printout of Elizabeth's letter. "Look. She says the answers are here if we can find them. She's telling us that the message has to be hidden – she has to be vague and she's struggling against barriers that nobody understands. Why? What or rather *who* could prevent her from telling us outright?"

Seth's expression showed his dawning realisation. "Her PT! That's it. She never once mentioned her PT. Remember, we sometimes talked about Nina? Dad's Russian doll, Mum called her. But we never heard anything about Mum's twin. Jeez, if you're saying he's the murderer, no wonder she broke down. Knowing who was doing this and not being able to tell anyone. Omigod, Dez. I used to get so annoyed when she was being moody." His excitement at finding the link was replaced with the guilt of misunderstanding his mother's behaviour. He sat with his elbows on the table and dropped his head into his hands. His shoulders shook as he tried to contain his sobs.

"Don't worry, Seth. She would've known you couldn't understand." I moved to sit beside him and tried to hold him. Being as clumsy as I am, I managed to stick my elbow onto the edge of a plate and it flipped up covering us both with left-over ciabatta pizza. It wasn't really that funny but we spent the next few minutes trying to control our hysterical laughing.

"You two look like you've been having a food fight."

Samuel's voice had us scrabbling to close down the Holo-Comms before he caught sight of the notes we'd made. I quickly slipped Elizabeth's *Handi* into my jeans pocket but wasn't fast enough to move the printed letter.

"What's this?" Recognising his wife's hand-writing, he reached for the page.

I looked at Seth as I tried to get there first but he shook his head and I held back. We stood silently watching Samuel read the long-lost letter. His reaction so similar to his son's earlier in the day that it felt like déjà vu. I looked at Seth again and gestured for him to pull out a chair for Samuel then I went in search of the brandy. When I'd poured a good measure and brought it to the table Seth had managed to persuade his father to sit down.

"I should go." I could hardly speak for the lump in my throat.

"No." Samuel's voice was surprisingly strong. "No, love, there's no need for you to go. Just give me a minute. Thanks for the snifter."

I couldn't believe how he was holding himself together so well. He'd looked ready to keel over and now he seemed in complete control.

"Really, Mr Wallis," I said, forgetting our first name agreement. "You and Seth have things to talk about. I should leave you in peace."

"Peace? You think there's been much of that about since Elizabeth took herself off?"

"Dad!" Seth looked at his dad in horror. Samuel was always such a quiet man – he'd rarely raised his voice even when we'd been naughty children. Yet now he'd snapped at me with such venom in his tone, it was unnerving. Although I tried to keep my mind occupied with the physical events, I heard Nina, Samuel's PT, asking what was wrong then scolding him for getting so unusually angry. I understood the conversation even though she was communicating in Russian and I recalled the time I'd heard Rosa. Ms Thorogood's explanation about the automatic translation came back to me and I realised that, of course, I couldn't speak Spanish or Russian – I understood Rosa and Nina because I heard them through their PT connection.

"Oh, love, I'm sorry. I don't know what came over me. I suppose it's all these years of not really knowing what happened and now this." He held up the letter as though he wished he could throw it away but was unable to let go of the last connection to his beloved wife. "I've been waiting for something like this to turn up. Thought it would make it easier. But it doesn't. It's like losing her all over again. Only this time I know for sure that she didn't intend to come home."

"No, Mr … Samuel! No apology necessary." I went to him and hugged him, breathing in the mechanical smell of nano-grease from his overalls. It brought back the memory of another Saturday afternoon – during the summer before Elizabeth died – Samuel came in from his workshop and she'd complained about his grimy clothes. He'd deliberately smudged the end of her nose with his grubby finger and she chased him out of the kitchen, shaking a wet cloth at him. Of course Seth had been hugely embarrassed by his 'rents' antics, but I'd thought it was so lovely that they still had so much romance in their lives.

Will Seth and I be as happy when we've sorted all this out?

CHAPTER 27

LONDON: May 2103

"Thank you, ladies and gentlemen." Dale Johnson raised his hand to stop the applause. When everyone had settled down he continued, "I can't thank you all enough for the wonderful support you have given to this project. Without your backing, both financial – still time to donate by the way –," A wave of laughter flowed around the room, "and hands on," A group of gap-year students cheered, "the Kalamoombi Community Hub would not exist. I hope this evening has shown you how important these facilities are to the region. In theory, the massive reduction in the world's population last century should have created a more equitable distribution of resources. In reality, the issues affecting the developing countries were simply compounded by the stalling of technological developments worldwide. The wealthier countries looked after their own problems and the poorer regions slipped further behind.

This evening I am pleased to announce that the recent G20 Summit confirmed its support of a new initiative, using our own model as the benchmark, and encouraging successful organisations to forge partnerships with those struggling across the globe. Exciting times lie ahead and we are looking forward to helping even more communities like Kalamoombi." He raised his glass. "To the future. To a truly 'Global Village'."

Images of the hub's construction were projected around the room, accompanied by wild cheers from the students whenever one of their friends was pictured.

"Hey, Beth, there's the one of you chasing off that meerkat."

"He kept pinching my lunch," Beth responded, sitting upright and imitating the staccato movements of the cheeky little creature. Just as she popped a spicy snack into her mouth a hand clasped her shoulder, surprising her. Her colleagues squealed with laughter as the hand that had caused her choking fit then slapped her on the back to ease her uncontrollable coughing.

"Sorry, Bethany. I didn't mean to startle you."

"That's okay, Mr Johnson," she croaked. She struggled to contain her coughing but the effort caused tears to stream down her cheeks. Could it be any more embarrassing?

"No, it's entirely my fault," he insisted, handing her a clean handkerchief to wipe her face and pouring a fresh glass of water.

Beth gratefully sipped at the cool drink and her spasms finally subsided.

"I'm fine thank you," she said, in a raspy tone.

"Hm, I'll keep you company for a moment just to be on the safe side." The others had wandered away from the table so Dale sat beside her. "I came over to offer my congratulations on your placement at Lloyd and Durleigh. How's it going?"

"You heard?" Beth was surprised that the man she respected almost as much as she did her grandfather would be following her progress.

"Yes. They asked me for a reference."

Beth felt her cheeks burn with embarrassment again. Of course – she'd put the details of her gap-year work on her application to the Sandridge Magna solicitors' firm. It wasn't anything to do with Dale Johnson taking a personal interest, although for him to have written the reference himself was a nice touch.

"Do you have a specific area of the law you want to pursue?"

So he was interested after all!

"I've only just qualified so I have to take what's handed my way," she replied.

"Qualified a year early and with honours, if I'm not mistaken. I'm sure you'll soon find your feet, Beth."

"Gramps has been bragging again hasn't he?" She glared towards the table where Lord Simpson was in conversation with one of the younger royals.

137

Dale smiled at her discomfort. "And why shouldn't he? If my girls grow up to be as talented, committed and beautiful as you, I'm sure I'll be well ahead of him in the bragging stakes."

"Are you flirting again, dear?" A tall, elegant and utterly stunning woman laid a perfectly manicured hand on Dale's shoulder.

"But of course, Geraldine, my love," he said, kissing her slender fingers, "I have to hone my skills so that I can keep up with you. I saw you giving Herr Nussbaum palpitations when you were chatting with him during dessert."

Geraldine Johnson gave her husband a playful slap on his arm and turned to Beth.

"I'm sorry to interrupt, Bethany, dear, but Dale needs to do the rounds. We have to sign up as many of these multi-nationals as we can."

"No, please. Don't mind me," Beth gestured towards her grandfather, "I need to catch up with Gramps, anyway."

As the Johnsons walked away from her table Beth heard them discussing a potential joint venture with a multi-national pharmaceutical corporation. Her interest piqued when she recognised the company name; Trevalyn. One of these days she really must dig out Great-Granny Julia's old notes. Several years too late for the deal to see 'Thorny Lyrics' but she had promised to help Gramps with the mystery of Julia's obsession. Although where she was going to find time amongst the heavy workload and extra studies was anyone's guess.

CHAPTER 28

Ellingham: 3 August 2110

Is there anything more cringe-worthy than the 'rents exchanging baby stories?

Mum, Dad and Samuel were laughing at another anecdote about Seth and me from when we were just kids and, whilst it was a relief to see them getting on so well after the initial awkwardness, it was becoming embarrassing to be the subject of their conversation. I looked at Seth and his pained expression showed he was feeling the same way.

"We'll clear the table," I volunteered.

"Thanks for a lovely meal, Mrs Hanson," added Seth, as he collected the plates.

"You're welcome, Seth," said Mum, smiling at the compliment.

It seemed odd to have such normality after our discoveries earlier in the day. Samuel's brief outburst was quickly forgotten and he, Seth and I had sat around the kitchen table trying to decipher Elizabeth's *Handi* entries. It wasn't an easy task. Often we'd break off when the reminder of their loss became too much for Samuel and Seth. Elizabeth could only make vague references to the killer and her device to guide us was to use literary quotes – some easier to understand than others. Through it all, I sensed Nina's presence sustaining Samuel as the revelations kept coming. For nearly four years he'd believed his wife had simply found life too depressing to carry on. He'd felt the guilt of not being able to make her happy, the anger that his love wasn't enough for her and the pain of never coming to terms with the loss of his soul-mate. Now he learned something of the truth. Elizabeth had loved him unconditionally and was devastated that she could no longer be with him. She'd struggled with a dark and awful secret that was impossible to share, even with him. Finally, she'd felt strong enough to take this horror away from her family, knowing that they wouldn't understand her actions. Knowing that she was going to break their hearts.

We were no closer to the identity of Elizabeth's murderous PT although we were convinced that all the entries in her *Handi* were significant and needed further consideration. I tried to focus my memory to see if I could connect to any more of the victims but merely sensed confusing, disjointed images and the voices became intrusive as I lowered my mental barriers. Seth noticed my grimace at the renewed noise and reached for my hand. He shook his head, silently telling me not to risk losing my control over the connections. I reluctantly 'closed the door' and the voices became quieter again. We hadn't told Samuel about my vivid recollections of two of the murders. We didn't think he'd want us to pursue things if he thought I was at any risk of following Elizabeth's path. There were still some of our own secrets that we weren't ready to share yet.

Unexpectedly, Mum had provided a welcome distraction by calling to insist that we all went back to mine for a 'proper Sunday roast'. Our light brunch and even the emotions of the day hadn't completely dampened our teenage appetites. Samuel was practical enough to want something to eat as he'd skipped breakfast due to the early call-out. So here we were, stuffed with roast beef, Yorkshire puddings and all the trimmings.

"I'm so glad you and Seth could come over this afternoon," Mum was saying to Samuel. "It's nice to cook a full family meal once in a while. Desirée's out most of the time these days."

My teeth clenched at her use of my full name. *Thought she'd got over that!*

"It was good of you to invite us, Celeste. Not often we get such splendid home-cooking, is it lad?"

"No, Dad," Seth replied dutifully, but I saw his eyes roll upwards. Despite the chirpy conversation and mutual appreciation going on, we could feel the underlying tension. There was an uneasiness between the adults – they were being too polite to put into words what they really wanted to say. I decided to push the bull into the china shop!

"Mum's really sorry that she didn't tell you about seeing Elizabeth that evening, aren't you, Mum?"

Her eyes opened wide in shock and her face paled. She swallowed the sip of wine that she'd just taken and licked her lips nervously. The look she gave me suggested I'd pay for that comment later.

"Y…yes. Of course I am, Samuel. I should've come straight to you when we found out she was missing. I'll never forgive myself." Tears were staining her face and I felt ashamed of myself for putting her in this situation.

"Don't worry Celeste," said Samuel. "We all feel we should've done things differently. We're only just finding out what happened and it doesn't look like any of us could've changed the outcome." He leaned across the table to pat Mum's hand. "Now we have to follow her advice and remember who she really was. She wouldn't want us to be beating ourselves up."

"No. She just wants us to nail the bastard who did this to her!" Seth's voice had an edge to it that worried me. It was one thing to work out the clues but, as Dad had suggested, it was another thing entirely to go after the killer ourselves. Seth's bad language went unchallenged as everyone seemed to be caught up in their own thoughts and I was trying hard not to hear them.

★★★

The 'rents had gone for a stroll to walk off their indulgent meal and make room for the cake Mum had promised us. Seth and I took a picnic blanket out to the garden and laid side-by-side staring up at the clear blue sky. Bees busily gathered pollen and we could hear a neighbour's children squealing with delight as they splashed about in their paddling pool.

I squeezed Seth's hand.

"Got an idea," I said.

"Oh-oh. That sounds ominous."

I squeezed his hand harder until he surrendered.

"Okay, okay. I'm sorry. What's your idea?" he said, rubbing his tortured fingers.

"I was thinking – if I remembered those murders as though I was the victim, maybe I can recall what happened to the others."

"We still don't know how you're getting these memories. Or whether they're accurate." Seth sat up and looked down at me, concern obvious in his eyes.

"It's not a good idea to go probing around in there," he tapped my forehead, "until you've got the all-clear from Alvin."

I sighed with resignation.

"You're probably right. It's just so hard to ignore all these connections, especially if one of them could help track down your mum's PT."

"Yeah, but who's to say he won't be able to track you down if you connect with him? You can't risk it, Dez."

"And that's another thing."

"What now?"

"Her PT – he'd know who your mum was. Why didn't he come to find her *Handi* to keep his identity secret?"

"A diary's such a private thing – maybe the Bloc keeps it hidden unless you really have faith in your PT. Anyway, even if he knew she was keeping a diary the entries are so vague he probably didn't put two and two together. He might have been flattered that she was keeping a scrap book of his killing spree. He'd feel safe enough knowing she couldn't refer to him explicitly." Seth's tone was one of revulsion.

No matter what Seth said, I was determined to use my abilities to follow Elizabeth's clues. Yes, I'd wait until I next saw Alvin, but once I knew how to control my open mind and target specific connections, I'd be going after the monster that killed all those people and drove my best friend's mum to her death.

"Come here," I said, lying on the blanket with my arms reaching up to invite him into them. "Let's try to be a normal couple for a while, eh?"

He grinned and lowered himself until his face was close to mine. "Like this?" he said and kissed my mouth lightly. "And this?" Kissing the tip of my nose. "And this?" Moving down the side of my neck.

"Oh, shut up!" I said, turning towards him to demonstrate the type of kissing I was really interested in. I felt his lips turn up under mine and I forced my tongue through his grin, savouring his taste and enjoying his slight hesitation before he responded. The sensations I'd experienced as the Parisian girl came rushing back to me. My breath came in short gasps, I felt my nipples tingle and the burning of extra sensitive nerves running through my skin. Every part of me fizzled and I pushed my body against Seth's, hungry for more. I gripped his buttocks and held him tightly to me, thrilled by the obvious effect I was having on him. I could feel his arousal and it made my desire stronger. I no longer had any control – my body writhed and throbbed with passion. My hands slid around Seth's hips reaching to undo his jeans.

"NO!" He rolled away from me. Breathing heavily and flushed red in his face. "Damn it, Dez. What's got into you?"

I was furious. My body still ached for fulfilment and he was looking at me like I was a sex-crazed slut. I was about to lash out with a foul-mouthed response, but the haze cleared and I came to my senses. The shock set in – I began to shake and tears filled my eyes, blurring the image of Seth standing well out of my reach. I felt sick with shame. I ran into the house, up to the bathroom and locked the door, only just managing to reach the loo before throwing up. Seth was right to be disgusted by my behaviour. We'd only just got together as a couple. Okay, we wouldn't be breaking any laws but why did I need it so early in our relationship and why so desperately? Was it even me wanting it or was it just that poor Parisian girl's cravings? I lay on the cool tiled bathroom floor and wept, sure that I'd lost Seth for real this time.

Eventually, I got my sobs under control and staggered to the washbasin. An occasional dry whimper escaped and my face was swollen, blotchy and particularly unattractive. *Serves you right!* I sneered at my reflection. *Might as well look as ugly as you feel!* Still, I splashed my face with cold water in an attempt to repair some of the damage. A tentative knock on the door interrupted my self-condemnation.

"Dez? Dez, are you okay?"

"Go away, Seth. Leave me alone."

"Dez. Please. Open the door. I'm sorry. You took me by surprise. That's all. Please, Dez. Let me in."

Oh, how I wanted to be strong. To send him packing with a flea in his ear for being so judgemental. But I agreed with his reaction. What had I been thinking? Never mind the moral issue – we were in my parents' garden in broad daylight *and* without any form of contraception! Jeez – the stupidity of it almost made it laughable. I released the lock but couldn't bring myself to open the door. After a moment's hesitation, Seth tried the handle and, finding it unlocked, he came in. I could see from the redness around his eyes that he'd been blubbing too.

"Desirée Hanson, you're dangerous to be with." His lop-sided grin was back again and it made me smile too. "How can I hold out under such an attack?"

"No. Don't," I said, the smile falling away. "Don't make fun of me. Please. I … I don't know what was going on. One minute it's fine and the next … well, I'm not surprised you're disgusted by what happened next. I just don't know if it was really me doing it."

"Dez, listen to me. I love you. I wasn't disgusted – no don't shake your head – I wasn't. Actually, I have to admit I was rather flattered that I could have that effect on you so quickly! I was loving it. Don't say you didn't notice. But I got scared. Scared at how fast we could go so far without realising it."

"You were angry with me, Seth. You were right to be."

"No, I just told you. It wasn't anger – it was fear. Fear of messing up. I want things to be done properly, Dez. We haven't even been on a date yet. You did say you wanted to be a normal couple, right?"

By now I was in his arms again, my head resting on his chest where I could hear the steady rhythm of his heart – *lub-dub, lub-dub*. He gave me a quick squeeze then steered me out of the bathroom, past my bedroom door and towards the stairs.

"Safer if we go sit in the lounge, yeah?"

"Suppose so." I agreed.

Although we sat together on the sofa, we merely held hands and avoided any serious kissing. My earlier reaction had created a reluctance to try anything more than an occasional peck on the cheek for now. I sighed and leaned my head back onto an over-stuffed cushion.

"What's it like to be normal?" I asked. "I've forgotten."

"Wouldn't know," he replied. He paused before continuing, "I'm a freak just like you." His grin softened the words and I knew he was trying to lighten the mood. "Maybe not *quite* like you," he added on seeing my raised eyebrow.

"Tell." I sat up straight, wanting to hear his explanation.

He hesitated for a moment then said, "I haven't connected to my PT either."

"WHAT?" I leapt to my feet and glowered at him, "You mean all this time I've been going through hell thinking I'm the only one with this … this defect, you've been the same?"

At least he had the decency to look ashamed!

"Seems I've got to apologise yet again," he sighed. "Sorry for not being up-front with you. Surely you, of all people, understand why I didn't let on straight away? Then you were all upset about your PT not connecting and I didn't get chance to say anything. And when you were going to see Alvin, I thought I'd see if it worked for you before I tried it. 'Course now you're open on all channels it's scared me off! I'd rather one of us had a reasonably empty head!"

I wasn't sure whether to be angry at his apparently selfish attitude in allowing me to take all the risks with the hypnotherapy, or to be happy that, at last, I knew he understood some of what I'd gone through since my Sixteenth-Eve Party.

"Yeah – your head is definitely the empty one around here!" I

145

grabbed the cushion and started to whack him with it – just as the 'rents came in from their walk. Luckily, the cushion was still intact so Mum's initial irritation quickly disappeared.

"Jennifer will be here soon. I'll go put the kettle on. Tea for everyone?" she asked, as she went through to the kitchen.

Trust Mum. Tea for all occasions!

CHAPTER 29

Ellingham: 4 August 2110

Is there something going on between them?

I surreptitiously looked at Alvin and Ms Thorogood as they settled themselves for our Monday morning session. When I'd answered the door they'd seemed startled and moved to stand further apart. *Mm – fancy that!* I resisted the temptation to try and listen in on their thoughts, but I could see from their body language that there'd been a shift in their relationship since our last meeting.

"So, Dez. What did you want to talk about on Saturday? Sorry I couldn't take your call – I left for a seminar after seeing you that morning." Alvin pushed his designer specs up onto the bridge of his nose and I briefly wondered why he hadn't had laser treatment or the latest ocular-implants to correct his sight. It was rare to see people wearing specs these days.

"I'm not sure if you can help but I've been having weird dreams – no, not dreams, more like memories. I can remember things as though they were happening to me but they never did." I could see the confusion in Alvin's face. "You think I'm crazy."

"No, not at all. Please don't label yourself, Dez. Tell me what you felt and we'll see if we can get to the bottom of it."

I looked at Ms Thorogood and she gave me an encouraging nod. Seth had transferred the news reports from Elizabeth's *Handi* to my current DataRoll and I passed it over to Alvin.

"I've had vivid memories of two of these, as though I was the victim – the girl in the Weardale woods and the Parisian girl. I felt and thought everything they did. I was there – I was them! How is that possible?" By the time I'd finished I was breathless and my heart was pounding making my temples throb with the rush of blood. I hadn't realised how tense I'd been, how worried I was about sharing this with anyone other than Seth.

Alvin looked thoughtful. He sat back in the chair, handed the DataRoll to Ms Thorogood then turned to me again.

"Dez, your extraordinary ability to connect with others is beyond anything we've come across before. I consulted with some of the therapists at the seminar to see if they've ever had anyone with similar abilities." I wasn't sure I was happy about being discussed – it must've shown in my face. "Don't worry," he continued. "I didn't refer to you by name, so you won't have the media beating a trail to your door. There've been very rare cases where an individual has been able to sense the feelings and thoughts of others besides their dedicated PT, but only when they are in close proximity to those other people. Your case is unique in that you seem to be able to connect remotely. Several of my colleagues would like to investigate your talent further but that, of course, is up to you."

"Not sure about that," I mumbled. "It's bad enough having it in the first place without becoming a lab-rat."

"No pressure, Dez. Just give it some thought and if you feel differently later we can always set something up."

"Don't push her, Alvin." Ms Thorogood came to my rescue. "She's got enough on her plate, don't you think?"

"Yes, sorry Dez. Debbie's right. My professional curiosity is getting the better of me. Let's take it one step at a time. These memories are very interesting."

"Frightening, more like," I interrupted.

"Indeed, indeed." But his sympathy didn't sound very convincing. Maybe I'd be better off trying to sort things out without him poking around in my head any longer.

"Alvin!" Ms Thorogood's voice was sharp as she reached over to shake him out of his thoughts. "Come on. Dez needs our help and you've gone over to the dark side – all scientist instead of therapist."

His head came up in surprise. "Oh! I'm so sorry. Please forgive me, Dez. I'll try to help – of course – but I *am* concerned that I'm working blind. I can't see the cause of the problem so we're going to have to be very careful. What's your main worry at the moment?"

"I spend most of my time trying to keep the connections locked away in that mental room we created last session, otherwise the noise gets too much. It's tiring and I've got a constant headache from concentrating so hard all the time. I'm getting used to it, I suppose, but it would be nice if it was easier to ignore."

"In that case, we'll try to reinforce your subconscious to do that for you in today's session. Anything else – other than these memories, of course?"

"What if I want to make a specific connection? Is that going to open the floodgates again?"

"That I can't answer, I'm afraid. Are you thinking about finding your dedicated PT this way?"

I didn't want to admit that I was trying to track down a killer and Alvin had, inadvertently, given me the ideal excuse. "Yeah. I'd really like to know who they are."

"Mm. I could try to suggest a mental key for you. So that your subconscious might allow you to make an individual connection whilst keeping the rest of them contained. Again, this is all new territory for me so I can't give you any guarantees."

"Understood."

"Right – I suggest we get on with that for now and, when I get back to my office, I'll research your memory phenomenon to see if anyone else has ever experienced it. Agreed?"

"Agreed," I answered and settled back into the chair for another relaxing hypno session.

★★★

"How'd it go?" Seth asked later that morning. "Did Alvin have any ideas about your memories?"

"No. He's gone off to see what he can find. He says I'm unique so I don't know how he's going to find anything of any use!" I was plumping up cushions in the lounge – thumping them more viciously than actually needed, just to release some of the frustration.

"Always knew you were one of a kind." Seth pulled me into a hug.

"Back off Wallis – I've a loaded cushion and I'm not afraid to use it!" I held it up, as though targeting his head.

He stepped back, hands up in surrender and we both laughed at my poor joke. I dropped onto the sofa, a picture of teenage dejection. Holding the cushion on my knee I sank my chin onto its velvet cover, the scent of Mum's favourite fabric freshener washed over me and I closed my eyes allowing the memory of childhood sick days to briefly comfort me. Days when I'd curl up on the sofa surrounded by those cushions and Mum would let me watch my favourite programmes while encouraging me to eat her homemade vegetable soup.

I woke to find myself lying on the sofa, my head on Seth's lap and his hand gently stroking my hair. I glanced up at his face – he was looking out of the window, absorbed in the antics of a cheeky squirrel trying to get at the birds' peanuts.

"How long have I been asleep?" I asked, sitting up and stretching.

"Not long. About an hour, I suppose. You must've needed it. I've never seen anyone go off so quickly."

"Sorry," I yawned. "I think the hypno sessions make me dopey."

"That and the sleepless nights you've been having, eh?"

"Mm. Well, let's hope this session has put my head-pals to sleep for a while." The voices were significantly quieter, a mere murmur that I could, *almost*, ignore. I would have to wait and see if that was a permanent change or just an immediate, short-term reaction to the hypnotherapy. "Yep, they seem to have dozed off for now. Come on, let's find something for lunch. Dad's in London and Mum's gone over to Aunt Jen's so it's just the two of us. What do you fancy?"

"You mean apart from you?"

"Ha, Ha!" I said, sarcastically though I couldn't stop the grin of pleasure and the slight blush his comment brought out. "I can do paninis, jacket spuds, or we might have some pizzas hiding away where Mum can't see them."

"Tell you what, I'll take you into town and we can try that new place – Muskrats, isn't it?"

"Kumquats!" I laughed. "You rich or something?"

"Not really. But if I can't manage the bill I'm sure my wealthy girlfriend can spare some of her birthday credits for a glass of water and some dry bread."

"Cheeky!" I punched him playfully and it was only when we were on the ecotram, half-way into town, that I realised he'd managed to get me away from home-turf for the first time since my stay at the clinic.

"I can't do this," I said. My vision blurred and I felt light-headed.

"You're okay, Dez." He squeezed my hand. "I'm here with you. Take a deep breath and you'll be fine."

Of course he was right. What was I afraid of? But I struggled to keep the panic attack at bay. I felt my forehead become clammy with sweat and my jaw ached from clenching my teeth to stop them chattering. Throughout the rest of the journey Seth soothed me and talked about random things to distract me. Some of the other passengers glanced our way, conscious that something was going on although not sure what. Finally, the ecotram got to our stop and Seth guided me out onto the pavement. I stood on shaking legs and took long steadying breaths to calm my nausea and slow my heartbeat.

"I'm fine now," I managed after a couple of minutes. "Sorry. Haven't done that in a while, have I?" I smiled weakly at him.

"Yeah, when you did it after jamming our Holo-Comms system I looked it up so I'd be better prepared next time. Seems to have worked." Seth smiled back at me, put his arm around my shoulders and steered me into the shopping centre.

As we settled into a cosy corner booth in Kumquats, a feminine squeal made me jump.

"DEZ! How *are* you? Heard about your accident at the lake. So glad you're okay."

"Thanks, Andrea," I replied, half-heartedly. The last thing I needed right now was the class bitch cosying-up to us, just to get her ammunition for Academy gossip. The little devil inside me reared its head and, without intending to, I was listening to her thoughts.

'What IS she wearing? He's no better. I wouldn't be seen dead looking like that. Maybe that's why she wanted to top herself – can't keep up with the rest of us.'

'Who're you bitchin' 'bout now, Andy-Pandy?'

'Don't do that! Keep out 'til I let you listen in. And don't call me THAT!'

'Not my fault I can hear you. Wish I couldn't, but your bitchin's so loud it cuts straight through the Bloc, sweetie!'

Andrea's PT hadn't flinched at the venom dripping from her vicious response. That wouldn't go down well with the girl who considered herself above everyone else.

Now that's what I call Karma! My own thoughts must've pushed the mental smile onto my face – Seth was nudging me under the table so I quickly rearranged my expression to look serious.

"Actually, Andrea, if you don't mind, we've just come out for a quiet lunch. Dez is still a bit shaky from her ordeal, as I'm sure you can imagine." Seth sounded so confident, so grown-up. I was surprised at his forceful tone and felt protected – my boy was looking out for me. And the look on Andrea's face when she realised he was giving her the brush-off – priceless!

"Oh. Oh, right. Well, I'll see you later then," she mumbled, turning on her four-inch heels.

When we managed to get our giggling under control, Seth went to order our lunch. He got back to the table and produced his DataRoll to study the notes we'd made from the news reports. He pointed to one in particular.

"Look here, Dez. We missed something. Dale Johnson, overdose in October 2105 – there's no DOM. The second report says he survived although he seems to have lingering brain damage. All his physical functions are intact, but he doesn't move a muscle voluntarily and he can't communicate."

I looked at the reports again. Dale Johnson was a highly respected businessman and successful entrepreneur. He'd been admitted to hospital with a suspected drugs overdose but this was completely out of character. Apparently, he was a clean-living, hard-working family man without a care in the world. The sentence that leapt out at me mentioned that his PT lost their connection shortly before Dale's collapse.

"Just like the two girls," I said.

"Two girls?"

"Yeah – the girls that I … remember dying with." I couldn't come up with a proper term for what I'd experienced. "They lost their PT connections before they died. I remember mentally calling out. What were their PTs' names?" I paused trying to bring back the last moments of those dreadful memories. "Simone, yes, Simone and Valerie."

We'd made a connection between the murders that wasn't just based on Elizabeth linking them. Could we take it further? Maybe if I could tune into the PTs of the victims they'd provide me with more clues to the killer's identity.

One problem. At the moment I can hear others but they can't hear me. How do I contact them?

CHAPTER 30

Central Africa: 8 October 2105

"This isn't what we agreed!" Dale paused his furious pacing. "We have a contract and I'll drag you through the courts if I must."

"Surely you wouldn't want the world to see the vindictive side of the saintly Dale Johnson?"

"You think that's what interests me? You don't know me at all, do you Trevalyn? My only consideration is for the people of this community. The people who trusted us to deliver on our promises and what do I find when I get here? You – using them to your own benefit. Like some kind of latter-day slave master." Dale was so angry he could barely get the words out. His felt his face grow hot with shame. He'd let these people down. He'd unwittingly introduced a self-interested oppressor and his conscience struggled with the cost of his naivety.

He pushed his sweat-dampened hair off his forehead in an attempt to cool both his temper and his temperature. By now this school building should have been in full use but Trevalyn had commandeered the work-force to complete his own suite of offices and laboratory. They were now meeting in a dusty, hot marquee where a solid, air-conditioned classroom should be.

"We needed to establish the clinical facilities first so that the community's health was safeguarded," Trevalyn said calmly, whilst pouring water from his flask and offering the cup to Dale.

Dale was too parched to refuse the drink. He gulped the lukewarm liquid before responding.

"Don't try to talk me round on this. Your laboratory is not the health clinic we'd planned. It's more a science facility than a medical one.

154

I want you off this site voluntarily by close of business tomorrow otherwise I'll be calling in the authorities to evict you and start a full investigation into what you've been up to out here." He banged the cup down onto a nearby workbench – the only evidence that some kind of construction was due to start. The question was; when?

"Tomorrow," he repeated as he left to face the villagers that had congregated outside.

Trevalyn nodded as he replaced the flask's cup, turning it slowly and deliberately until it clicked into place.

London: 9th October 2105

Dale hated working into the evening. He was a family man and always tried to be home to read the girls their bedtime story. The Holo-Comms, realistic as it was, could never replace the warm, delicious smell of his children snuggling close to him in their cosy onesies, after their nightly bubble-bath.

During the flight back he'd been feverish – probably an emotional backlash after his run-in with Trevalyn and dealing with the subsequent anguish of the Lipostzi people. His travel inoculations were up-to-date so he wasn't worried about any exotic illness. He stretched, rubbed his neck and took a couple of paracetamol. He scoured the fine details of the contract with Trevalyn. Knowing how persuasive Trevalyn could be, Dale would need a watertight case to take to the court on Monday morning. He grinned thinking that if Asil had been able to reach beyond their Bloc he'd have been off to deal with Trevalyn on a more personal level! The Turk's temper was legendary once he'd been riled enough to lose it.

The cramps came unexpectedly. One minute Dale was scrolling through holo-screens of contractual jargon, the next he was sprawled on the floor in agony. His jaw clenched so tightly he couldn't call out for help. Even his PT link to Asil seemed to have disappeared in the fire of pain blistering through his body.

CHAPTER 31

Ellingham: 4 August 2110

One-step at a time, Dez.

I needed to track down the PTs of the murder victims before I could think about how to contact them. Even if I found out who they were, it wasn't going to be easy getting in touch – "Hi. I'm Dez and I heard your PT's dying thoughts." Not a good opening!

After our lunch, I persuaded Seth that we should go straight home to continue our research. I think he would've rather spent the afternoon mooching around in town, trying to do what ordinary couples do, but now I had a focus I needed to make some real progress before I lost the momentum.

"And anyway," I argued, "you still owe me big time for keeping schtum about your non-existent PT!"

"You're gonna keep bringing that one out every time you want your own way, aren't you?" Seth groaned in defeat.

"You bet!" I grinned and ran off towards the tram-stop.

"Have you decided what you're gonna do about it?" I asked as he joined me in the queue.

"About what?"

"Your PT." I lowered my voice so that the other people in the queue couldn't hear.

Seth scowled and whispered back, "Not yet. And let's not discuss it in public, okay?"

"Sorry." I stretched up to kiss his cheek in apology. His scowl vanished and he reached for my hand. We got all the way to his house before he let go.

We started up the Holo-Comms system to study the full-sized chart that we'd created. The kitchen table once more reflected the register of death and loss. Was the killer showing Elizabeth that he was unstoppable? Had he become so proficient that he could organise these killings without worrying about being caught? And how did he manage to subdue multiple victims? The Parisian couple; four backpackers lost in the Romanian Alps; and, the last news entry in Elizabeth's *Handi*, a minibus full of Austrian schoolchildren travelling home to Innsbruck. They were returning from an outing to the quaint village of Vipiteno in northern Italy. The mandatory speed restrictor and impact warning devices which automatically cut the vehicle's power if a collision is imminent had been inspected prior to the trip. Despite these, the bus had plunged from the New Europa Bridge. There was no explanation other than the suggestion of a freak malfunction of the safety equipment. No survivors. This final entry seems to have been the tipping point for Elizabeth. The attached pop-up quote, from 'The Scarlet Pimpernel', seemed to say it all:

'The weariest of nights, the longest of days, sooner or later must perforce come to an end.'

"Still wanna convince me she didn't set out to kill herself that night?" asked Seth, sombrely.

"I'm not sure, Seth. Maybe she was going to confront the bastard. Maybe she thought she could stop him somehow."

"Come on, Dez. Read the letter again. It's obvious she wasn't expecting to come home."

"She may have thought she wouldn't survive – she *was* going to see a killer."

"That's if your theory is right." Seth was dismissive of my alternative to his belief that Elizabeth had taken her own life. Did he *want* her to have done so? I preferred to think she'd gone out to stop the murders by any means possible and committing suicide wouldn't achieve that.

"Sorry if it sounds callous but that's a side issue at the moment. It's more important to nail the killer then we can think about what happened to your mum," I said, hoping he wouldn't think that I didn't care about Elizabeth's death. A brief flash in his eyes showed how he felt about my calling it a side issue but he nodded in resignation.

"Share your deductions then, Sherlock," he said, putting his arm around my waist and leaning over the table to study the notes with me.

I squeezed his hand where it rested on my stomach then pointed to the reports about Dale Johnson.

"How about we go see him? Maybe we can find something out about his PT from his wife. The report didn't identify the PT but he came forward at the time to try and help. He might be willing to talk to us if Mrs Johnson asks him."

"What makes you think she'll want to speak to *us*?"

"Wouldn't you want to try anything to find out what happened to your partner?" I asked.

"Yeah. But – as your dad so ably put it – we're kids! Why would she think we can do anything to help?"

"We might be kids – but I have a super-power, remember?" I took up the classic Superman stance – hands on hips, head thrown back, chest thrust forward. Seth's eyes fixed on my boobs which were now brushing his shoulder as he leaned over the table.

"A-hem." He cleared his throat. "Do you mind moving those out of my line of vision please? You're distracting me!"

After a brief giggling and kissing interval, we turned our attention back to the problem of getting to Dale Johnson's PT. Seth tapped a few commands into the Holo-Comms system. Its blisteringly fast net access meant that, within seconds, we could *Swift-Search* the Johnsons. We watched holograms of Dale accepting business awards, with his pretty wife by his side. There were corporate events where he gave motivational speeches and sponsorships for young talent, charitable organisations and sports fixtures. As the timeline progressed the holograms showed the growth of his family with the final video being of Dale, his wife and their three gorgeous little daughters at a party. They were laughing and hugging – not a care in the world.

"HELP ME!"

I staggered and almost threw up as my stomach reacted to the intense pain that suddenly filled my head. Seth reached out to catch me as I sank to the floor, moaning and holding my throbbing temples.

"Dez! Dez can you hear me? What's the matter? Hang in there." He ran to the sink, filled a glass and brought the cool refreshing water to my lips. "Here, try to take a sip."

I felt completely drained but the pain had gone by the time I'd finished drinking.

"Thanks," I said, handing the empty glass to Seth and manoeuvring myself onto a kitchen chair. "Phew, that was … well, bloody awful actually. But I think I heard Dale Johnson."

"What do you mean? I thought he'd lost his telepathy with the brain damage he suffered."

"I'm sure it was him, Seth. It was a man's voice, desperate and loud – very loud!"

"What did he say?"

"Just 'Help me.' He's trapped. Lost inside himself and I could sense his fear that he'll never find a way out. We've got to help him, Seth. We've got to bring him home." I was crying, possibly from the adrenaline rush of that unexpected connection or from the feeling of desolation that Dale projected.

"Jeez, Dez. You never do anything by halves do you? Let's see if we can find any contact details for the Johnsons." Seth slid his finger-stylus across the Holo-Comms screen and scrolled through the pages of information. "Here we are. A blog from Mrs Johnson. She's keeping all his good works going whilst he's incapacitated. She's convinced he's going to get better one day and wants things to be ready for him to take up the reins again."

"Is there a private contact? I don't fancy leaving a message on her blog for everyone to see."

"No. But there's a link for funding applications. Apparently, Mrs Johnson personally looks at each request. If we apply for a grant, maybe we could put something in to catch her eye."

I wasn't sure it would work and I had the feeling of it being not quite right, but Seth was so enthusiastic about the idea that I couldn't refuse to follow through. After all, it *was* my suggestion to contact the family in the first place. I couldn't back down without good reason.

"What do you think she'll be most interested in?" I asked.

"I suppose she'd be keen on anything to do with researching brain injuries. We could say we're students doing a thesis on 'connective tissues and nerve pathways researching a consistently successful treatment to by-pass the damage and get the brain accessing previously redundant areas thereby restoring lost functions.'"

"Dammit! You sound like you've swallowed a medical textbook. How'd you come up with all that so quickly?"

He looked down, nervously and started picking at a loose thread on his t-shirt. I clamped my hand over his to stop his fidgeting. "Come on, Seth. What's up?"

"The usual … Mum," he sighed. "When she was getting more and more of her 'moody-blues' I thought she had something wrong in her head. I started looking up stuff about brain malfunctions, injuries and diseases. For a time I thought I'd try to go in for medicine – I'd even thought up that title for my university thesis – but I'm not really clever enough. I'd never get the grades to go to the right uni. When my PT didn't start up I started to think I'd inherited some mental illness so I've been reading up again."

"Why didn't you talk to me?" I knew from my own recent experiences what Seth must have been through. Why hadn't he felt able to confide in me?

"It was something I needed to sort out for myself. I didn't want you to know about Mum's condition and I certainly didn't want you to think I was going bonkers!"

"Wallis, you've always been bonkers to me!" I pulled him into a hug. "In a silly let's-find-out-if-bolognese-sauce-makes-worms-taste-like-spaghetti way – not a mentally-ill-needing-brain-surgery way." I hastily added. He laughed at the reference to his first attempt at cooking – left-over pasta sauce dribbled over a bowl of worms harvested after a heavy downpour. Elizabeth had caught us halfway through the banquet. She'd given us salt water to make us throw up then she brought out the ice-cream to placate the tearful four-year olds.

"So are we gonna fill in this application or what?" Seth said.

We entered the required contact information and an outline of Seth's suggested thesis. The funding request was in respect of the costs involved in travelling to major specialist clinics and surgeries throughout the world to gain first-hand interviews and materials as evidence for the project findings. It seemed a bit flimsy to me but Seth had a point – Mrs Johnson may grasp any opportunity to find a cure for her husband. With a flourish Seth pressed the "Submit" button on-screen. As he did so, I felt a sharp tightening in my stomach – the sort of feeling you get just before the rollercoaster starts its first dive.

I hate rollercoasters!

CHAPTER 32

Ellingham: 5 August 2110

Right you lot, behave yourselves.

It was silly talking to the voices in my own head, especially as I knew they couldn't hear me, but it was the only way I could handle the weirdness. I was going to try to isolate individuals and was scared that I'd be opening the floodgates and letting all the connections out at once. I remembered the first time they had hit me full-on and I didn't want to experience *that* again. Seth had insisted that I wait until the morning following our application to the Johnson Foundation before I attempted anything. He wanted me to be fully rested after that unexpected shout from Dale had all-but floored me. Rested? Who was he kidding? I hadn't slept a wink all night. My mind churned, trying to work out how we were going to find the murdered victims' PTs and what I would say to them when, or even if, we did.

"You look worn out this morning," said Mum, as she passed a plate of scrambled eggs to me.

"I'm fine." The yawn turning my assurance into a lie. "Just miles away."

"Have you got any news for your father? He's beginning to fret about that diary of Elizabeth's."

"Mum, we've only just started to look at it properly, but I really don't think Dad's got anything to worry about. It's not like we're about to jet off to some secluded castle and confront a megalomaniac holding the greatest weapon of mass destruction!" I joked, to cover my own doubts. I was nervous enough about playing around in my head and that was before I considered what we were going to do if we ever did find out who the killer was.

"Mm," she muttered. "Well, keep us informed and don't do anything silly will you?"

"Yes we will and no we won't, Mum!" I said, grinning cheekily to lighten the mood.

I knew that Mum would continue to fuss over me if I didn't finish my breakfast so I struggled to get the eggs down and swigged my lukewarm tea before dashing off to get ready for Seth. He'd promised to come around as soon as Samuel had gone off to work so I needed to get a move on. In my room I rooted around to find a decent top and was half-way through applying make-up when I heard the doorbell. *Damn!* Then I gave my reflection a quizzical look. *When have you ever worn make-up for a day with Seth? Who are you and what have you done with Dez?* This romance thing was all a bit unnerving. I wanted Seth to think I looked good but I'd never been a girly-girl so why start now? He'd probably be in his tatty jeans as usual. I grabbed a wipe and smeared the eyeliner down my cheek – *oh, very attractive!* By the time I'd finished my cheeks were red and my eyes watering from the excessive rubbing. *To hell with it,* I thought and ran down the stairs to find that Mum had already let Seth in.

"Oh!" I skidded to a halt, taking in the vision of manliness waiting in the hallway. Seth had washed his hair and slicked it with gel so that it framed his face like a fiery halo – for once the curls were staying in place. He was wearing a new shirt with the top two buttons undone but I was sure I could see the tip of a tie peeping out of his pocket. His jeans were pristine, not a pinprick of oil to be seen. He held a large bunch of flowers and a box of chocolates in outstretched hands as though he couldn't wait to get rid of them.

"These are for you, Mrs Hanson," he said, presenting the chocolates to her, "and these are for you." He pushed the flowers into my arms, blushing furiously.

"That's very kind of you, Seth," said Mum. "Isn't it, Desirée?" she added, pointedly.

I realised I'd been standing there with my mouth open and shut it quickly, licking my dry lips as I did so.

"Yeah … yes. Thanks Seth," I managed. With a quick glance at Mum to make sure she wasn't going to interfere, I reached up to kiss his well-scrubbed cheek. I smiled as, beneath my lips, I felt the stubble that he'd missed when he'd shaved.

"Shall I put them in water for you, Desirée?"

"Muuuum!" I wailed.

"All right, all right. I'll try to remember. Although why you have to shorten that beautiful name I've no idea." A touch of the old irritation came into Mum's tone but she smiled as she took the flowers and gave Seth a nod of approval before disappearing into the kitchen.

"Wow. Don't you scrub up well?"

"If you're gonna make fun, I'm off," he said. "I knew it was a bad idea."

"No! No, it wasn't. It's lovely that you dressed up for me, Seth. Thank you. Sorry I didn't manage it. I tried, but make-up and me just don't get along together."

"I thought we could go on one of those dates I mentioned and I wanted to surprise you."

"You certainly did that!" I kissed him again. "But now you're gonna have to wait for me to get ready after all. Can't have people thinking you're dating a down-and-out, can we?"

I pushed him through to the kitchen where Mum was busy trimming the flowers and arranging them in one of her favourite vases – *Hey, remember they're mine!* I thought – aloud I said, "Will you look after Seth while I get changed, Mum?"

"Yes, yes." She waved me away. "But hurry up. You shouldn't keep the poor boy waiting." *Poor boy?* He must've made a big impression with those chocs to get her sticking up for him.

"Mu-um!" I called, after half an hour. "Help!"

What sounded like a herd of elephants came charging up the stairs.

"Dez, are you all right?" Seth shouted as he rattled the handle of my bedroom door.

I leapt towards the door and leaned against it to stop him getting in – I was only wearing my bra and pants and they didn't even match!

"Excuse me, Seth." Mum's voice cut through Seth's attempts at breaking and entering.

"Oh. Er, sorry Mrs Hanson. I thought something was wrong with Dez."

"I'll let you know if she needs anything." Mum knocked on my door and I opened it just enough to let her in. "What on earth's the matter?" she asked.

"Look at me," I wailed. "I'm no good at this."

Mum looked around the room – clothes strewn all over the floor and my bed, make-up tipped out of my drawer onto the dresser top and a sickly mixture of all the perfumes I'd been trying. How did she always manage to look so damned gorgeous even first thing in the morning? She gave me one of her smiles – the ones so full of love that they made my heart squeeze – and I didn't need to hear her thoughts, I could see them in her expression: *Dizzy still needs me after all.*

This was a first – Mum and I spending girly-time together – and I was surprised to find myself enjoying it. I'd expected her to go for sensible stuff and no make-up at all but she dug through the clothing to find a lacy little number that actually gave me a decent cleavage, matching knickers, a silky strap-top that I'd forgotten about, and a pair of skinny jeans with beaded embroidery. Finally, she produced a pair of strappy sandals from the back of my wardrobe. She turned up the bottom of my jeans so that my ankles were showing and put the sandals on for me as though I was Cinderella and she was Prince Charming's side-kick. Once she was satisfied she turned me around so that I could see myself in the mirror.

"Oh!" I lost my breath in that one word. Mum was a miracle worker! She'd managed to tame my hair into a smooth curtain of black silk, a single understated diamante clip holding the fringe to one side. Although she'd applied make-up it was difficult to see where the cosmetics started and my natural colour ended, so subtle was the effect. I'd always thought my eyes were a dull slate blue but now they shone like a sparkling clear ocean.

"Thanks Mum." And my sight blurred slightly.

"Ah-ah," she said, quickly grabbing a tissue. "None of that, you'll spoil the effect." Although I could see she wasn't far off a few tears herself.

Mum went downstairs to assure Seth that I'd be down soon. I looked around for my small, cream shoulder bag – the big retro-denim one was a definite no-no today. I transferred my Comms kit, and Elizabeth's *Handi* into the smaller bag, dropping in a couple of tissues and my lip-gloss for emergencies. When I finally made it down the stairs Seth was, once again, waiting for me in the hallway, pacing impatiently. It was his turn to stop mid-stride and look in wonder.

Ooh, this feels good! I thought and decided that I'd ask Mum to give me some more lessons.

"Shall we go?" I asked sweetly.

"Y-yes. Yes, of course." Seth opened the door and almost bowed as I walked past him. I'm sure I heard Mum quietly chuckling behind us.

***

I didn't know what to expect from this date and was rather nervous. And irritated – why was it now so unsettling merely being with my best mate? The shift in our relationship created a wariness that had never been there before. We'd had arguments in the past but they hadn't felt like our world was crumbling. We'd had rolling around on the floor play-fights but that physical contact hadn't felt like bolts of electricity whenever we touched. Now everything was so much more concentrated, more intense. I briefly wondered if we'd made a mistake taking this step. Maybe Seth was feeling the same way as he gave my hand a squeeze and took it to his mouth for a reassuring kiss.

"What's the plan, Stan?" I asked, trying to lighten my own mood, at least.

"Stan? Who's this Stan? Let me at him!" He jumped about, shadow boxing and grinning as I rolled my eyes in mock irritation. "I don't want to tell you the plan. It's a surprise."

"Ah, Seth," I sighed. "You know I hate surprises."

"No you don't. You just say that 'cos you think it's modest. But deep down you love 'em really. Everybody does. It's shocks that nobody likes."

"I'll reserve judgement." I had to admit he'd got me tagged. I did think I wasn't supposed to like surprises, being the centre of attention, but it was exciting to think he'd planned something exclusively for me.

We walked towards the park and headed up the path to the wooded hill. I was glad we weren't going to the lake, it held too many memories old and new that I wanted to avoid for now. As we reached the peak of the hill, Seth steered me towards the little woodland café. One of the outside tables was set with a checked table cloth, matching napkins, and a small vase of wild flowers. Seth guided me to the table and gestured for me to sit. He headed into the café and eventually reappeared carrying two enormous ice-cream sundaes with sparklers fizzing so brightly that I worried his face would be burned.

"Ta-da!" he sang as he placed them on the table. "Pistachio *Surprise* Sundae." He emphasised the surprise with a wink, but I knew that wasn't the end of his planned date. I laughed and stood, leaning across the table to kiss him.

"Whoa!" he said and held me at arm's length. Just as I was about to protest, he nodded downwards. I followed his glance and realised I'd been about to scorch my silky top on the still fizzling sparklers.

"Oops!" I grinned, self-consciously. Only a moment ago I'd worried about his lovely face being injured by the fireworks and there I was almost setting fire to my assets! "Thanks," I added. "Thanks for this." Sweeping my arm over the safe areas of the table. "Thanks for that." Indicating his spruced-up appearance. "Most of all, thanks

for always being here for me." I lifted my ice-cream glass in a toast –
the sparkler had fizzled out by now so my eyebrows were safe.

"Cheers!" he replied, mirroring my gesture.

It seemed the most natural thing in the world to sit there
dawdling over our ice-cream whilst it melted. We talked about the
little stuff – how we thought we'd done in our end of year exams,
which of our Academy pals had got together and whether they still
would be when we went back to class in September, and the latest
mischief that Jeremy had been creating. The turmoil of the last few
weeks was put to one side and I realised I'd barely a whisper of
telepathic connections to cope with. Either the hypno treatment was
doing the trick or relaxing with Seth was the best therapy to keep
them quiet. But thinking about them brought to mind that I was
supposed to be working on isolating individual connections.

"Seth," I said, reluctant to break the mood. "This is really lovely
but don't you think we should be getting back to work on your
mum's *Handi*?"

A frown creased his face. "I wish I'd never let you see that," he
grumbled. "Maybe we should just give it to the authorities and be
done with it."

"NO!" He looked up, surprised by my outburst. "I mean, not
yet. Please Seth," I said more quietly. "I need to sort through it before
we do, not just for your mum's sake but to clear my own head."

"You see?" He threw his arms up in frustration. "That's why I
shouldn't've got you involved. Now your head's all messed up too."

"I think it would've been whether or not I'd seen the *Handi*. But
now that I *have* seen it I can't ignore your mum's letter any more
than you can." I reached across the table and took his hands in mine,
squeezing them tightly to make him see my point.

He shrugged and stood up from the bench, resigned to my
suggestion. "Come on then," he said. "The rest of the date'll have to
wait."

"Sorry," I said.

There I go spoiling things again!

CHAPTER 33

Paris: 12 February 2106

Nicole's latest research was throwing up more questions than answers at the moment. She wriggled her shoulders to release the building tension. At least it was Friday and she was sure Tomas had something planned for the weekend. She smiled, allowing herself a moment to fantasise about what it could be. She'd heard rumours about reallocating staff in the labs. Perhaps Tomas had been considered for a promotion – oh, but maybe he would have to move to another site. She didn't like that option! Dare she even think about what else he could be thinking of? They'd been together a while now. She knew it was old-fashioned to want a ceremony but her great-grandmother's wedding dress was so beautiful, so delicate and Mama had promised that she could use it when her turn came.

"Nicole?" Her supervisor's voice cut through her reverie. She tapped her Comms headset to respond.

"Bonjour, Madam Barteau!"

"I'm calling regarding the report you are submitting, Nicole. Your data seems contradictory to the expected outcomes."

"Oh? In what way?" Nicole answered slightly less politely. It was disconcerting that her supervisor could watch her work in real-time.

"I believe you and Tomas have been collating evidence? It appears several of your test subjects are not listed on the master register. Not only that, but, their response to the treatment is inconsistent with that of the registered individuals. Perhaps some rogue data has corrupted your figures?"

"I'll look into it, madam."

"I do hope that it is not a personal distraction interfering with your work? You came to us with high recommendations from your university tutors." The query in Madam Barteau's voice was clear. Nicole and Tomas had been very discreet about their relationship but the French can always sniff out any whiff of a romance.

"Oh no, madam," she replied, a shade too quickly.

"Mm." Madam Barteau didn't sound convinced. "I'll be consulting the Test Board to check whether any other anomalies have been noticed. In the meantime, please re-check your information and forward your findings to me first thing Monday morning."

"Absolutely, madam!" The click of disconnection seemed louder than normal. Nicole had struggled to develop a good rapport with the prickly Madam Barteau. This issue with the data could provide the supervisor with the means to dismiss her. The trouble was that Nicole herself couldn't understand why the data seemed so far off the norm. That was what she'd been researching before her musings about the weekend. She'd simply have to go over it all again to make sure it wasn't her own error skewing the figures.

She didn't want to risk dragging Tomas into a potential career-killer but she needed to confirm the information they had gathered. She opened Tomas's Comms connection. Within seconds his smiling face filled the holo-screen.

"Bonjour, ma petite! Could you not wait to see me?"

"Sh! Stop that," she replied, instantly ashamed to see his reaction to her tone. "I'm sorry, Tomas. But this is serious. Madam Barteau is concerned about our data. It's contradicting that of the other test groups."

"I expect ours is the placebo group and that's why the results aren't consistent."

"Surely she would account for that? And she mentioned that not all our testers are on the official list. How could that be?"

"I'm sure it'll all be fine, cherie. She could be right thinking it's rogue data. We just need to find where it's crept in. Maybe another lab's work has seeped into our system."

Nicole breathed more easily. Tomas was probably right. Laboratoires

Lisle was only one section of a huge conglomerate, many parts of which were running pharmaceutical tests. Despite the best monitoring systems that money could buy no integrated technology was guaranteed to be completely failsafe. She'd trace the data back to its origins and filter out the errors. She glanced at the clock, 11:30am – no lunch today! She worried that she might need to work on this all weekend.

CHAPTER 34

Ellingham: 5 August 2110

Let's get on with it.

I sat on the sofa with my eyes closed and Seth trying not to sulk beside me. No need for me to read his thoughts, they were plain enough – his straight-back, arms-crossed pose and the occasional sigh that he indulged in. *Tough!* If I was to have any chance of succeeding I had to ignore Seth's disappointment and concentrate on the babble of voices in my head.

As I'd expected, my probing had caused the volume of noise to increase. It was like the mental equivalent of poking a mouth ulcer – uncomfortable on its own and when your tongue investigates the sore spot the pain sharpens, but you keep going back to it! My forehead tightened and Seth must've spotted the change as I felt his arm move to wrap around my shoulders and give me a reassuring hug. The trouble was that I didn't know how to latch onto an individual when they had no way of hearing me. When you're in a crowded room with lots of conversations going on you can make someone aware of you with a wave of your hand or by touching their arm. How was I going to achieve that telepathically when nobody could sense me? I tried moving my eyes under my closed lids, as though I was looking around that crowded room. It had some effect as I could grasp occasional snatches of thought: *Wish they'd just get on with it … Where did I put those keys? … Nice cold glass …* Not all of them came through in perfect English but the translation brain-gadget that Ms Thorogood had talked about in class did the trick and I understood the thoughts of a foreign origin as easily as those from English-speaking connections. But no matter how hard I tried to hold onto a single connection, I would soon lose it amongst the general murmur.

I concentrated on the remembered image of Dale Johnson, thinking about his shout the previous day. It sort of worked – in a distant corner of my mind I heard his fearful cry for help or maybe it was just the memory of that first connection. I reached out with my thoughts trying to reinforce that link and that's when I heard it for the first time: ... *if she's always open. What a perfect opportunity. Ha! I'll be ...* I lost it and was grateful that I had. I opened my eyes in horror and grabbed Seth's arms so tightly he cringed in pain.

"Omigod, he's here," I panted, my breath coming in ragged, fear-driven gasps.

"Who? What's the matter Dez? Did you connect with someone?"

"It was *his* voice. I recognised it from my memories of the murders. The killer, Seth, and he knows I can hear him." I couldn't contain my sobs any longer and I clung to Seth until I managed to get my fear under control. "I don't want to do it like this. There must be another way." I sat and chewed my nails, rocking myself back and forth on the sofa while Seth gently rubbed my shoulders and mumbled soothing noises. Eventually the shock faded and I calmed down enough to sit back in Seth's comforting arms. He kissed the top of my head as it rested against his chest.

"Don't worry, Dez. I'm here. You're safe with me," he said.

"Yeah, I bet that's what Nicole thought about Tomas," I muttered.

"Who's Nicole?"

"Oh! I don't know ... No, hang on. It's the girl in Paris. Tomas was her fiancé."

"You've never mentioned her name before and it wasn't in the news report."

"I know. It just came out of nowhere. I'm sure that was her name and that Simone, her PT, lives on the south side of the Seine in Paris, but that's it." Without a thought, I raised my hands and shoulders in a very French style shrug. I realised what I was doing and laughed self-consciously. But it gave me an idea. I reached into my bag to find my Comms kit. Ignoring Seth's puzzled expression I keyed Aunt Jen's number and hoped she was able to pick up.

"Hello, Dez, love. What can I do for you?"

"Hi, Aunt Jen. Are you really busy at the moment or could you spare some time for your favourite niece?"

"Always got time for my favourite niece," she quipped back.

"Great. We'll be round at yours in half an hour or so. See ya!"

"See you soon, love."

As I stood up from the sofa, Seth looked at me with his brows pulled together in query, "Aren't you Jen's *only* niece?" he asked.

"Ye-es."

"Well, you do realise that makes you her least favourite niece too, don't you?" He laughed and pulled his arms over his head to defend himself from the cushion I was using as a missile. "I'm gonna ask your mum to remove all soft furnishings from the premises! Anyway, what are we going to Jen's for?"

"Henri," I replied. "Aunt Jen's PT. He's a Parisian too. Don't know why I didn't think of it sooner. Maybe he could track down Simone for us."

Seth's face registered his doubts.

"Dunno, Dez. Do you think we should get anyone else involved? We were trying to keep it to just us, weren't we?"

I hesitated trying to work out how we were going to get any further on our own and coming up blank.

"Sorry, Seth. I can't face opening up my head to that creep again. I've only just managed to get the connections quiet." I rubbed my temples to relieve the pressure that had built up. "Jen and Henri will be discreet. You know we can count on them to be on our side."

Seth smiled reluctantly and nodded, no doubt remembering the many times that Aunt Jen had played advocate for us when we'd been in trouble. Some of her expertise came from Henri himself – he was a senior magistrate in the French criminal court.

"Come on, then," Seth said, grabbing my hands and manoeuvring me towards the door. "Let's go see what Henri can do for us this time."

Aunt Jen's farm was a good half-hour walk from home. The afternoon was still warm and sunny and the stroll gave us chance to rekindle some of the romance from earlier. We held hands and swung our arms like little children skipping along on a school nature trail – the difference being that we got to stop every so often for a bit of canoodling, as my dad called it. The last opportunity was by the kissing-gate at the top of Jen's drive and I was determined to make the most of it. The rhythmic squeaking of a neglected bicycle interrupted us.

"Whatcha doin' here?"

"Playing I-Spy! What d'ya think, Baby Boy?" I snapped.

"Aw, get real," wailed Jeremy. "I'm only a coupla years younger than you. I'll be starting PT Prep this year."

Seth and I winked at each other – *as if that's gonna make a difference!*

"We're just here to say 'Hi' to your mum," Seth said. He tried to sooth the friction between Jeremy and me, probably remembering how awkward he'd felt at fourteen.

"She's in the ménage with Dick and the latest nag." Jeremy gestured down the path then stood on the pedals to push his bike off in the opposite direction.

"You really shouldn't be so harsh on him. Poor kid." Seth nodded towards the dust cloud that Jeremy had created with his speedy exit.

"You're calling that spawn of Satan a poor kid? He wouldn't think twice about spiking your tea with laxative or sneaking itching powder into your underwear drawer!" My face burned with embarrassing memories – spending an entire Saturday evening a couple of years ago locked in Jen's loo after Jeremy *kindly* made me a cup of herbal tea and, another time – wriggling throughout my French Oral, trying hard not to scratch my bum! I could see Seth found my embarrassment highly amusing although he was doing his best not to smile too broadly. I scowled at him to remind him he was supposed to be on my side and we set off down to the ménage.

"Hello," I called as we reached the sturdy boundary fence. The horse that Jeremy had called a nag was a magnificent stallion, a rich chestnut colour, jet black mane and tail, long elegant legs and a big opinion of himself! He tossed his head around but couldn't break Jen's grip on the reins as she took him through his paces. Dick sat on the fence with a tense expression on his face.

"She always has to go for the most temperamental," he sighed, as we climbed up to perch beside him. "One of these days she's going to meet her match."

I smiled. "Don't worry, Dick. There isn't a horse born yet that Aunt Jen can't handle."

"Thanks for the vote of confidence," Jen panted. "Give me a few more minutes to wear him out then we'll head in for a drink. Jeremy will be pleased to see you, he's getting bored being out here alone." she added.

Seth snorted in amusement and almost lost his balance as I prodded him with my elbow. Dick looked puzzled but left us to it, he was more concerned about Jen keeping *her* seat.

In the coolness of Jen's stone-floored kitchen we drank her home-made lemonade and nibbled some of Mum's ginger biscuits. Seth's blissful expression prompted me to think I would have to learn how to make them. Dick excused himself when he'd finished and went to feed the various animals that Jen had accumulated over the years. Maybe she'd told him we'd need some privacy or maybe he'd picked up on the tension, but I was grateful for his tact – usually Jen wanted to do the rounds and check on the livestock herself.

"So, what did you want to talk about? You're not pregnant are you?" She looked at our linked hands and Seth quickly drew away. I grabbed his hand back again and glowered at my aunt.

"Why does everyone keep thinking that? No I am NOT pregnant." I heard a snigger from the open window. "Bog off, Jeremy!" I yelled. The diminishing squeak of his bike assured me he'd taken the hint.

"Okay," said Jen, gesturing for me to calm down. "Tell me, what *is* the problem?"

176

I tried to start at the beginning and work my way through but found myself back-tracking several times to explain what had been going on since my birthday. Seth helped out if I got too wound-up or if he felt I'd forgotten something and eventually I got to the point.

"Let me get this straight. You didn't have an PT to start with and now you're connected to every PT in the world. You can hear people's conversations with their PT. You're having memories of being murdered but you don't know who it is that kills you. Elizabeth left clues in a journal on her *Handi* because it was her PT that committed the murders. And you want Henri to track down the PT of one of the murdered girls so you can talk to her about … Nicole, was it?"

"Yeah, that's about it. Can you help?" I asked.

"Does your father know about this, Seth?" Jen turned to him and he blushed, looking like a naughty child caught doing something he shouldn't.

"He knows about the *Handi*," he admitted. "But not about Dez's memories."

"And I can't imagine Celeste being very happy about it?" Jen made the statement sound like a question.

"Mum and Dad have said we can have some time to figure out what Elizabeth's *Handi* can tell us," I answered, bringing it out of my bag as evidence that we were being genuine. Seth's face clouded with uncertainty, he still wasn't keen to involve Jen and Henri despite knowing that we needed help to get any further with Elizabeth's riddles.

"Are you listening to Henri and me now?" Jen, like the others who'd heard about my 'open mind', seemed upset that I might be eavesdropping.

"No," I said. "I've managed to shut the connections in a sort of mentally sound-proofed room – my personal padded cell – so that I can't hear them as much. It's only in particularly stressful situations that a voice might get louder and attract my attention."

It wasn't my fault the damned thing had gone haywire. Why did my family and friends automatically think I was listening in on their own thoughts when I had millions of conversations vying for headroom?

Jen picked up on the weariness in my voice,

"Sorry, love. I got a bit fazed by it all. No doubt that's an understatement for how you feel, eh?"

I managed a wry smile and nodded.

Yeah, the mother of all understatements, I'd say.

CHAPTER 35

Ellingham: 5 August 2110

Why am I complicating things like this?

"Hang on. I don't need to listen in to your thoughts, Jen. Just ask Henri if he's available to talk privately and I'll Comms him." I saw the look of relief cross her face before she managed to get it under control.

"Why are the simplest solutions always the hardest to find?" Jen laughed, trying to cover her reaction.

I shrugged half-heartedly. I suspected that everything I'd been going through had clouded my judgement, making normal options seem too easy. Things needed to be sorted out soon though – I was exhausted from the constant changes and mental onslaughts. Sensing my mood, Seth squeezed my hand and gave me a reassuring kiss on my cheek.

"Come on," he said. "Let's go count chickens and give Jen some privacy."

"Only those that are hatched," Jen twisted the ancient saying to lighten the atmosphere. The joke was bad enough to do the trick – I followed Seth outside, shaking my head and groaning at the pun.

We found Dick surrounded by noisily clucking fowl as he threw the feed to the ground for them. I've never been a big fan of chickens but Jen and Dick kept them looking sleek and healthy, some of them looked quite beautiful with their russet feathers shining in the late afternoon sun. Suddenly the chickens scattered, some running in the odd rolling motion that seems so unbalanced, others tried to fly away but could only manage such short distances that they looked as though they were riding pogo-sticks. The source of the commotion came to a standstill in the middle of the yard.

"Did ya leave any biscuits for me, Seth?" Jeremy pointed at the stray crumbs still clinging to Seth's shirt. I would've been annoyed but Seth just laughed, swiped away the crumbs and assured Jeremy that there were still plenty of Aunt Celeste's gingers in the tin.

"Dez," Jen called from the kitchen door. "Henri is in a meeting but he said he'll call you as soon as he's free."

"Fine. Thanks Jen."

"Why d'ya wanna talk to Frenchie?" Jeremy was going through a rude stage of belittling all those that didn't fit with his idea of perfect – so – everyone but himself, of course!

"Jeremy, behave," sighed his mother. "Dez just needs some first-hand anecdotes for an Academy project." She winked at me. "Let me know how you get on with it, wont' you, Dez?"

"Sure. Thanks for the help, Jen." I smiled at her, grateful for her discretion. "See you later then."

"Thanks for the lemonade and cookies. Bye," added Seth.

A chorus of "Bye," "Cheerio," "Whatever!" followed us out of the farmyard.

"Don't fret, he'll grow up one day," said Seth when I cringed at Jeremy's parting shot.

"He's such a spoilt brat. I can't understand Aunt Jen letting him get away with it all the time." I spotted a grin creasing Seth's cheeks and halted mid-rant. "Okay, okay. Who am I to talk? Is that why you're struggling to keep your face straight?"

"Well, you have to admit Dez, it does seem to be a family trait. Your dad spoils you rotten too." And before I could respond, he pulled me into a hug, pinning my arms by my side and kissing away my indignation. When he felt me relax he released me. "Better now?" he asked.

"Don't push it Wallis," I warned, but I took his hand and we set off back to his house to wait for Henri's call.

We didn't have to wait long. As Seth opened the front door my

180

Comms kit buzzed and I had to root around in my bag to find it. Why do things disappear even in the smallest of handbags?

"Bonjour, Henri!" I chimed, mangling the rs in my attempt to sound fluent.

"Good day to you too, Desirée," he crooned in accented English. His voice is so silky smooth, so sexy, so French! He's the one person I really don't mind using my full name, he makes it sound sophisticated and chic. "Jennifer tells me you and the gorgeous Seth need my 'elp. What can I do for you, cherie?"

"Firstly, dear Henri you can stop flirting with the gorgeous Seth – he's mine!"

"Oh, 'ow could you do this to me, cherie? I no longer 'ave the reason to come to England. I am desolate." I could visualise him dramatically stroking his forehead with the back of his hand and I was tempted to switch to holo-vid to check it out. *"Stop teasing her Henri. Just get on with it."* Oops – I didn't mean to overhear Aunt Jen. I launched into my explanation of the last few weeks to distract myself from the connection, finishing with my request for Henri to track down Simone.

After a short silence Henri replied, "Under normal circumstances, I wouldn't even consider this but I suppose these are 'ardly normal circumstances. I may be able to access the coroner's reports for Nicole and Tomas and see if their PTs were identified. If so, I shall approach Simone myself to see if she is willing to talk to you."

"Thank you so much, Henri. You're a star." I felt the lump of anxiety soften in my chest – *at last we might be getting somewhere.*

"Au revoir." He chuckled at my gushing gratitude. "We'll speak again soon."

"Bye, Henri and thanks again." I put my headset back into my titchy bag.

"It's nearly six, Dad'll be home soon. What do you fancy for tea?" Seth asked.

"Do you ever think of anything other than food?"

"Not if I can help it," he laughed as he rooted through the fridge to see what was on offer.

Henri's call had filled me with nervous energy and I couldn't keep still. I hovered around the kitchen getting in Seth's way until he lost patience and handed me a packet of radishes, telling me to top and tail them while he prepared a green salad.

"Now that's what I like to see – co-operation in the kitchen," said Samuel on his arrival home. He smiled at our domestic tableau and the realisation that this could be our future came as a bit of a surprise. I was so distracted, in fact, that I managed to top my finger instead of the damned radish! After quite a few scrapes and bruises over the years I'm usually fine with the sight of blood. I turned to the sink and doused the end of my finger with cold water, but the bleeding didn't ease up. The next thing I knew I was on the floor. Seth was holding up my legs and Samuel was patting a cool, damp cloth on my forehead. My first random thought was, *Glad I'm wearing jeans!* Then *Ouch!* as Samuel pressed a cloth firmly onto the injured finger. It bloody well hurt! I also felt sore on my shoulder, *Must have hit it on the way down.*

"All right, love," Samuel said when he noticed I'd opened my eyes. "Take it easy, now. We'll drive you down to the clinic for them to check you over, eh?"

Before I could protest, Seth had me in his arms and we were heading to the car. For the second time in a week I was admitted to the Ellingham clinic emergency department. I shuddered at the feeling of déjà vu and glanced around nervously looking for that awful nurse, sure that she'd be lingering with the dopey juice at the ready. A cute male nurse stuck the tip of my finger down with medical grade nano-glue that stung like hell. When I winced at his friendly pat on my shoulder he sent me for a full scan to check that I hadn't done any further damage during my less-than-graceful faint.

After a few more prods and tests I was discharged. Nurse Bridges joked about staying away from sharp implements as he handed over a set of instructions on wound-care and a single-dose tube of the glue for home treatment in the unlikely event of the cut splitting again. Instinctively showing a possessive streak, Seth wrapped his arm tightly around my shoulder. I gritted my teeth when the developing bruise protested – I didn't want to spoil his macho-moment.

Samuel insisted on taking me straight home to put my parents' minds at ease. He'd called them from the clinic to say what had happened and to assure them that it wasn't serious.

Mum was waiting at the front door,

"Oh, thank you. Thank you so much Samuel," she gushed.

"Don't mention it," he replied, looking very embarrassed by Mum's fussing. "We'll let you get on," he added and turned to leave but Mum grabbed his arm.

"No. Please come in. Don't rush home." Mum guided us all into the lounge and started piling up cushions until they looked like a squishy Leaning Tower of Pisa.

"Here you go, love," she said as she deposited the pile on my lap. "Prop your arm up on there to keep the blood flow light." This was an unexpected reaction, especially after the restrained welcome home the previous week! *But we do seem to be getting on better these days,* I thought, *Best make the most of it in case it doesn't last.*

Dad came in, balancing a huge tray filled with a selection of drinks, sandwiches and cakes.

"We thought you might like some supper, having missed your evening meal," he said, as he offered the refreshments to Samuel and Seth. When appetites were satisfied, the men started discussing the latest cricket results and Mum kept glancing my way to make sure I hadn't quietly expired. In spite of my best efforts, I did start to wilt fairly quickly. I was drained from the excitement of the latest trauma, even if it was only a cut finger – I was sure I'd lost half my body's blood supply at least! Some unspoken gesture alerted Seth and I was in his arms again as he carried me to my room. Mum climbed the stairs ahead of us, no doubt feeling we needed a chaperone now that we were a couple.

"See you tomorrow," Seth whispered as he kissed my forehead. His fingers swept down my cheek and I grabbed his hand to kiss his palm. Mum was standing by the door and couldn't have seen the gesture but her expression was one of mixed feelings. I allowed myself to sense her thoughts – it was wrong of me, I know, but I'm not perfect. Surprisingly, she had no negative thoughts about Seth, she was very fond of him, but she was worried about me becoming sexually active and she was concerned about the possibility of an unplanned pregnancy. *Why can't parents trust their kids?* The memory of my sudden hunger for sex with Seth the other day answered the question for me.

But that wasn't really me! Was it?

CHAPTER 36

Sandridge Magna: 21 April 2106

"No, Gramps, the campaign's going fine. Don't worry, L and D are enjoying the kudos of having the youngest independent candidate coming from their firm."

"Are you sure you're prepared to break off your career if you're elected? Even a back-bench MP has a huge responsibility to their constituents." Matt Simpson's hologram features creased with his concern.

"The law and politics – what could be a better combination? When I did my gap-year with Johnsons I saw how difficult it was to make real change happen. Politicians lost their passion a long time ago. Maybe having PTs tones it down for some people but I'm lucky – mine's as committed as I am. Come on Gramps, you and Great-Granny Julia made your mark funding the tele-prep introduction. It's our generation's turn."

"Okay, okay!" Matt waved his hands in surrender. "We Lords do our bit for King and Country too you know," he laughed. "I don't need your rallying speech, young lady."

"Sorry." Beth shrugged her shoulders. "I get carried away sometimes."

"Your mother has invited us all for Sunday lunch. Will you be able to join us?"

She grinned at her grandfather's attempt to steer the conversation onto safer ground.

"Love to," she said. "And I might have something to share with you by then." She winked and watched the hologram of Matt's puzzled face dissolve as she broke the connection.

She turned to the pile of papers strewn across the floor. Great-Granny Julia's notes, cuttings and old official documents from her great-grandfather's time in the House of Lords held the clue, she was sure of it. As a lawyer she'd learned that there were few truly significant coincidences in life – or death. She had a talent for finding patterns that revealed the connections of apparently unrelated incidents.

Her interest in Julia's obsession with the Trevalyn family had been reignited when her mentor Dale Johnson fell ill. He and Victor Trevalyn had been working together on a project in Lipostzi at the time. The media reported that a suspected drugs overdose had caused Dale's collapse but Beth wasn't prepared to accept that, despite the evidence of the leaked medical records.

She slid from the sofa to sit on the floor, picked up a sheaf of handwritten notes and began to read through them – again. Three hours later she sighed, straightened her stiff back and rubbed at her eyes. This was proving to be a toughie. She opened the Comms system and began trawling the InfoNet for any references to items that Julia had listed. Despite their global presence the Trevalyn Corporation had very little press – good or bad. Victor was a virtual recluse and she had to rely on her memory of him from that reception almost three years ago. The last time she'd seen Dale face-to-face too. It would've been nice to call him for advice but the twist was that without his sudden collapse, Beth wouldn't have been looking through Julia's files.

"Coffee!" Beth needed a break but didn't want to go to bed just yet. She wandered into the kitchen, pausing to look at her digi-snap board. Her gap-year group grinned through the dust and sweat of their hard work. E-cards from friends now living abroad framed the collage of family events. One of those snaps gave her a renewed burst of energy. She tapped the board and the picture enlarged to show Beth as a child, dressed in a peach bridesmaid dress and lacy tights. She was standing with the bride and groom, slightly forward of the happy couple and straining to be the centre of attention – then, she'd thought their smiles were just for her. She knew better now of course.

"Uncle Jonny and Aunt Ce-Ce," she whispered. Maybe it was the time to test her theory about their professional past.

CHAPTER 37

Ellingham: 6 August 2110

No, it was left-over feelings from Nicole, wasn't it?

Alvin had arranged for us to meet at his office and I hoped that he'd have the answer to my shared memories and feelings. If my new sexual appetite was merely Nicole's unfulfilled desires, how would I know when it was *me* wanting to be with *Seth* rather than *Nicole* wanting to be with *Tomas*? Not that I was about to ask Alvin to solve that little problem for me!

Seth had come over to mine in the morning as promised and, to appease Mum, we'd had a very sedate few hours watching classic holo-films and having lunch with her. She'd done her mother-hen bit and checked my finger countless times to make sure the wound hadn't split. It was nice to feel loved again after our cool relationship of recent years, but it was beginning to suffocate me. I was glad that Alvin had suggested we went to his office this time – it gave us chance to escape Mum's fussing.

"How's the finger?" Seth asked.

"Don't you start."

"Only asking," he responded, in a peeved tone. "You were swinging your arm as we walked so I thought it might've made it throb again."

I had to admit to myself that my finger did feel a bit uncomfortable but I wasn't going to own up to it. "No, it's fine. Thank you."

"Liar," he said and gently gave the offending digit a make-it-better kiss.

I laughed and moved closer to him as he draped his arm around my shoulders. I wondered if we were just going through a teenage crush, whether we'd still be together after the Academy, after University – if we got there. The simple concerns of a 'normal' teenager were a pleasant diversion from all the other stuff we had to think about so I indulged myself with a few more carefree, romantic daydreams of our future.

Alvin didn't have a receptionist at his office which was situated above 'Bloomin-Marvellous', Ellingham's most expensive florists – the sort where a single, exotic bloom would be elegantly displayed in the window. We climbed the stairs to the half-glazed door and buzzed the intercom.

"One moment, please." A recorded female voice replied. Then the auto-lock hummed and the door opened. "Please take a seat. Mr Grey will be with you shortly," the voice advised. I just managed to stop myself saying an automatic thank you to the disembodied assistant.

The room was clean and functional with modern furniture, a water cooler, pristine vertical blinds at the window and a holo-vid currently showing the options menu for the latest cricket tournaments. Seth's eyes lit up as he headed towards the screen.

"Hi guys." Alvin's voice stopped Seth in his tracks. "Come in. Come in. I've got something I want to discuss with you," Alvin continued. His excitement was catching and I felt buoyed-up, expecting some good news to come from the meeting. Seth looked longingly at the holo-vid then followed me into Alvin's inner office. This was a distinct contrast to the waiting area. It was still clean and tidy, but it was furnished with antiques and decorated in a classical style. Alvin's desk was a huge, dark-wood affair with a well-worn, green leather insert on the top. Both the wood and the leather shone from centuries of polishing. There was a chaise-longue to one side of the room and I looked at it warily.

"Don't worry, Dez. You don't need to sit there," Alvin said, having spotted my discomfort. "Not many people use it these days but some, like the client I told you about, feel that hypnotherapy isn't genuine without the stage-props. Anyway," he added. "I didn't ask you here for a hypno session. I've come up with a theory about your memories."

At last! I thought as I sank into a large Chesterfield-style club chair. The arms of the chair were so high I couldn't reach over them to hold Seth's hand and although the seat was comfortable I felt isolated inside its hugeness. I pulled myself forward so that I was perched at the front of the chair. Seth's hand found mine and I relaxed knowing I wasn't alone after all.

"I spoke to a number of my colleagues," Alvin began, "and did some InfoNet research. I believe I have an explanation for your memories of those murders. I think you are experiencing them third-hand."

"Third-hand?" Seth and I asked in unison.

"Yes. Dez, you have these remote connections, don't you? So it's possible – even *probable* that you can link to the murderer. Now, what if that murderer is one of those people who can sense others beside their own PT? Someone who can feel and hear everything that the victim does when they are in close proximity? The murderer absorbs the victim's last few moments as though the experience is their own. You come along and tap into the murderer's thoughts and feelings, but from the view point of the victims." Alvin sat back in his chair and waved his hands over his desk as though presenting a tray of jewellery for inspection.

We all sat in silence for a few moments, considering the theory, thinking through the logic and finally agreeing with the argument. There couldn't be any other explanation – well, another was that I'd suffered a mental breakdown but that wasn't an option I wanted to consider.

"So, if I can perfect the closing off of the connections, I could break that link and not have the memories any more?"

"It's possible," Alvin replied. Then he frowned. "Dez. The other day when you spoke about isolating connections you were talking about the murderer weren't you?"

If there was one time I wished I could lie convincingly it was then. Poor Seth – he'd kept his mother's secret for four years and in less than a week I'd managed to get my parents, his dad, Aunt Jen and Henri in on the act. Now Alvin was getting suspicious and I didn't have a good enough explanation handy to sooth his anxiety. My hero stepped into the breach.

"Mr Grey," Seth said. "Dez simply wanted to clear up why she's been having these flashbacks. When we started to look up the news archives we discovered she'd experienced two real murders but only one was reported as a murder. There's a long list of incidents that she feels could be linked to one killer. If she's able to identify the killer we can alert the authorities."

"What if the killer finds you first? Remember he or she can also link to people other than their own PT."

"But you said they're only likely to hear someone they're close to at the time." I protested. Alvin still didn't look convinced. He removed his specs and rubbed the bridge of his nose.

"This really goes against my better judgement, but I can't stop you experimenting in your own head, can I? Although I urge you not to do anything that puts you in any kind of danger – mentally as well as physically. Think what this person is capable of and then consider if it's worth the risk to your own health, Dez."

I saw Seth nodding in agreement with Alvin's assessment. They both looked at me as though I was a condemned prisoner on my way to the executioner's block. As if I wasn't already scared to death, having experienced the killer's cruelty first – *or third* – hand.

"Don't worry, Alvin," I said. "I've no intention of letting him get close to me in any sense." I saw his quick intense glance as he heard me put a gender to the killer.

"What makes you think it's a man?" he asked.

"I remember his voice from the murders. I can't remember his face clearly but I'd definitely know his voice if I heard it again." I shuddered – the spine rattling shiver of someone walking over my grave.

"Fascinating," Alvin leaned forward over his desk. I'd piqued his professional curiosity again. "He must be able to interfere with the victims' sensory receptors. Or maybe this is a demonstration of the theory that the last sense one loses in death is hearing. Therefore, that's the strongest memory for you during these flashbacks."

I began to worry that Alvin was going to ask me to try to remember another murder so I stood up and, without thinking held my out arm for a parting hand-shake.

"Thank you for your help, Alvin. I need to think things through before I decide what to do next. I'm managing to keep most of the connections under control in the subconscious room that we built and I don't want to jeopardise that," I said.

"You're welcome, Dez," he replied, taking my hand in both of his and shaking it vigorously.

"OUCH!"

"Oh! I'm so sorry, Dez. I didn't notice your injury. Been in the wars again?"

"Mmph. S'okay. Just a slip whilst cutting radishes," I managed between lips pressed together in a grimace of pain.

"I hope I haven't set back the healing." He frowned and I could sense his concern that he'd hurt me. "Please do let me know how you get on and if there's anything else I can do for you. I'm sure I speak for Debbie, too." The softening of his expression and the lilt in his voice as he said her name confirmed my suspicions of the other day – they were definitely a couple too.

Ooh, wait 'til we get back to class!

CHAPTER 38

Ellingham: 6 August 2110

Hope Henri can find Simone.

I didn't want to connect telepathically to the murderer ever again. At the moment our best lead would be Simone, assuming Henri could convince her to talk to us. And if Mrs Johnson also contacted us about our 'thesis' there was a chance we could find some solid evidence to help solve Elizabeth's clues. Otherwise, it seemed the only way we'd discover the murderer's identity would be for me to hunt him down in my own head – despite my promise to Alvin.

"Penny for them," Seth said, as we walked along the High Street towards the ecotram terminus.

"You couldn't afford 'em. There're far too many,"

"I meant just yours." His mildly hurt tone reminded me that he hadn't yet connected with his own PT. Maybe he was feeling isolated despite his sympathy for my own opposite affliction.

"Sorry," I said. "I was thinking about Simone and Mrs Johnson and hoping that we'll get a breakthrough from what they might be able to tell us."

"Don't you think we're getting in a bit too deep here?"

"What do you mean?"

"Dez, we have no back-up if things start to get heavy. What if you do identify the killer? If Mum couldn't tell the authorities who he was, what makes you think you can?"

"There doesn't seem to be anything stopping me telling you who I can hear, does there?"

Seth paused as if he was about to argue but realised that I hadn't had any problems talking about my connections so he tried a different approach.

"What if he can hear you and he works out we're on to him?"

"He'll only hear me if he's close to me and I'm not going to stand around next to a complete stranger waiting to see if he pounces, am I? Besides, I've got my big, brave Seth to protect me!"

The frown remained on Seth's face.

"All right," I said. "Let's see if Simone and Mrs J give us anything new to go on. If not, we're at a dead end anyway and, if they do have something useful, we'll assess whether we should go further with it or pass everything on to the authorities, okay?"

He gave a begrudging shrug but tightened his grip on my hand – luckily it was my left hand. The summer afternoon heat was building and my finger was throbbing. I slipped my thumb through my bag strap to keep that hand close to my shoulder. It helped ease the pain a little but I still felt uncomfortable and I wasn't convinced it was all down to the weather. Seth was right. What hope did we have of exposing the killer if he'd managed to keep ahead of the authorities all these years? At the time, there'd been no reports of a man-hunt for a serial killer so there couldn't be any tangible evidence to unite the murders that Elizabeth had linked in her *Handi*. Would the police take any notice of us if we did go to them? I felt a twinge of bitterness towards Elizabeth. Why did she leave that damned diary? I had enough to cope with, having all those multi-channels in my head! The feeling passed quickly, though. Elizabeth had merely wanted someone to put a stop to his killings if she failed in her attempt and the only way she could help expose him was via the clues in her *Handi*. It must've been hard for her, knowing that Seth or Samuel would end up with this responsibility and I was ashamed for my brief indulgence in self-pity.

"You're off again," Seth said.

"Sorry. Did you say something?"

"No." He laughed at my concerned expression, "Don't worry. I'm getting used to you having your internal conversations."

"I wasn't listening to anyone," I replied, stung by his assumption. "I'm not permanently eavesdropping, you know."

We didn't speak again during the journey home, until I hesitated at the end of the driveway to Seth's house.

"Aren't you coming in?" Seth asked. "Look, I'm sorry if I upset you earlier. I didn't mean anything by it."

"Maybe we're spending too much time together," I replied. "We seem to be bickering all the time."

"Dez, we've always bickered. Just 'cos we're a couple now that won't change, will it? It's simply part of our relationship – we get annoyed with each other but know that we'll always be there for each other."

"Yeah, but recently it's got worse."

"No. It's just recently we've had a lot more to deal with. Come on, Dez. We'll check for messages from Mrs J and see if we can sort out this mess. Once we can move on from finding Mum's PT, things'll get better, I promise."

Seth could always win me round with his confident promises, even if they didn't always come through. I slipped my arm around his waist and stretched up to kiss his cheek.

"Thanks," I said, feeling safe in his strong, warm embrace.

***

Mrs Johnson had responded to our query and was keen for us to get in touch with her. She'd given us her personal contact details and suggested we arrange to meet as soon as possible. I felt guilty for stringing her along but we had to speak to Dale's PT and the only way was through Mrs J. As I can't lie to save my life, Seth made the call and, without flinching, continued the subterfuge that we were students looking at developing treatments for brain injuries. It worried me that he seemed so good at it – what if he lied to me, how would I know? Mrs J had a two-hour gap in her diary for the next day and invited us to go down to London – at her expense – to see the Foundation and discuss our proposal. Her enthusiasm for our 'project' was heart-breaking. I hoped that we'd be able to repay her in some small way by putting Dale's attacker in jail for the rest of his life.

"It'll be fine," Seth assured me when they'd closed the call. "I'm sure she'll understand when she hears the full story."

"I feel so bad raising her hopes like that. What if it doesn't do any good? She'll hate us."

"Try not to worry. Let's take it one step at a time, yeah?"

My Comms kit was buzzing – Henri calling. I connected the call through Seth's Holo-Comms equipment so that we had video. The suave Frenchman waved at me from his office in the Paris Judiciary Centre. It was hard to believe he matched my aunt in age – his forty-eight years had been much kinder and he could easily pass for a man of thirty.

"Bonjour, ma cherie," he said. "'Ow are you today?"

"Could be better." I wiggled my injured finger at the web-cam.

"Don't tell me, it was a right-handed knife," he joked, referring to a time when he'd been visiting many years before. In frustration at not being able to cut an apple at the age of six or seven, I'd complained that the knife I held in my left hand didn't work because it was right-handed.

"Ha-ha," I responded, sarcastically. "Never mind the sympathy. Have you got any news for us?"

"But of course!" Henri gave the time honoured French shrug, as though it was an insult to doubt him. "I spoke to Simone moments ago and, although she is still 'aunted by the events of that night, she is willing to talk to you." He quoted her contact details and reminded me to be careful, both for her sake and ours.

I sat and looked at the information for a long time after my conversation with Henri had finished. Suddenly, it became much more real being so close to contacting a victim's PT. Especially when, via the killer's memory, I'd been more connected to Nicole in her last minutes than Simone had. Would she be jealous? Angry that I'd had those final few moments when she'd been cut-off from her own PT?

"Come on," Seth interrupted my thoughts. "We'd better list the questions you want to ask."

It wasn't as easy as the detective shows make it seem. We had some information from the news report so we tried to expand on that. Eventually, we felt we had enough to make a start – maybe more would come naturally out of the conversation with Simone. I made the call via Seth's Holo-Comms centre but only used the audio connection to allow her some privacy.

"Bonjour?" Simone's voice was quiet, almost timid, a contrast to Henri's brash, confident attitude. Having Henri as my only example, I'd expected all Parisians to be self-assured cosmopolitans.

"Bonjour, Simone. Je m'appelle Desirée Hanson. Parlez-vous l'englais?" I couldn't imagine trying to explain everything in my school French.

"Ah oui. Monsieur Cartier told me you would be calling. It's about Nicole, yes?"

I looked at Seth and he gave me an encouraging nod.

"Yes, thank you for agreeing to talk to me, Simone. I hope that, with your help, we can discover the identity of the man who killed her and Tomas. Do you feel able to answer a few questions?"

"Please, go ahead," she replied. "I'll do whatever I can to help."

I looked at the list we'd made and began the interview.

"The reports mentioned that Tomas worked for a Research Laboratory. Do you know which lab that was?"

"It was Laboratoires Lisle. He was researching new drug therapies for psychological problems, especially for those unfortunates who don't have a … jumeau télépathique … er, in English I think you say Psyche-Twin?"

Unfortunates – *ouch*, that struck a chord! Although it now seemed a dim and distant past when my own PT connection had failed.

"And Nicole was helping him with her own research as a post-graduate. She was studying the evolution of the PT connection. They enjoyed working together very much. It was how they met and fell in love." Simone's voice caught as though she was trying not to cry. She'd answered my second question which had been about Nicole's studies so I skipped to the next one.

"Thank you, Simone. Do you have access to Nicole's study

materials at all? And, if so, would you be willing to allow me to see it?" I sensed her initial reluctance. It was the last remnant of her unique connection to Nicole. To share it was to sever the tie completely. I was aware of another presence comforting her and I felt even more like an intruder. Simone had connected to a new PT, as sometimes happens when a PT dies.

"I shall forward her notes to you," she finally replied and, although I had a couple more questions on my list, I didn't have the heart to ask more of her.

"Thank you very much, Simone," I said. "You've been a great help. I'll let you know how we get on. May I call you again?"

"Yes, yes. Please do. I hope you find the bâtard and he rots in Hell forever!" Simone's hatred was startling, coming from her timid, quiet tone.

"We'll do our best," I promised.

"Before you go," Seth spoke for the first time and gestured towards the list, "could you please tell us about your experience on the night of Nicole's death, if you feel up to it?"

The silence lasted so long that I thought Simone had hung-up on us and I tentatively reached out for her in my mind. Yes, I could still sense her there – she was simply gathering her thoughts.

"It was cold," she began, "I never like February it always seems to me an unlucky month." She laughed briefly as though ashamed of her superstition. "Earlier in the day Nicole was worried about something at work, I'm not sure what as it was confidential, but by the evening she seemed better. She was very excited. I could feel it as though I was going to dinner myself. She had a suspicion that Tomas was going to propose but she tried not to think about it too much in case she was wrong. Sometimes she would holo-vid me to get my opinion on how she looked. She was always gorgeous, very beautiful. I'm ashamed to say I was jealous of her good looks and her relationship with Tomas. That night she was so nervous, she just kept chattering to me through our link and, in the end, I became annoyed. I asked her to leave me alone for a while." Simone's voice broke again and we waited for her to regain control of her emotions.

197

"She was hurt by that and she tried to be quieter. When Tomas gave her the ring, her feelings overwhelmed me and I cried with joy for them. During the meal Nicole was like a warm, happy feeling hovering in my mind but a little after they left the restaurant she disappeared. Our connection was broken … no … it was smothered. As though a thick blanket had been thrown over my head. For a while I couldn't move, I was paralysed and my heart was racing so fast that I was afraid I would have a heart-attack."

"It's all right Simone," I soothed, as her voice began to rise in panic. "You needn't go on."

"Yes, I must. I'm fine. Thank you, Desirée. From that moment I never heard Nicole again. I now believe that the effects I suffered were similar to what Nicole was going through but, at the time, I didn't realise what was happening. I thought it was me that was ill. If only I'd known, I could have called an ambulance for her."

Now she couldn't hold back her sobs and I again felt Simone's new PT trying to comfort her. She was fortunate to have someone who understood her feelings – her new PT must've been bereaved too to be available for the connection at their age. I wondered how many of the connections in my head were lone voices looking for a replacement PT. Not everyone who lost their original PT wanted a new one, not everyone *could* re-connect. Although we'd had all those months of Tele-Prep with Ms Thorogood, the reality was much harder to handle than the theory.

I swallowed the lump in my own throat.

"Thank you, Simone," I croaked. "Please don't blame yourself. I'm sure Nicole knew you would've helped if you'd realised what was happening." I couldn't tell Simone that I remembered the terror Nicole felt at not being able to contact her but I was convinced that Nicole didn't blame her PT for the broken connection. "Don't worry, we'll find the bastard." I made the same promise as I had for the girl left to die in the Weardale forest.

I just hope I can deliver!

CHAPTER 39

Sandridge Magna: 22 April 2106

"It's difficult to pinpoint the exact cause of the explosion at this point, Marie, but authorities believe that a faulty connection may have allowed gas to build up to such dangerous levels."

"Surely the building had a current safety certificate, Mahmood?"

"Well, Miss Simpson's certificate was due for renewal last month but there seems to have been a backlog and her apartment had yet to be inspected. We're currently waiting for a comment from the Health and Safety Exec on this.

However, Miss Simpson was due to stand in the Sandridge Magna by-election next month and her supporters say that her reluctance to bow to pressure on key proposals made her unpopular in both political and commercial arenas. Her passionate campaigning as an independent candidate was according her a certain notoriety and she didn't shy away from being a thorn in the side of those she considered to be bullies in society.

It's not the official line but it seems that foul play might not yet be ruled out. Back to you, Marie."

Ellingham: 22 April 2106

"Jonathan. JONATHAN!"

"Whatever's the matter, Celeste?" Jonathan ran from his home-office into the sitting-room to find his wife shaking and holding her hand to her mouth, trying to stifle her sobs.

"Beth — Bethany." She waved towards the holo-screen and the headline banner. An archive video of Bethany Simpson campaigning for the by-election ran behind the newsreader's shoulder.

"Oh, my lord!" Jonathan pulled his wife into his arms and struggled to control his own grief. He comforted her while wondering how he could face Matt after this tragedy. Their relationship, once so close, had slipped to an occasional call. A catch-up once in a while, rather than the regular gatherings when Jonathan and Celeste were younger. It happened to many friendships – it was nobody's fault – but Jonathan felt he should've tried harder to keep in touch. Dare he approach Matt and Jade now, almost out of the blue? Would they still think fondly of him or feel he's just being morbidly curious?

Stop being so self-centred! he thought.

Aye. I was just about to say the same laddie! Claude's telepathic prompt jolted Jonathan out of his shock.

"We'll see if Jade or Matt need us over there," he said. "Will you be alright while I call them?"

"Of course." Celeste nodded and took a deep breath as Jonathan closed his office door. She was relieved they'd have chance to settle down before their daughter came home from her after-school visit to the Wallises. It was not to be. The front door flew open and two giggling children charged down the hall towards her.

"Mum! Can Seth come here for tea instead? His mum's got a migraine. She looks really poorly but she says she just needs to lie down … What's the matter?" Dez's insistent chatter died away as she saw her mother's blotchy, tear-stained face. Celeste prided herself on always being perfectly groomed.

Ah! Celeste chose a convenient response to her daughter's query, "I've just had a dreadful sneezing fit, that's all." She turned the children towards the kitchen so that they didn't notice the News showing the macabre holo-vid of a body-bag being removed from a burnt-out building in Sandridge Magna. As Jonathan came out of his office, a glance passed between them. They didn't need telepathy to communicate after all the years they'd been together. It had helped them in their field work and now she needed his understanding to shield the children. A slight nod told her he'd picked up her meaning and he slipped in to the sitting room to power-off the holo-screen.

CHAPTER 40

Ellingham/London: 7 August 2110

Jeez! What time d'ya call this?

I waved in the direction of the morning alarm sensor. The projection on the wall flashed brightly to remind me that I'd set it for 6am. If I didn't get out of bed the pressure transmitter would re-set the alarm to ring again in three minutes. Sometimes I hated modern technology!

When I'd mentioned our proposed trip to the big city, Mum insisted that we travel with Dad – he was due in his London office that morning. He still wasn't too happy about us playing amateur detectives so, although I'd normally kick up a fuss about getting up this early, I tried to be cheerful at the breakfast table and his coolness gradually thawed. Maybe he felt more comfortable knowing that we were keeping them informed of our plans – though I'd only given a vague explanation about how we'd got an appointment with Mrs Johnson, avoiding the underhand method we'd actually used. If some omnipresent authority was keeping score I hoped our motives for lying would be taken into consideration – I'd heard about the road to Hell being paved with good intentions!

Hiding my jaw-breaking yawns behind my hand, I answered Seth's knock at the door.

"Come in," I groaned, irritated that he could look so wide awake and handsome whilst I had bed-head and puffy eyes. He grinned and gave me a quick but thorough kiss anyway. He was lucky – I'd just cleaned my teeth!

The journey to London was uneventful – at least I think it was

– I slept through most of it! Keeping the voices quiet was now almost at a subconscious level and I only needed to concentrate on reinforcing the room in my head if one of them became too rowdy. I'd been waiting for the memories of another murder victim to surface, but even that phenomenon seemed subdued. Despite the relief, it was like circling a sleeping tiger – afraid that, at any minute, it would wake and attack. I was always wary of dreaming in case it allowed the monster to spring, but with Seth's arm around me and my head resting on his chest, hearing the comforting rhythm of his heartbeat, I dozed peacefully.

As we joined the city commuters jostling down the platform, Dad reminded us to be back at the station by five so that we'd have plenty of time to meet him for the five-fifteen. I told him not to worry and waved him off to be carried along by the determined crowds. Seth and I managed to side-step the throng and walked at a more leisurely pace. Our appointment with Mrs Johnson wasn't until ten o'clock so we had a good two hours to fill. We headed for the nearest coffee-shop and studied the interactive A-Z.

"Where are we heading?" Seth asked, leaning closer to me to look at the map.

"The Johnson Foundation offices are south of the river, near Guy's Hospital," I replied.

"We've got time to spare. Shall we walk down?"

I looked at the clear sky. "Yeah, why not? I can pick out my city home on the way."

London was still full of ancient architecture – not only the ugly tower blocks of the 20th century but also the old magnificent structures like the Georgian mansions and the Regency crescents. I loved soaking up the history that seemed to radiate from them. I imagined the people and the events they lived through, for which the buildings stood as a backdrop. Only the extremely rich could afford to live in these magnificent homes and I often tried to think of ways that I could become wealthy enough to join them. I was always disappointed! It was probably time I started to think about where I was heading after the Academy. Indeed, our summer break should've been endless discussions with Seth about what we wanted to do with our lives but circumstances had changed all that. I couldn't think about the future when the past was holding onto us so tightly.

We arrived at the Johnson Foundation with three minutes to spare – my numerous architectural diversions having taken up all the extra time we'd had in hand.

"Please scan your ID here," said the receptionist, indicating an electronic scanner set into her desk. "The security system will register your presence so that we have an accurate record of who is in the building should there be a need to evacuate." She smiled broadly as though to reassure us that this was never necessary, but I checked the exit route, just in case. "Mrs Johnson is expecting you. Please take a seat."

I was too restless to sit so I wandered around the room looking at the wall-mounted monitors that were silently scrolling through images of various medical aid facilities around the world. They'd all been set-up or supported by the Johnson Foundation. Pristine clinics and research centres filled with smiling staff, patients and visitors. One image gave me a strong feeling of déjà vu but I knew I'd never been to that centre myself. I must've caught it on a monitor when we'd first arrived.

My pacing brought me to a large window and I squinted against the morning sun glistening on the silver ribbon of the Thames. The distinctive buildings of The Tower of London dominated the far bank. Clusters of tourists were trying to get closer to the Yeoman guides. Maybe we'd have time for a quick visit before we left.

"Good morning."

I turned at the greeting to see Mrs Johnson approaching us, her hand extended in welcome and looking more beautiful in the flesh than in the holograms we'd watched.

"Good morning," we replied in unison.

"I'm delighted that you could come today. I have a visitor who would like to meet you. I hope you won't mind him being part of our meeting?"

I looked at Seth for his input – he was better at this than me and he stepped in without a pause. "Of course we don't mind. Do we, Dez?" he said, with perfectly straight face.

"No, no. Not at all," I replied, knowing that my own face was quickly colouring up.

Luckily, Mrs Johnson had turned to lead us to her office and didn't seem to notice my blustering. She opened the door to a large bright room. One wall was made up of floor to ceiling windows. They'd been programmed to counteract the glare of the sun and were currently tinted, giving a sepia tone to the room. No doubt there would be fantastic evening views of the city through the cleared glass when the daylight faded. Along an adjacent wall stretched a huge synth-leather sofa and at the far end of this sat a handsome, swarthy man. He looked up as we entered and stood to offer his hand in greeting.

"This is Asil Kaya. He's Dale's PT and is as interested as I am in your research," Mrs Johnson said. "Asil, this is Desirée Hanson and Seth Wallis – the young people I told you about on Monday evening." She turned back towards us. "Asil booked the first available flight from Ankara so that he could be with us today."

She gestured for us all to sit down. Seth and I sat closely together on the sofa leaving the majority of its length free for Asil. Mrs Johnson sat on an adjacent armchair, within reach of her husband's PT. Without consciously seeking her thoughts, I sensed that she was as nervous as I was and that Asil's support was as necessary to her as Seth's to me. It helped me to relax and from that brief connection I was convinced that she would be sympathetic towards our intentions. I swallowed my nerves and began to explain.

"Mrs Johnson, Mr Kaya. Please bear with me while I tell you how we ended up coming to see you today. Your security system will show you that we're not actually old enough to be studying for such an advanced thesis as we proposed but it was the only way we could think of to approach you. We're truly sorry for that subterfuge."

Asil leaned forward as though to stand up but Mrs Johnson held up her hand.

"It's all right, Asil," she said. She turned back to me, her face now pale and her lips a tight line of disappointment. "I did wonder when your chips registered your personal details but I was willing to give you a chance. I suppose I was hoping you were some kind of scientific prodigies. Please continue."

"At my Sixteenth-Eve, my PT connection didn't work ..." I told them the whole story; about my hypnotherapy, the voices in my head, the memories of the murders and, finally, the sense that Dale was trying to come home, calling me to help him. Seth occasionally interrupted with information from his mother's *Handi* and why we believed that Dale's collapse was connected to the murder reports that she'd tagged. I forced myself to keep going through the resurfacing emotions, although I frequently had to wipe away my tears.

When I finished we all sat in silence for a few moments. I could hear Asil's quick, short breaths and I was afraid he was going to lose control of his temper. Mrs Johnson stood and moved towards her desk intercom. I thought she was going to have us thrown out but instead she asked for some refreshments to be brought to her office. She returned to her seat and we continued to sit quietly, waiting for her reaction. The door opened. A young man, not much older than us, brought in a tray, placing it on the coffee table by our knees.

"Thank you, Ross," said Mrs Johnson. "Please give my apologies to all concerned but I need to cancel my appointments for the remainder of the day. This is going to take longer than I expected."

"Certainly, Mrs Johnson," Ross replied.

"You must be exhausted," she said to me, as the door closed behind her assistant. "Please, help yourself."

I was astounded at her composure and my hand shook as I poured a glass of water. My stomach wouldn't take anything else for the moment.

"I'm so sorry," I whispered.

"I admit I'm disappointed that you're here under false pretences, although I admire your tenacity in coming to see me. I just don't know what it is you want from me."

"We weren't sure about that ourselves," said Seth. "We hoped you'd be able to put us in touch with Dale's PT so that we could ask him about his experience of the night of Dale's collapse. Mr Kaya being here is a great help." He looked at the Turk who was pouring a strong, black coffee.

"Asil," he said in a thick accent. "Call me Asil. The French girl's twin say like blanket over head?" he asked me.

"Yes, as though their connection was smothered. Is that what happened to you?"

"Mm." He nodded then waved his arms in frustration, searching for the English words to convey his feelings. "Same then, same today. Like thick fog. I know Dale is there but I can't get through. Like talking underwater, you know?"

I heard Mrs Johnson's sharp intake of breath,

"I can't imagine how awful it must be for you Asil, and the horror that Dale is suffering … It's too much to contemplate sometimes." She dabbed a delicate handkerchief to her eyes. Her cheeks glowed with suppressed emotion. I so wanted to help her.

"How's Mr Johnson's general health?" I didn't know why I asked the question but it seemed important at the time.

"That's the irony," she said. "He's in good physical shape. He's had blood cleansing and marrow boosting treatments. He has regular physiotherapy so that his muscles don't atrophy and he can breathe without assistance. There's no known medical reason for his paralysis." She finally gave in to her sobs and Asil reached for her hand, squeezing it between both of his to reassure her.

I had a strange sensation at the back of my skull and I reached up to scratch my head. But it wasn't anything external – it began as an itch then became more intense like a slight electric shock. Just as it was beginning to feel uncomfortable it stopped but it left me nauseous. I gulped another mouthful of water.

"Would it be possible for me to see Mr Johnson sometime?" Another question I hadn't planned!

"Actually, he's here today." Mrs Johnson stood and walked towards a panelled door at the rear of the room. "The children are on summer break and, as we have an apartment on the top floor, we occasionally stay here overnight." She pressed her hand to one of the panels and the door slid open to reveal a large hidden elevator. The four of us barely filled a quarter of the space but I felt overcrowded – emotions were high and I heard the disjointed thoughts of both Mrs Johnson and Asil as they tried to take in all that I'd told them. Mrs Johnson was anxious but willing to listen, Asil was sceptical and ready to lash out if we weren't genuine.

We stepped out of the elevator into a large open-plan living area. Near the window-wall the family were sitting at a long table playing the old-fashioned game of Scrabble. Dale's wheelchair was at one end of the table and the girls sitting on either side of him leaned towards him, looking at his Holo-tiles as if playing on his behalf.

"Mummy!" squealed the youngest of the three girls, and she ran into her mother's arms. "I made a seven letter word on a triple score and it had a q, so I got squillions of points."

I could see the word she'd made – a strange mix of letters that didn't make any word I knew but her sisters had obviously decided to indulge her. Mrs Johnson winked at her older daughters as she hugged the baby of the family.

"That's lovely, poppet. Well done. Now just let me introduce these visitors to Daddy then you can help me make something for lunch, okay?"

"'K. Hi, Asil." The little girl waved at him and his answering smile smoothed away the brooding frown he'd worn since meeting us. It was as though he was the guardian of the family, looking out for them until Dale could retake his place as their protector. *Very patriarchal!*

Mrs Johnson bent to kiss her husband's cheek.

"We have guests, darling," she said. "Asil will tell you all about them." She turned to her daughters. "Come on. Let's see what we can rustle up for lunch." With sidelong glances in our direction, the girls followed Mrs Johnson to the kitchen area.

Asil began the introductions and without conscious thought I placed my hand on Dale's arm. Asil reached out to pull me away but as his hand came into contact with my shoulder an excruciating pain swept through my head and I almost collapsed. My vision cleared. I was still upright, holding Dale's arm in a tight grip and leaning towards Asil, my other hand pressed against his chest to steady myself. Seth hadn't joined us at the table and now hovered in the background, unsure whether to come forward. I tried a reassuring smile but it probably looked more like a grimace. The pain had subsided to a loud buzzing similar to that I'd had after my first hypno session. I closed my eyes trying to concentrate on pushing the noise away – back into the padded-cell. Instead, the hissing subsided and I could decipher the words,

"Dale? Can it be?"

"Asil? What happened? Who's this girl? Where are Geraldine and the children?"

Both men were staring at me. Dale with curiosity and bewilderment, Asil with a mixture of joy and horror: *How did you do that?*

"I ... I don't know," I answered aloud. I had a tingling sensation all through my body and my hands felt hot. "I'm going to let go now," I said and pulled away from both men. The buzz of their shared communication died away in my head but not completely. I looked at Asil for confirmation and he nodded, smiling so broadly that I could see almost all his teeth. I sank into one of the dining chairs and Seth quickly came to sit by me, taking my hand in a duplication of Asil's earlier reassurance of Mrs Johnson.

Yeah, Asil. How did I do that?

CHAPTER 41

London: 7 August 2110

I'm gonna be sick!

"Over there." A hoarse voice answered my plea. I looked up into Dale's eyes. Although there was a trace of the horror he'd been living, they were full of life, sparkling with happiness and gratitude. His hand was on my arm and he was jerking his head towards a door across the room. I covered my mouth, biting my lips to keep them tightly closed and made a run for it. I just made it in time, throwing up everything I'd had that morning until my stomach ached from the retching. Drained, I lay on the bathroom floor, my knees tucked up into my chest and shaking from the aftershocks of the head pain and sickness.

"Can I come in?" Seth's muffled question followed his tentative knock at the door.

I straightened my legs and sat up with my back against the wall.

"Yeah, s'open," I croaked through my raw throat.

He looked like he was about to be sick too. His face was tinged green-grey and his eyes were screwed up with worry.

"Jeez, Dez. Could you try to stop scaring me every five minutes?" He wrapped me in his arms and kissed the top of my head. "What just happened?" he asked.

"Dunno for sure. It was like an electric shock going through me. My head felt like it was gonna explode then I heard both Dale and Asil, and they were talking to each other."

"What did you do?"

"Nothing! It came out of nowhere. I wasn't even thinking about anything in particular at the time. Wait ... It was when Asil held my shoulder and I was touching Dale's arm at the same time." I looked at my hands. They were still pink from the heat of that reaction.

"You must've channelled their connection." Seth seemed awed by my apparently supernatural powers. His reverent tones made me giggle with embarrassment. I half-heartedly punched him and staggered to my feet. I splashed cold water onto my face, ran my damp hands through my hair and took a steadying breath.

"Come on," I said. "Let's go find out what havoc I've caused now."

Mrs Johnson and the girls were taking turns hugging Dale and each other. Asil stood by the kitchen counter looking on. He turned to smile at me.

"Come," he said. "Say hello properly."

We joined the happy group at the table and were greeted by our own hugs and kisses from Mrs Johnson and each of the ecstatic daughters. Even Asil gave me a brisk Arabic triple peck on the cheeks. Every time someone touched me there was a slight fizz of energy at the point of contact but I seemed to be the only one who noticed it. Maybe the excitement gave everyone else their own buzz.

"Dale Johnson. So very nice to meet you," he said, reaching forward to shake my hand.

"Dez, and this is Seth," I replied.

"Hello Seth. You've got a remarkable girl there. I'd keep hold of her if I were you."

"Don't worry sir. I intend to."

Mrs Johnson had tactfully withdrawn to the kitchen and taken the girls with her. We could hear their excited chattering as they made plans for the summer now that Daddy was back. Dale shuddered, looking at the wheelchair he still occupied. Recognising the unspoken request, Asil helped his PT while Seth pulled the wheelchair away, replacing it with a dining chair.

"Thank you, Seth," Asil and Dale said simultaneously. That was all it took to send us all into fits of hysterical laughter. It was a while before we got ourselves under control again.

"You want to ask about what happened," Dale said, serious once more. "But I'm afraid I can't remember anything from that time. There are a lot of blanks that I'll need to fill in. If anything comes back to me I'll let you know."

"Thank you," I said, trying to sound grateful despite the disappointment. I'd thought we were so close to solving everything now that Dale could communicate again. He seemed to sense my feelings and reached forward to take my hand.

"You're a very special individual, Dez. I can't thank you enough for finding me and bringing me home. I'll try my best to remember, I promise. Anything we can do to help otherwise – just ask and it's yours." I realised he wasn't speaking aloud and I looked at Asil, worried that their telepathy held been lost again but he was nodding in agreement with Dale's words.

Seth looked curiously at the three of us.

"Sorry, Seth," said Dale. "I've spent so long trapped in here," he pointed at his head, "that it'll take some time to remember to talk out loud."

Seth's nonchalant shrug didn't convince me and I made a silent promise to try and help him establish his own PT connection.

"We'd better leave you in peace," I said. "As you say, you've a lot of catching up to do."

"You stay for lunch?" Asil asked then looked at Dale as if remembering that it was no longer his place to extend the family hospitality.

"Yes, do stay," Dale said, smiling and nodding at Asil – reassuring his friend that he hadn't overstepped the mark.

"No, thank you. It's very kind but I think we all need time to take everything in," I answered.

They accepted the reasoning even though I sensed they wanted us to join their celebration. Asil went to fetch Mrs Johnson and the girls to say goodbye to us and we left after many more hugs, kisses and promises to keep in touch.

As we stepped into the bright midday sunshine I felt a sudden shiver. A spectral shadow brushed through my mind. I turned back to see the automatic doors closing and through the diminishing gap I glimpsed a man striding confidently towards the reception desk. Something held me there, watching through the tinted glass. The man shrugged at something the receptionist said. As he began to turn back towards the door, I felt Seth tugging at my hand.

"Come on slowcoach."

I was still uneasy but I put it down to the aftershock of what had happened with Dale and Asil. I squeezed Seth's hand as we walked towards the City.

★★★

By the time we got back onto more familiar streets of London I was exhausted! We didn't manage that tour of the Tower. I felt like an extra from 'The Night of the Living Dead' so we walked slowly, looking for a quiet street-side café to sit and watch the world go by.

"You all right?" Seth asked when I'd been quiet for a record length of time – for me anyway!

"Yeah. Fine. Just knackered. Can't believe how tired I feel when I haven't done anything!"

"You haven't done anything? You've only gone and reconnected a couple of PTs when one of 'em's been almost comatose for nearly five years – that's all!"

"Shh! Someone'll hear you." I looked around hoping that Seth's loud response hadn't attracted eavesdroppers. Luckily most people were listening to music or news through their earpieces, or were too busy gossiping to their colleagues to take any notice. I leaned closer towards him.

"Seth, you know I was wondering how to isolate telepathic connections? I think it helps if I'm touching the person – I could hear Dale clear as anything when he was holding my arm. I know it won't help find the murderer, but it's one more thing I've discovered about my own capabilities."

"Mm." Seth shrugged. I didn't need any telepathy to know that he was still struggling with his own lack of an PT compared to my constantly evolving talents. I squeezed his arm.

"Don't be mad at me," I pleaded. "Tell you what – let me see if I can connect to you."

I closed my eyes to concentrate but he pulled his arm out of my grasp. I tried not to let my disappointment show. Why did he want to keep his distance from me? We were supposed to be a couple.

"Not just now, Dez," he said. "You've had enough excitement for one day."

He tried to make light of it but I knew there was something more going on in his mind – his eyes gave him away even if I couldn't hear his thoughts.

We still had plenty of time before we had to be at the station so we spent the afternoon window shopping in Oxford Street and Regent Street. When we finally got onto the train home my feet and legs were aching. Dad, ever the diplomat, resisted the temptation to ask me how things had gone – he knew I'd tell him when I was ready. The rhythm of the train made me drowsy and I struggled to keep my eyes open. Just on the edge of sleep I heard it.

"Can you hear me Miss Hanson? So, you knew Elizabeth. What a lucky coincidence!" I leapt up, grabbing Seth's hand tightly and looking around the carriage to check whether the man was in there with us.

"Dez, are you all right?" Dad asked, leaning forward from his seat opposite and putting his hand on my knee. I felt a jolt of energy from the contact and Dad's eye widened slightly. He pulled his hand away and rubbed his finger tips together. *"Bit of static."* I heard him thinking.

"Yeah ... yes, I'm fine Dad. A bad dream, that's all." He accepted the reassurance and we continued our journey without further incident.

Once we were home, however, the 'rents insisted on hearing all about our visit to the Johnson Foundation and Dad's frown of concern deepened as we finished our report.

"Dez. I really think we should get you checked over at the clinic. You keep having such violent reactions to these phenomena and nobody seems to understand what is going on. We're worried for you, sweetheart."

A vision of that awful, drug-wielding nurse came to mind.

"No, Dad, please. I can't stand that place. It gives me the creeps. Anyway, Alvin is researching my condition and I'm sure he can take care of my mental health if needs be."

"We'll see. But at the very least, I want you to take a rest from all this diary business. I am sorry Seth, I understand how important this is to you but Dez's wellbeing has to come first."

"I agree, sir, I've asked her to drop it but she just won't ease up."

They were ganging up on me! I looked at Mum hoping to find some female support but her expression made it clear that she was on their side too. I held up my hands in surrender.

"Okay, okay. I'll try to back off but I can't leave the job half-done. You said yourself, Dad – if Elizabeth's *Handi* can give us information to put away a murderer we can't ignore it."

"Yes, young lady. And you will recall that I said it should be in the hands of the authorities who are better equipped to deal with it!" Dad's voice had taken on an edge of irritation, I shouldn't push my luck but I continued to heckle him.

"Please let us do as much as we can before handing it over. I feel like we're so close to solving the puzzle. If the authorities had anything to go on they'd've caught him by now."

"I'll keep an eye on her, Mr Hanson." Seth finally came to my rescue and tipped the balance in my favour. Dad wavered then finally crumbled under our joint pleas.

"One more episode of sickness, fainting or even a bad dream and I'll take the bloody thing to the police myself," he grumbled. He never used bad language – this was a big deal for him. Despite my ability to hear the numerous communications in my head I was still a long way off being empathetic to the emotions they carried. I didn't understand my dad's feelings of uselessness and hurt – I merely felt relieved that I'd got my own way. I gave him a big hug of gratitude and felt him stiffen at my touch.

"How are you doing that?" he asked, hoarsely.

I stood back and looked at him, puzzled at his reaction. His face was pale, his lips blue as though all his blood had drained away. Suddenly I realised what it felt like to watch someone you love suffer and not know what to do to make it better.

"What is it, Daddy?"

"Jonathan?" Mum's voice sounded brittle with worry.

"I sensed you. When you hugged me. I felt I could telepath with you. How?" My normally erudite father seemed at a loss for words but I gathered his meaning. When I'd touched him he must've heard my thanks telepathically. *Oops* – that was something I'd forgotten to mention when we'd been talking about the events of the day.

On the plus side – it proves my theory about how to isolate my links!

CHAPTER 42

Wiltshire: 6 May 2106

"I know I said it yesterday but I'm so glad you're here, Jonny." Matt grasped his godson's hand tightly, seemingly desperate to find an anchor in this sea of misery.

"I only wish it wasn't for such a dreadful occasion." Jonathan imagined how he would cope if he'd lost Dez in such a tragedy, but realised he couldn't truly comprehend the family's despair – particularly that of Bethany's mother. He glanced towards Jade, sitting with Laura and Eddie – all three straight-backed and stoic. Yet, beneath the calm exterior he knew their hearts were breaking. When he and Celeste had arrived the previous day he'd seen the raw agony in their eyes. They'd spent the evening together, recalling the vibrant young woman who'd had such a lot to give, such a lot of living still to do. It helped that they'd had time to shed their private tears so that, today, they could face the world with a degree of calm.

The funeral director approached and touched Matt's arm, "Sir?"

"Mm? Oh, yes. Yes, we'd better make a start." Matt joined his family. Laura smiled and nodded to Jonathan as her husband reached for her hand. Jonathan's chest tightened and he struggled to keep his emotions in check – a struggle made harder as he felt his own wife's hand slip into his.

"They said it was a freak accident, Jonny. Some ancient fault in the gas line that had been undetectable during the normal inspections. Pah!" His scornful reaction drew attention from some of the mourners. He led Jonathan to a secluded corner of the room where his granddaughter's funeral tea was being held. "I don't believe it. I can't.

But I mustn't drag Laura and Jade through this. Even Eddie seems to accept the lies. I'd've thought he'd want to find out what really happened to his niece." His agitation grew and Jonathan tried calming him before the lurking media started to take an interest in Lord Simpson's erratic behaviour.

"I'm sure he's just as keen as you are, Uncle Matt, but why are you so sure it was anything other than accidental?"

Matt's shoulders slumped. "It's just a feeling." He sounded defeated. "My memory's not what it was but I can't shake the feeling I ought to know what's behind all this. Will you help me, Jonny? I know you have your own family to look out for but I don't have anyone else I can trust."

Jonathan looked towards Celeste, who was deep in conversation with Laura and Jade. He could sense her empathy towards the family as if it was something solid. She seemed to know his thoughts — she turned her gaze towards him and smiled. It felt like she was giving him her blessing. He readily offered his help in whatever way Matt deemed necessary.

London: 12 May 2106

Jonathan looked at the crate that had been delivered to his London office. He'd expected a few files not realising that this research had begun with Matt's grandmother almost a century ago. Could this simply be a family feud between the Simpsons and Trevalyns? Something built from nothing all those years ago during the Nuke War and the 'flu pandemic? But Matt had been adamant.

"My grandmother was convinced Benjamin Trevalyn was a villain. She believed it to her dying day, Jonny. I've let her down by not getting to the bottom of what she was trying to prove. It bothers me that Bethany had been looking at it again and now she's ..." He couldn't finish but Jonathan got the gist.

The trouble was that all the Trevalyns, past and present, were notoriously private, vastly wealthy and extremely powerful in both business and politics. They'd had governments worldwide begging for their services and advanced technologies. Hell, even he and Celeste had relied on Trevalyn gadgetry during their field operations. He was going to have to keep this work well under-the-radar. It would mean a long hard slog, working virtually alone and the old-fashioned way without relying on the Department I.T. He couldn't tap into the resources he'd normally use – they were too entrenched in Trevalyn's systems and he needed to avoid drawing any attention to his investigations.

He hoped he'd quickly discover it was a wild goose chase but he couldn't erase the image of the sweet little bridesmaid in the peach dress. He wouldn't shy from the truth if he found anything to prove Bethany's death was not an accident.

CHAPTER 43

Ellingham: 8 August 2110

Come on Dez, it's staring you in the face.

Seth had brought all our research, notes, and Elizabeth's *Handi* to our house. It was a way to reassure the 'rents that we were being careful – and Mum was baking again so Seth was staying close, taking no chances at missing out on the results! Dad was allowing us to use his study so we'd have access to his interactive wall-screen – much easier than sifting through hundreds of *Handi* pages.

I still had a thumping headache from the day before but I wasn't going to let it interfere and, while Seth set everything up in the study, I went in search of painkillers. I keyed the code to the medicine cabinet, a precautionary measure that Dad had installed when I was little, and looked at the array of pills, sprays and potions that had accumulated over the years. I grinned at the sight of the calamine lotion, remembering its lovely coolness and unique pink, powdery smell when I'd needed it to sooth a particularly bad heat rash one summer. *Surely, it's out of date now?* I picked up the bottle to check the label. It was past its best-by date by six months and I couldn't resist a twinge of satisfaction that something had slipped through Mum's super-efficient cleaning regime. I replaced the bottle and took out the packet of painkillers, turning the box over to look at the instructions. My brain gave a nudge as I read:

PL Holder: Lisle Pharmaceuticals EU, Paris, Subsidiary of Trevalyn Corps, Regd Office: 264 Lisle St, London, Distributed by Deveaux International, Boulevard de Sébastapol, Paris.

"Seth," I said, as I rushed into the study thrusting the package towards him. "Look. Lisle. Isn't that the same name as the lab Tomas worked in? We need to check the notes that Simone sent though."

"Steady on!" Seth took the box from me and gestured for me to sit down. "Now, tell me calmly what you're on about."

"It's beginning to come together, Seth. I wondered why one of the photos at the Johnsons' looked familiar. It wasn't really familiar to me but it was to Nicole 'cos it was the lab where Tomas worked – Laboratoires Lisle."

"And ..?"

"And in the Johnsons' photo they were with the head-honcho from Trevalyn Corps – oh, what was his name?"

"Trevalyn, by any chance?"

"No need to be sarcastic, Seth. Anyway, we can look that up easily enough."

"But, Dez, what's the connection? I'm still not following."

"It's just a hunch at the mo, but let's look at the other victims to see if there're any links to Trevalyn Corps. I don't know why, but it feels like the right track." A sudden shiver went down my back and for no apparent reason a vision of that rotten nurse at the clinic flitted across my subconscious.

We powered up the wall-screen and linked Elizabeth's *Handi* and our home Comms kit so that we could trawl the InfoNet and run several apps simultaneously. After a couple of hours or so we had a list of the victims and any noticeable link to Trevalyn Corps:

1. Weardale girl – A follow-up report of the girl's death identifying her as Sally Mathers, an office worker at the local Trevalyn Laboratory. (A celeb-gossip site had a photo taken at a Christmas party which gave me a déjà-vu moment, as though I'd been there myself. A man was trying to shield his face but the caption named him as "Victor Trevalyn, CEO of Trevalyn Corps, enjoying himself with his employees.")

2. Dale Johnson – his Foundation had joint projects on the go with the Trevalyn Corps.
3. Nicole and Tomas – Lab Lisle, Trevalyn's subsidiary.
4. Bethany Simpson – MP candidate, died in explosion at home. No apparent link.
5. Backpackers in Romania – went missing in the summer of 2106. No apparent link – but other news reports of their disappearance mentioned that they were paying for their holiday by volunteering for drugs tests – were these Trevalyn pharmaceutical products?
6. School bus – plummeted over the Europa Bridge in Austria. No apparent link.

I pushed the hair out of my eyes and straightened up in my chair.

"It looks so much worse when it's laid out like that," I said, struggling with the lump in my throat. Seth pulled me into his arms and gave me a reassuring squeeze.

"Hang in there," he said. "We're making great progress."

"How can you say that?" I asked. "We can't find something that links all of them to Trevalyn's so it can't matter can it?"

"Just 'cos we can't see 'em yet doesn't mean they're not there. Come on, Dez. Don't give up now. You were the one all gung-ho to get the bastard and it looks like we've got a number one suspect here."

I looked at him to check he wasn't just trying to cheer me up but I saw his expression and knew he was taking this all very seriously. My mouth dried up as the pieces started to fall into place in my own mind. A fleeting memory from Sally's trip to the Weardale Forest showed me the face of the man she was with – he'd tried to hide from the media but I still recognised him: Victor Trevalyn!

"You're right, Seth. It's him. It's Victor Trevalyn. I remember him from the forest but how do we convince the police? And what connects those other victims?"

"Let's look at Mum's quotes again. Maybe they'll make more sense now."

"Can we ask my mum to help with that?" I asked. "She's good at cryptic clues and she knew your mum so well that she might have a better idea."

Seth paused, his brows drawn together in a tight frown. I could see he still struggled to let others see his mother's *Handi* but he finally gave a sigh and nodded his acceptance.

In the kitchen, the smell of home-baking was comforting and Mum was humming one of her favourite tunes as she tipped the latest batch of muffins onto the cooling rack.

"Mum."

She jumped and nearly dropped the baking tray, then laughed nervously to hide her embarrassment. I apologised for the scare and asked if she had time to give us a hand with something. I saw the brief look of surprise then she smiled and nodded, wiping her floury hands on her apron before turning off the oven. Although I didn't catch her thoughts I could see that she was pleased to be included in our activities even if she didn't fully approve of them. Her smile soon faded when she saw the list of death on the wall-screen and she held her face in her hands as though trying to stop the horror showing in her expression. Seth brought a chair forward for her to sit down and she patted his arm in gratitude as she sank onto the cushioned seat.

"So many," she said in a hushed tone. "I didn't know. Poor Elizabeth." I sensed Rosa's protective reaction to Mum's distress and I felt a moment of jealousy that I couldn't experience that closeness, that comforting presence of a genuine PT. I reached to hold Seth's hand and consciously opened my mental door to allow all the connections through. The sudden onslaught of psychic noise threatened to floor me but I managed to tame it, searching for the one voice I desperately wanted to hear. Seth's subconscious remained locked to me. He didn't even react to my touch. Why couldn't I get through to him like I had with Dad, Dale and Asil the day before?

"Mrs Hanson," Seth was speaking to Mum and I had to force the voices in my head back into their padded-cell so that I could concentrate on the problem of Elizabeth's riddles.

"Mrs Hanson, we're hoping you can help with the clues that

Mum tagged onto the news reports of these incidents," he explained. "Dez thought you might have a better insight as you were good friends. And you're an ace crossword puzzler." He turned and winked at me, oblivious to my inner turmoil.

Mum's cheeks, already pink from the heat of the oven, turned a deeper shade. *Omigod, is she simpering?*

"I'll see what I can do," she said, as Seth added Elizabeth's quotes to the list.

"We can see the first one is self-explanatory now that we know Sally worked for Trevalyn," said Seth. "'*He just had the power*' seems simple enough."

"Yes," Mum agreed.

As Mum looked towards the wall-screen her enthusiasm to solve another clue seemed to disappear. She was looking at the entry for Bethany Simpson and her face drained of colour so that she was almost as white as the screen she was staring at.

"What is it, Mum?" I tried not to probe mentally to find out what had suddenly struck her dumb, but I couldn't avoid hearing her desperate thoughts.

"Oh dear lord, Jonathan, what have we let them get into?"

CHAPTER 44

Ellingham: 8 August 2110

What was all that about?

Mum made an excuse to leave the room – something about burning the scones, but I'd seen her turn off the oven earlier. Seth and I exchanged puzzled looks then turned back to the wall-screen.

"What is it about Bethany Simpson that got her going?" I mumbled.

"Pardon?" Seth obviously hadn't noticed Mum's reaction was to a particular incident.

"I overheard Mum's thoughts just as she saw Bethany Simpson's entry. She was worried about what we'd got ourselves into."

"Your dad's been saying that all along, so it's nothing fresh."

"Yeah, but this was different. She was really frightened. I bet she's out there right now trying to get Dad home early to put a stop to this."

As I was about to march out to the kitchen to confront Mum I heard my personal Comms kit beeping. I sensed who the caller was but checked their I.D. to be sure.

"Hi, Alvin."

"Hello, Dez. I thought I'd check to see how you're getting on."

"I'm fine thanks." I glanced at Seth who was shaking his head and mouthing 'liar' to me. I wasn't sure I wanted to share the latest revelations of my condition but Seth had different ideas.

"Tell him about Dale," he said, loudly and, as I didn't have the privacy filter activated, Alvin heard Seth's comment.

"Dale?" Alvin asked. I threw a furious look at Seth and he

grinned back at me knowing I couldn't attack him while I was on the call.

I told Alvin about the spectacular result of my physical contact with Dale and Asil. I had to recap several times as Alvin kept interrupting to ask for more details – I was sure he was taking notes for his next offering to the annual medical shin-dig. I felt I was being treated like an interesting lab-rat rather than his client.

"Fascinating," he said, when he eventually allowed me to finish. "You certainly push the boundaries of what we currently know about psychic connections, Dez. These abilities have never manifested in anybody before. You're a real trailblazer." His excitement didn't help my mood but his next comment stopped any sarcastic reply I had in mind. "Victor will be very interested to hear about your latest exploits."

"V-Victor?"

"Yes, Dez. Victor Trevalyn. He's the current President of The International Alternative Therapist's Association. He was the key speaker at the conference last weekend and he heard some of the delegates talking about you – not specifically of course, it was all anonymous – but he searched me out to ask if he could follow your progress."

I struggled to respond. I was shaking with the shock of hearing Alvin talking about that monster Trevalyn with such respect and excitement. Seth couldn't hear Alvin's side of the conversation but he'd heard me say Victor's name and he saw my reaction. He grabbed the Comms kit from me and disconnected the call.

"Dez. What's wrong? What's happened?"

"Trevalyn's on to us," I whispered through parched lips. "He'll pick up what I know if he gets close enough." An image of the man going into The Johnson Foundation flashed across my memory. "Omigod, he was there."

"Where? Dez, what are you talking about?"

"Yesterday. He was at Dale's offices. Maybe that's how he managed to connect to me. What are we going to do?"

"Time for the police," Seth said.

"It's gone beyond that now." Mum was standing by the door. All my preconceptions about her being a silly, stay-at-home mummy disappeared as I saw an old-fashioned pistol in her hand.

"Mum!"

"Mrs Hanson!"

"Shush. I'll explain later. Right now, please, just do as I ask for once." She looked at me with pleading eyes. I nodded, unable to find a smart answer. "We've got to back-up all this data and keep it hidden securely until Jonathan can deal with it." Mum rarely called my dad Jonathan when speaking to me, it was usually 'your father' or in good times 'Daddy'. Why the sudden change – in fact, who was this woman and where was my mum? She must have sensed my anxiety and her expression softened. "Don't worry, Desirée. We'll look after you." Ah, yes there she was, using my full name again!

Seth adjusted to the new Mrs Hanson a lot quicker than I could and she soon had him following her orders with military precision. For a while I stood mutely watching the activity around me. Files were backed-up onto Elizabeth's *Handi* and a separate copy onto a mini-pin-drive that Mum stuck into the underside of her jacket collar. The home hard drive was scoured with a programme I'd never seen before. It wiped the system spotlessly clean – as clear as the day it was installed and every trace of data removed. I worried about Dad's work but Mum kept reassuring me that things would be fine.

She programmed all the house windows to the privacy setting. We could see out but nobody could see in. Seth kept checking what was going on outside. It wasn't helping me to calm down and I sobbed quietly, feeling that I was responsible for bringing this terror to the people I loved and I was helpless to divert it. Why hadn't I just accepted that I didn't have a bloody PT? Why did I have to open the floodgates and get Alvin interested in my unique abilities? Why did I think two teenagers were any match for a cold-blooded killer?

"Stop it now Desirée. That's enough self-pity."

"That's rich coming from you," I retorted, instantly regretting it but surprised to see Mum smiling.

"That's better," she said. "That's more like my Dizzy." We hugged briefly before she sent me off to pack. "We'll need a few days' worth of clothing, Dez. Sensible stuff, mind."

When I returned to the study I found a very confused Samuel in deep conversation with Seth. Mum guided me into the kitchen and gestured for me to set out some of the fresh baking while she made a pot of tea.

"Samuel and Seth aren't safe either," she said. "We're going to a secure location until we can get the data verified and the right people involved to help us."

"Mum, what's going on? This … this is all so much bigger than I thought."

"You're right. It *is* much bigger. I can't tell you more until we're safely away and have time to talk about it. Pass the milk, there's a dear."

This was surreal. One minute we're in fear of our lives and the next we're calmly sitting in the lounge and complimenting Mum on her delicious cakes. We were still sipping our tea when Dad came charging in.

"Everyone all right?" he asked, and he grabbed both Mum and me in a fierce hug.

"Fine, fine. I'm merely suffocating at the moment." Mum struggled to free herself from his grip.

Dad's eyes were full of concern yet there was also a hint of approval as he looked at the preparations we'd made before his arrival. His emotions crept into his speech.

"I see you've got it all under control, Celeste. Any chance of a quick cup of tea?"

That broke the tension and we all laughed as he stacked a plate, trying to catch up on his share of the cakes. When the silly moment had passed Samuel turned to Dad.

"What happens now then, Jon?" Samuel was the only person I'd ever heard abbreviate Dad's name. It sounded nice. He trusted Dad to get us through and it made my chest ache with pride.

"Victor Trevalyn is a nasty piece of work," Dad said. "But he is

227

very well connected and we are not going to convince the prosecution service until we have concrete evidence against him. And that is not easy to find, believe me. I've been investigating him for a number of years now." He turned to me, "When your mother saw Bethany Simpson on your list and read the quotation that Elizabeth had attached she knew we were in trouble."

"*'The true men of action in our time, those who transform the world, are not the politicians and statesmen, but scientists.'* It's by W H Auden. I can't remember the essay it's taken from, but I don't think Elizabeth was using it as a compliment to scientists," Mum said. Her knowledge of 20th century literature always astounded me. I wasn't a big English-Lit fan myself, maybe 'cos I knew I could never compete with her phenomenal knowledge.

"What does it mean?" Seth asked.

"Elizabeth was reminding us that the scientists have been the real forces behind global changes. Think of the atomic bomb and how that affected the entire world," Mum replied.

"Amongst some family files, Bethany had discovered a number of archived documents written by her great-grandfather during his time in the House of Lords," Dad continued. "They mentioned meetings with the Trevalyn Company – a small player in pharmaceuticals back then."

"Trevalyn? The same family? It goes back so long?" Dad nodded at my questions.

"In the early 21st century – a period of serious civil unrest – Benjamin Trevalyn, Victor's grandfather, developed a mood suppressant that he presented to the authorities. The financial crash of 2008 was still affecting the global economy. The numerous uprisings in the Middle East made everybody nervous. Governments around the world were seen as corrupt and elections were being regularly dismissed as rigged. Things came to a terrible climax in October 2015 when nuclear war broke out in the Far East. It was brief but devastating. The 'flu pandemic hit during the Nuke War so, between the two tragedies, a significant proportion of the world's population was wiped out."

"Apart from the Nuke War and the 'flu, we never heard any of this in History," I said.

"You wouldn't. The response to the situation could never be made public."

"Response?" Samuel asked.

"When the volatile situation was at its peak, the most powerful world leaders – not just politicians, but industrialists and religious leaders too – were fearful of a complete break-down of society. According to Simpson's notes they were convinced that this mood suppressant from Trevalyn was safe enough for worldwide use. The bio-agent was to be distributed via nano-particles released into the atmosphere. It would multiply and survive for up to a year so by the end of 2016 the vast majority of the population would be treated."

"Infected more like! Surely that's biological warfare?" Seth interrupted.

"I agree," Dad answered. "But the need to restore calm and the assurances that the product was safe reassured the decision-makers that the benefits outweighed individual human rights. Even sworn enemies shook hands on the deal. After all, the distribution method meant that they would be taking the drug themselves."

"This happened so long ago. Why is Victor Trevalyn killing people now?" I could barely speak. It felt like I was calling him into the room by saying his name aloud.

"We are not entirely sure, sweetheart. I've been trying to uncover what really happened in the years following the dispersal. According to the established history a new, more-virulent mutation of the swine 'flu brought the anticipated pandemic and affected ninety-five percent of the global population. Of those who survived a large proportion had residual depression and mental health problems. The latest theory that our medical historians have come up with is that the phenomenon of telepathic-twinning was emerging and people were finding it difficult to deal with this new psychic ability."

Mum had been constantly pacing around the room, checking through the windows, nervous about our delay but she'd listened to all Dad had been saying. Her puzzle-solving mind sifted through the details.

"So," she said, "the bio-agent probably provided the catalyst for the PT evolution."

Dad smiled at her. "You always did manage to find the answer quicker than the rest of us. We've missed your talents. I'll insist the department re-commission you as soon as we sort this out."

Mum's eyes flashed a warning at Dad then she glanced my way as though checking to see if I was probing her thoughts. Under the stress of the situation, I was struggling to keep the door shut on all those telepathic connections so, despite the temptation to see what was hidden in Mum's past, I stayed out of her head.

"Why the sudden fear for our own safety?" Samuel asked. We hadn't had chance to fill him in on our suspicions about Victor Trevalyn being Elizabeth's PT, but before I could answer, Mum spoke.

"The current Lord Simpson is Jonathan's godfather. He was convinced his granddaughter's death was suspicious and he asked Jonathan to help prove it. And now we know he was right. Elizabeth's *Handi* lists Bethany amongst Trevalyn's victims. Dez and Seth used InfoNet searches to link the incidents in Elizabeth's *Handi* with Trevalyn Corps and we're assuming Victor Trevalyn has in-built tracers which will have alerted him to their enquiries. It would explain how he was able to trace Bethany when she was conducting her research."

"Now I remember! Your bridesmaid – little Beth? Oh my god, I'm so sorry. I didn't make the connection." Samuel rubbed at his forehead, frowning while he struggled with the complex relationships. "But what has Elizabeth's *Handi* got to do with Trevalyn?" he asked me.

"The murdering bastard was her PT," Seth answered on my behalf.

Well done, Seth. Why use tact when a sledge-hammer will do?

CHAPTER 45

Ellingham: 26 October 2106

Trevalyn had threatened to take Seth from her unless she came to him. *"I merely want to meet you face-to-face after all these years? Don't be afraid. You're my muse, I couldn't harm you."* He sensed that Elizabeth was utterly drained. The school bus tragedy was the last straw. She'd agreed to meet him on the Memorial Bridge at the lake.

***

"I wasn't sure you'd come," he said, as he emerged from the shadow of the lakeside woods. He approached the bridge cautiously, half-expecting her to turn and run. "Your Bloc seems to have reinstated itself. Fascinating. I didn't know it could do that."

"What do you want?"

"Is that any way to greet the one who's shared your innermost thoughts and feelings all these years?" He grinned maliciously then added, "To tell you the truth, I'm bored, Lizzie, darling."

"Don't you dare call me that," she screamed at him.

"Calm down. You'll draw attention to us and you wouldn't want your precious Samuel to hear about you meeting a strange man by the lake would you?"

Elizabeth's tears shone in the clear October moonlight and he felt something totally unfamiliar as he watched the silver drops flow down her cheeks. An overwhelming sadness blended with hints of sympathy and apology seeped into his mind. He wasn't entirely sure if these sensations were his own or those being experienced by Elizabeth. Was he the object of her pity? He almost abandoned his plan to take her with him. Almost.

"I need you to come with me now Elizabeth," he said. "I'm sure I could stop the slaughter if you helped me. I tried to distract myself with the relationship thing. Sally Mathers – remember? How could I not see she was only interested in hooking the boss to impress her PT? So shallow, don't you agree? I could have been so much more. A loving husband, a proud, doting father. Alas it was not to be." He sighed dramatically.

"Your Bloc may still keep some of your secrets, but I know you've never loved anyone other than yourself. What would you know about the strength of family bonds?"

He was surprised to hear her vehement response. He'd thought that she was drowning in the despair that he'd inspired, no longer able to react so passionately to his torments. Her comment brought the unwelcome recollection of his childhood. One dominated by the ambitious men of the family with the women brought in only to keep the gene-pool healthy. *Well that didn't work so well for Father did it?* Once they'd produced the required son the female Trevalyns seemed to step aside – whether by choice or under duress, Victor was never sure but he remembered his grandfather's stern dismissal of any conversation regarding his own missing wife.

He realised his self-indulgence was allowing Elizabeth access to his weakness – his loneliness. His experiments to enhance psyche-links had reaped some benefit – for him if not the poor, now-demented, people he'd used as test subjects. He had been able to connect telepathically to people other than his PT but only if he was within a few feet of them. It wasn't enough. Despite numerous versions of the drug he used to establish his additional telepathy, he couldn't sustain a remote or lasting connection. No matter what risks were involved, he needed to understand the mechanics of his psyche-twinning with Elizabeth.

He lunged towards her but she leapt backwards to avoid his grasp. The momentum carried her over the rail into the dark water below. As the lake closed over her, her weariness became overwhelming and she embraced her fate. She projected final bitter thoughts to bombard her tormentor whilst the stinging cold lanced down her throat and the weight of her woollen coat dragged her to the murky depths. *Without his muse there would be no art in his killing. Without her he wouldn't be able to torment another soul with his monstrous thoughts. Without her he'd become one of the 'Empties' that he so despised, a freak without a true PT.*

"NO!"

This was one shared death he hadn't planned, that he wasn't prepared for. He felt the physical pain of his mind being ripped apart, the loss of half his soul – the better half.

Ha! She thinks I'll stop just because she's gone? No. Now there's nothing to hold me back – no whining voice of conscience to keep the monster at bay.

CHAPTER 46

Ellingham: 8 August 2110

He's gonna have a heart attack!

Samuel's face had turned a dreadful shade of grey and Seth pushed a cup of lukewarm sweet tea into his hands.

We all struggled with the implications of Trevalyn cropping up in our amateur sleuthing. I realised that as soon as he'd been in contact with Alvin, Trevalyn was able to lift my identity from the therapist's thoughts. During his brief visit to The Johnson Foundation he'd have picked up that we'd been there too. In the heavy silence that followed Seth's bomb-shell announcement I wondered how to start explaining the situation.

Dad got to his feet and began gathering the rucksacks in preparation to leave. I watched the people I loved most in the world being uprooted from the security of home, work, and school and all because I'd brought us to Trevalyn's attention. I didn't need to look for him in my head, I could feel him probing, sending waves of hate towards me and suddenly the link was full on and I had to stifle a groan of pain. He had his hands around my neck – no, it wasn't me, it was that awful nurse from the clinic and he wasn't strangling her, well not fully. *Omigod, she's enjoying it!*. I tried to tune out – I didn't want to sense any part of the action but the connection was too strong.

His recent memories came flooding through. He'd checked up on Alvin's location and guessed that the therapist had initially visited his unique client at the Trevalyn clinic in Ellingham. It was easy for Trevalyn to check admission records from his own facility. When my name cropped up, not once but twice – and that the second time my stand-in parent had been Samuel Wallis – he knew he was onto something more than an interesting telepath with exceptional talents. He'd found a link back to his lost PT. His lost soul. His Elizabeth.

I felt an intense fury to hear her name in his mind. *He's no right to even think of her!* I wished I could halt his thoughts – silence them like he'd silenced her.

The hateful nurse was only too keen to fill in any details about me that hadn't been officially noted.

"You've been a great help, Marion," he said. "Now you can have your reward."

Her giggle was cut short the instant he twisted her head and I almost vomited when I felt her neck break as though it was my own.

A strange calm came over me – I'd had enough! The last few weeks had been one disaster after another. My head constantly ached. I was bad-tempered. I was tired. And I kept dying for godssake! Victor Trevalyn might've liked that sort of experience whenever he killed someone but I didn't.

I now understood what had happened to Elizabeth – I felt the same desperation that she'd had on the night she went to meet him at the Lake. He had been constantly goading her, enjoying her agony whilst he replayed his murders in her mind. The details became clear to me in a sudden rush of information. In his privileged position Trevalyn had access to all the latest drugs and digital gadgetry. His own concoction of drugs had killed Sally Mathers in the Weardale forest. With his new digital toys he'd overridden the safety devices on the Austrian school-bus – just to see if the technology worked.

He was now projecting these images especially to get my attention. Well, it worked! I had to get away from the others and face him alone. I wasn't going to give him the satisfaction of tormenting Seth and Samuel with details about the night he'd lured Elizabeth to meet him.

More of his memories flashed through my thoughts.

Although he hadn't lost the ability to sense another person's thoughts and feelings whilst in close contact Trevalyn hungered for the relationship he'd had with his unique PT. That was all about to change. He'd heard about me and he was looking forward to getting up close and personal so that I could replace Elizabeth. With my ability to hear his thoughts, he would make me suffer the same horrors that she'd felt as he tormented her with his killing plans. And, of course, he'd be able to enjoy my suffering because of his own extra telepathic talent.

Not if I can help it! I thought, although I had no idea what I was going to do to stop him. I tried to clear my head – difficult even under normal circumstances. Breathing slowly and deeply, the way Alvin had taught me, I detached myself from the frantic activity surrounding me. Everyone was so caught up in the preparations for our escape that nobody noticed me slipping out of the back door. Silent sobs tore at my throat and tears blurred my vision as I realised I might never see my family, Samuel or my dearest Seth again. I hadn't even left a message to say goodbye. At least Elizabeth had had the chance to do that, even if it had been hidden.

"Alvin," I coughed to cover the sob that escaped. "Sorry… Alvin…Hello."

"Hello Dez," he replied. "Are you all right? Our call earlier got cut off and now you sound …"

"Just a frog in my throat," I interrupted, trying to sound more cheerful. I needed to pull this off. "I was calling to say I'd be happy to speak with Mr Trevalyn if you have his contact details."

"Oh! Yes, I'll send them through to you straight away." Alvin seemed put out. I gathered from his stray thoughts that he'd expected to be present at any meeting between Trevalyn and me, so that he would get the credit for 'finding' me. Whilst I was annoyed that he still saw me as an important medical anomaly, I sensed his professional ambition was not entirely selfish.

"I'll make arrangements to meet him at your office tomorrow if that's okay?" I offered. For once my lie was convincing enough and Alvin's grin was obvious in the tone of his voice as he said goodbye. Immediately after the call was disconnected, my Comms kit pinged to alert me to his message. Before I could lose the courage to do it,

I sent a text to Trevalyn. Calling would be too hard, I couldn't face speaking to him knowing his voice would destroy my resolve. The message? LAKE – NOW.

No going back, Dez.

CHAPTER 47

Ellingham: 8 August 2110

What the hell am I doing?

The residual memory of that October night when Elizabeth confronted Victor clung to me and sent shivers through my body.

The sun was beginning to sink behind the trees surrounding the lake. Starlings swirled in vast living black clouds as they came back to their nests amongst the hedgerows along the park boundary. In the distance, the lake attendant finished chaining up the pedal-boats for the night although in the morning he'd find one or two adrift in the middle of the lake – a favourite pastime of local couples, night-time boating.

How could life continue so serenely, so normally, when the world held horrors such as Victor Trevalyn? Had that bio-agent made us all oblivious to the violence that we were still capable of? Three weeks ago I'd been a naïve teenager, angry with my mother for making me wear a frilly dress at a stupid party that I hadn't even wanted. How I wished I could go back to those innocent, safe days. But had they ever really been innocent or safe? Victor had been there in the background all my life, through my relationship with Seth and his family. He'd caused Elizabeth's death and its effect rippled through our lives on a daily basis. I had to find a way to avenge her and to complete her intention. I had to let Seth and Samuel know that she'd died trying to protect them. It was my turn now. Trevalyn must be stopped.

"Good evening, Miss Hanson." I'd sensed his approach before he spoke so I didn't jump with fright as he'd hoped although I couldn't stop my stomach from clenching as I finally met the man who'd been such a malevolent presence in my life for the past few weeks.

Trevalyn in the flesh was somehow less than the shadow he'd cast in my mind. If I hadn't known that he was around forty-four years old I'd have put him in his sixties. He was slightly stooped and his hair was completely white, trimmed close to his head so that I could see his pink skull beneath. Even so, he exuded a strength that belied his apparently frail body – probably due to him being so close to me. Too close. I could hear his thoughts clearly.

He was mentally gloating that he'd brought me here – a re-run of the last meeting with Elizabeth. This time he wouldn't be distracted and lose his prize.

"You didn't bring me here. *I* sent *you* the invitation." My voice sounded petty to my own ears but he was surprised that I'd managed to speak at all.

"I see that the rumours about your talent are well-founded," he said, acknowledging that I'd understood his thoughts perfectly. A frown briefly crossed his face – he'd been trying to hear my thoughts but he hadn't been able to connect. I hadn't expected that myself and I tried to keep the relief from showing in my own expression. He stepped forward as if to grab me.

"Hello there Dez. Are you feeling better?" a neighbour called, as he approached with his Labrador trotting obediently alongside. He eyed Trevalyn suspiciously as though he could sense the tension between us.

"Fine, thank you, Mr Marshall. I'm just showing Uncle Vic around. He's visiting us for the first time – all the way from Australia." My false teenage enthusiasm soothed Mr Marshall's worries but I didn't want Trevalyn to register anything about our friendly neighbour. I patted Mr Marshall's arm briefly and, by pure instinct, I tried to build a telepathic barrier around his mind to keep Trevalyn out.

"Nice to meet you." Mr Marshall nodded at Trevalyn and rubbed his arm absentmindedly as he continued his evening dog-walking duty.

The interruption reminded Trevalyn that the area was too public at this time of year. The late night meeting with Elizabeth in October had been private – secluded. Now, on a warm August evening too many people, out enjoying the late sunshine, could become potential witnesses, so he had to keep control of his violent tendencies. He sat down at the far end of a bench, gesturing for me to join him. I still had no idea how I was going to deal with the situation, although I was quickly discovering more about my psychic talents. For the moment, I had to make it up as I went along. I sat as far away from him as I could. I didn't trust what might happen if we came into contact physically. At least I now knew I could hold him at bay telepathically.

"That was neatly done," he said. "Marshall, was it? He should be grateful to you for trying to save his life. Although you realise, of course, that I'll track him down later."

"Not if I stop you right now." *Yeah and how am I gonna do that?* I wished my thoughts were more positive and was relieved that Trevalyn couldn't read them to see how useless I felt. He didn't need to hear my thoughts to respond with a sarcastic laugh. He was mega-rich – a murdering bastard with the will, the power, and the gadgets to do whatever he wanted and to get away with it. I was a sixteen year old Academy student *with a mental problem – and a girl at that!*

"Please don't underestimate me simply because I'm a girl. And, I don't consider my open telepathy to be a mental problem," I said, amazed that I'd found the courage to retaliate. "I can handle it now. I can use it for the good of others."

"Ah, yes. When I visited the Foundation yesterday, I heard about dear old Dale making a miraculous recovery and, although they're keeping your involvement secret, I could easily pick up the details. Shame he can't remember what happened that night."

"You're what happened. You were testing your unlicensed and illegal drugs on the people that Dale was trying to help through his medical aid projects. Trevalyn Corps was supposed to be assisting the Johnson Foundation but you were just using it as a cover. When Dale got suspicious he had to go."

"You've already proved you can read my thoughts, Miss Hanson. Are we going to spend the entire evening listening to you regurgitate my past activities?"

"I'm simply letting you know that we have the records to connect you to your victims and with my psychic links to them and to you, we'll be able to put you away for the rest of your life." I was stalling. He knew that, but he played along – he wasn't in a rush and he was curious about what I had in mind since he couldn't read it.

"I see," he said, nodding as he drew his own conclusions. "Via your telepathic connection to me, you sense their death throes because I was able to absorb them myself. How very interesting. No wonder Grey was so excited about you. I'm going to enjoy breaking into that pretty little head of yours to see how it all works."

His tone of voice sliced through my resolve. The calmness that had kept me stable was weakening. He projected a vision of me being strapped to an operating table; he was drilling open my skull and prodding my brain with his shining surgical instruments whilst he chatted to me about his numerous murders. I felt sick and struggled not to retch.

"Lay one finger on her and you're dead right here and now."

No, Seth. Why did you come? I tried to shield his mind but without touching him I had no chance and Trevalyn's response showed I'd failed.

"Seth Wallis. Elizabeth's boy. How nice to finally meet. I'll thank Mr Marshall later for pointing you in the right direction."

I could hear Seth's teeth grinding with fury and fear. Why could Trevalyn hear his thoughts but I couldn't? *It's not fair!* I stood and ran to Seth's side, reaching towards him, trying to make that elusive connection. Seth held both arms rigid as he pointed Mum's antique pistol at Trevalyn. The expression on his face terrified me and I stood apart from him, held back by his anger. The pain and anguish from the past four years had hardened into absolute hatred for the man in front of him. He was ready to kill and that was what scared me the most. Trevalyn didn't seem fazed at all.

"Where did you find that antique toy, Wallis? Think you'd stand a chance with that peashooter, do you?"

"Don't listen to him, Seth." Mum's voice came from the gathering gloom. "Don't let him push you."

"Celeste, my dear. I suppose that undeserving husband of yours isn't far behind you."

"No, he's behind *you*." I almost cried with relief at Dad's one-liner. We'd got Trevalyn surrounded. He didn't have any way to escape now. So why was he smiling and what had he brought out of his pocket? As each of my loved ones had arrived, I'd let my attention wander and lost focus on his immediate intentions. I furrowed my forehead as I pushed back into his thoughts.

"NO!" I wailed.

"Are you going to tell them or shall I?" Trevalyn said. Then, without waiting for my reply, he continued. "This handy little device is a remote link to one of Trevalyn Corps' many satellites. From anywhere in the world I have control over all of our facilities – pharmaceutical plants, laboratories, bio-hazard storage dumps, even small town clinics." He couldn't resist a wink at me. "I hope you appreciated the treatment during your stay at my clinic, Miss Hanson. Our mutual friend Marion was so eager to share her thoughts about your condition."

"No, Dad," I warned as he moved closer to Trevalyn.

"That's right, Hanson. Keep your distance. This little beauty can trigger the instant release of my latest pharmaceutical concoction." He waved the control casually, but I sensed he was being very careful not to hit the release button by accident. He didn't want to lose his advantage too soon. He turned back to Seth.

"Biological warfare? You'll think 2015 was a blessing compared to what I can unleash now. Go on, tell them." He jerked his head, instructing me telepathically and I recoiled at the hatred in his thoughts.

"He's made a more powerful form of the original mood-suppressant. The tests showed it was almost one hundred percent effective. It completely overrides free will and the few people who are unaffected will be *dealt with* in due course. He's immune to the drug himself so he's not bluffing. He'll release it if I don't go with him."

"And what good will that do you, Trevalyn?" Dad asked. "Megalomaniacs always forget they need healthy, hard-working people to produce their food, work in their industries, and worship at their feet." I'd never heard my dad speak so derisively and I worried that his mocking would encourage Trevalyn to push the button.

"You imagine I haven't thought this through? Don't worry, Hanson. I'll have enough people to do what's needed to keep the world turning. But I'm not going to waste my time sharing my plans with you. This isn't one of those dreadful vintage Bond films where the villain tells all while the hero works out how to get away. I'm weary of talking. Come along Desirée. Say bye-bye to your folks."

The noise in my head exploded as my failure to stop this evil became too hard for me to bear. I heard snatches of my parents' tormented thoughts, their internal struggle between the need to save their only child and the duty to safeguard billions of strangers. Among distant voices I heard Alvin wondering if it was too soon to ask Debbie to marry him. Claude, far out in the North Sea, looking for a good stock of cod, and Rosa, in sunny Argentina, hanging out her daily washing – both halted in their actions by the anguish they felt from their PTs. It was all too much. I screamed with the pain not caring that the screech merely added to the agony.

Everything happened so quickly but I felt like I was bystander watching from the side lines.

Trevalyn reached forward to grab me. Seth leapt towards me to hold him back. The force of Seth's action threw the three of us off balance and Trevalyn lost his grip on the digital device. A pistol shot rang out and the roosting starlings flew up into the darkening sky squawking their anger. I felt something leap from my mind and lodge deep in Trevalyn's subconscious.

I lay on the ground, panting, dry retching and sobbing all at once. It seemed that hours had passed but it must've only been minutes – seconds even. Mum was pulling me into her arms and rocking me like a baby, soothing my hair and whispering that it was all going to be fine. Dad was using packing straps to tie Trevalyn's hands behind his back, although Trevalyn wasn't responding in any way. His eyes stared unseeing, his limbs were floppy and he couldn't even sit upright without Dad supporting him.

"SETH." I heard the shriek. The cry of a father whose grief can't be contained.

NO. No, no, no.

I scrambled out of Mum's arms and turned to where Seth had fallen during the scuffle with Trevalyn. Samuel was on his knees beside his son, his hands hovering over the prostrate body, not daring to touch. Seth's eyes were closed, his pale face almost luminous in the dusk, his auburn curls turning a deeper, terrible, shade of red where the blood flowed from a head-wound.

Don't you dare die, Seth Wallis. Don't you bloody dare.

CHAPTER 48

Ellingham: 26 October 2107

He'd believed that he could escalate his murdering without the restraints of Elizabeth's telepathic personality but the killings no longer satisfied him. He still disposed of those who got in his way but he didn't waste his time on any that would be just for fun. And some were simply unavoidable side-effects of his work. Casualties of the battle he was fighting – tragic but necessary.

***

"It's our anniversary, Lizzy. A year since I took you away from that snivelling family of yours. You should've heard their wailing when they finally found the bloated body. They say time heals but Wallis and your brat Seth wouldn't agree. I saw them earlier this evening, throwing flowers into the lake. Shame I couldn't get close up to hear their thoughts. Then again, it was pretty obvious what they were feeling." Trevalyn checked that the area surrounding the bridge was clear of any other late night visitors then emerged from his hiding place amongst the drooping branches of the weeping willow.

He walked to the middle of the ancient bridge – to the spot where Elizabeth had flinched from his touch. His anger at the memory matched only by the grief of his loss. She would rather die than be with him.

Did she really think it was so easy to slip away? He ran his hand over the smooth wood of the bridge's guard-rail. In his imagination he sensed the impact of her body as she'd fallen backwards in her hurry to escape

245

him. He smiled at the irony. In trying to escape she had become entirely and exclusively tied to him.

The others will never know what really happened that night, will they, my love? One day they might even thank me for it. But not yet. I'm not prepared to share yet."

CHAPTER 49

Ellingham: 8 September 2110

I can't do this without you, Seth.

The empty seat next to me feels like a black hole, pulling me into its nothingness, blotting out the classroom and muffling the buzz of the kids around me. I'm impatient with their chatter. They're all just children. The horrors I've seen and experienced over the summer break have made me grow up fast. I've left my Academy schoolmates behind and they'll never understand what I've been through.

My arrival that morning had brought a ripple of excitement to the Academy. Classmates fell into two categories; one group kept their distance, unsure about what to say or how I would react; the other group were over-emotional, hugging me and crying on my behalf, telling me how sorry they were. I preferred the first group.

During lessons I often noticed someone looking at me. Their reactions, when caught out, varied. Darius was quick to smile reassuringly; Frankie gave a brief nod of encouragement; Melanie's eyes filled with tears and Davy and Jing-Wei held onto each others' hands as if their lives depended on that physical contact – it turns out their PTs were complete strangers to them. With the late summer sun blazing through the windows and the underlying tensions, the room became stifling and when morning break finally arrived I ran for the door before anyone could stop me. I didn't stop running until I reached the bench, half hidden by the large beech tree, at the far end of the sports field.

I didn't care about not having an individual PT. I'd stopped trying to find The One amongst all those connections in my head. It would've been nice to be 'normal' but I'd accepted that it wasn't my fate to be normal. My newly-discovered abilities were frightening and I still shudder at the thought of my head-to-head with Victor Trevalyn. Some would say it was poetic justice – he'd trapped Dale Johnson in a mental prison for all those years after the mixed-drug overdose failed. But Trevalyn's condition wasn't drug induced – I'd done that to him, simply with the power of my teenage mind. We'd been told during our PT-prep lessons that our brains would continue to develop for several years after our initial connection. What was mine going to develop into? *Will I become a monster like Trevalyn, feeling superior to everyone around me, disposing of those who get in my way?*

"Penny for them?" Andrea sat beside me and asked the most tactless question of the century. But it made me laugh!

"A penny wouldn't make a dent in them," I said. "You've no idea how many there are in here." I tapped my head and crossed my eyes. When I brought her face back into focus I realised she was looking at me with real concern.

"How do you do it, Dez? I couldn't have come back after the summer you've had. First your accident, then that loony Empty bashing poor Seth senseless. It's weird, I'm telling you. I'll never walk by that Lake on my own again!"

It was as close to an apology for her snide behaviour at Kumquats as I was ever likely to get and I couldn't understand why the class bitch being sympathetic was more comforting than the supportive words and loving embraces that I'd had from my family.

***

Seth had noticed I'd disappeared that evening. He'd snuck out too, taking Mum's pistol while she was distracted with the travel preparations. He guessed I'd head for the lake and Mr Marshall confirmed it when he'd met Seth on the way.

"Yes Seth, Dez is with her Uncle Vic by the lake. If you run you'll catch up with 'em, no problem."

And why did Mum have an antique pistol in the first place? I don't think anyone expected it to work. Trevalyn certainly didn't. Later Mum explained that only a simple mechanical weapon stood a chance against Trevalyn. He'd developed his handy little digital gadget to control anything electronic. She'd always kept the 20th century pistol cleaned and primed – just in case.

"In case what?" I'd asked, but she wouldn't tell me more. There were secrets in our family that I'd been protected from and that wasn't going to change anytime soon, even if I had just put down the world's most dangerous man!

Dad was no help either. Surprisingly, he hadn't got into serious trouble at work for hiding his Trevalyn inquiry. I suppose the fact that Trevalyn was now safely locked away in a secure hospital meant the whole thing could be hushed up. The events of that evening were related to the press as a vicious attack by a drug-addled MPT. Seth would've been furious about another government whitewash but I could see Dad's point of view. The world wasn't – and, maybe still isn't – ready to hear the whole truth yet. Dad went back to work as usual, spoke impeccable English as usual, and treated me like his little princess as usual. How could everyone go on as if nothing had changed?

No, I was being unfair. I saw how the last few weeks had affected them. Their smiles were tainted with sadness. Mum's apparently self-centred behaviour was fast becoming a fading memory as she treated us with tenderness and pride. Her over-protectiveness didn't skip a beat though. I still had to tell her exactly where I was going and when I'd be home. I don't think she realised that I had the greatest weapon to protect me inside my own head.

Samuel was distraught, although he tried to stop me wallowing in guilt. He told me over and over again that nobody was to blame other than Trevalyn. But even a visit from Nina, his PT, couldn't bring him out of his depression. She'd insisted on taking a sabbatical from her work as Museum Curator in Kamrovskij. She said she could research Icons that had surfaced in Britain over the past couple of centuries and that would keep her bosses happy. I liked Nina. Her no-nonsense, practical approach kept us all afloat, heads just above the flood of despair that would sometimes threaten to swamp us. She quickly became good friends with Mum and Aunt Jen. And Jeremy was never far away when Nina called at the farm. His schoolboy crush on the exotic Russian was sweet to see.

Aunt Jen never said a word about what had happened. She knew there was nothing that would help yet. She was simply there when I needed her; a long pony trek with a good gallop at the end to blow away the tears; a kitchen smelling of horsehair, tack and polish while I rubbed the leather to a mirror shine; a shoulder to cry on, no need for apologies.

And here, on my first day back at the Academy, Andrea's tactless sympathy was surprisingly welcome. She wasn't trying to gain any kudos. She was merely letting me know she didn't have a clue how I was holding it together. Having done so, she stood up straightened her skirt and threw a "See ya later," over her shoulder as she headed back to her group of cronies.

Seth would've been amazed to see that.

EPILOGUE

I wish you could hear me, Dez.

He destroyed Mum, I had to stop him getting to you too but it wasn't supposed to end up like this! I'd give anything to go back – to start the whole story again. We got carried away didn't we? Thinking we could save the world, catch the bad guy and walk into the sunset hand-in-hand. Real life never works out like the movies though, does it? Guess it's right what they say: 'Life's a bitch and then you die!'

I know you wanted a connection with me. For so long after Mum died, I was scared to let anyone get too close. Maybe that's why my PT didn't hook up. And I never said the right words to make you understand, did I? Now the chance to put it right has slipped away. We could've been good together, couldn't we? I realise now that I've always loved you. And I always will. I hope you know that.

My head aches so badly – the throbbing drives me mad.

It's getting dark and cold. So lonely. Now I can understand Dale's fear when he was trapped inside his own head. What if this is it for me too? Shit, I'm frightened!

Maybe if I have a rest, things will be better when I wake up. But promise me – promise you'll be here when I do, Dez, promise?

ECHOES OF THE SOUL

coming soon!

December 2110: Seth lies comatose in Ellingham Clinic.

Unknown to all but a select few, Trevalyn is being held in a secret, secure area of the same clinic – also in a state of mental lockdown.

Dez searches through her 'head-mess' for clues to Seth's PT's identity, hoping that a link might help her break through and bring him out of his coma. However, from the depths of her psyche, she senses a more familiar voice calling to her – not one that she could ever have expected to hear!

Before she realises the implications, Dez is once again gathering clues and racing against the clock to save her loved ones from Trevalyn's evil machinations.

And would finding Seth's absent PT help or hinder her?